FLORIDAWORLD

Steve Welch

This book is a work of fiction. Names, characters, and incidents are products of the author's imagination or are used fictitiously. Any resemblance to actual events or persons, living or dead, is entirely coincidental.

Copyright © 2023 Steve Welch
All rights reserved
ISBN: 978-0-9968014-4-7 paperback
ISBN: 978-0-9968014-5-4 ebook

Special thanks to story development editor Caroline Knecht

Cover design and artwork by Luísa Dias

Published by Cave Branch Press

About the Author

Steve Welch grew up in Daytona Beach and now lives in Winter Garden, Florida.

He's had the good fortune to travel the world performing waterski shows with a roving band of aquatic warriors and renegade cultural emissaries known as The Stars of Florida. The lucky cuss also enjoyed years of adventure and discovery as part of the entertainment creative teams at various theme parks.

Those unusual experiences inspired FloridaWorld.

Many people helped bring FloridaWorld to life, but the author extends a special laurel and hearty handshake to Shannon and Ryan Welch for their efforts to make the skiing elements as accurate as possible. Shannon's sharp eye for detail was also invaluable in the editing process. Thank you both.

To Tim "Skippy the Flying Banana" Miller - thank you for laughter beyond measure.

And much love to everyone involved with the waterski shows and theme parks I've known through the years. You are the inspiration, and your spirits live in the pages of this book.

This one's for Cindy and Gumbo.

1

Winter Paradise, Florida, October 31st, 1929.

Two Days After the Great Wall Street Market Crash.

Count yourself lucky if you missed the invitation to the Halloween orgy on the night Sir Reginald Williams slaughtered the broken gods of Bacopa County.

What if you'd received that invitation?

Well, you would have made a beeline for the front door of the old mansion because Sir Reginald never did things halfway.

You'd have gone to Old Reggie's romp because the Crash brought your world low, and you'd be in a mood to burn away your troubles.

You'd have made your way through the groves and along the dirt roads to that great place on Lake May because this party promised to be a real ripper, a wingding for the end of days.

Later, you'd have been pissed to find yourself just another corpse bleeding out onto the mansion's beautiful cypress floor as the rain fell hard outside.

But hey, FloridaWorld was born that night and that's why we're here.

#

The Williams Plantation House was constructed in 1846 by wealthy Englishmen, fresh to America, who used the blood labor of slaves to build their gentile new home nestled like a castle in Central Florida's orange groves.

The Williams family didn't see things quite that way, of course. In their minds, they were kind and decent people, but horror is horror and truth is truth. War changed some things, but not as many as you might expect. This was the heart of Florida's agricultural bounty, so the plantation continued on in much the same way through the years, gathering ghosts and echoes of terrible things as it went.

It was everything you could want, if palatial Southern estates were your taste. The tall columns, the gabled roof and cupola, the wide balcony that ran the length of the place, the towering windows and bright white paint. She was framed by oaks that stood along the shore like monuments. There was Spanish moss on the limbs, fireflies came to life in the night, and lightning crackled in the distance over Lake May.

On this night, the fireflies were dark because the air was pregnant with the coming rain. Florida thunderstorms can be bad, and this one was moving fast and looked dangerous.

Gas sconces warmed your way with golden light as you entered through the great doors flanked by the thin colonnades. Beyond the wide foyer was the sweeping staircase.

Everything was so clean on the surface and so bone white.

The music was loud, the storm was near, the Crash was two days past, and Esther Jones was more than happy to let Jane's husband drink the cold champagne from her shiny kicks. She even let him run his hand along her thigh and up to her jewel bedazzled panties because it gave her a thrill and thrills would be scarce soon, thank you Wall Street.

She would be dead in just a short time, but in that moment Esther was never more alive.

Esther laughed, blew smoke, and spilled champagne. Joe, the husband, was wet with the stuff, which might have been a problem had he been wearing anything other than the small wrap of white silk around his waist.

Joe laughed then, too, and his wrap twitched.

"Looks like you're pitching quite a tent there, Sheik," she said.

The Duke was an Airedale, meaning he was a dog, but he tossed a swell party. This wasn't just your ordinary petting party.

No. This was something different.

Something special.

Something secret.

There was the band, local boys, playing some swing in the side parlor and playing it hard enough to shake the walls in the banquet room. There was the booze, and plenty of it, the wine from France and the bourbon from Kentucky and the beer from St. Louis. The heat of summer was still high, even now in late October when the days were long and Florida saw a dip in temperature, so there was ice everywhere for drinks and for cooling and for touching. There was food, great mounds of it, seared steak, chilled crabs, shrimp from the Gulf, candies from New Orleans, and the citrus.

Oh, there was citrus, of course.

The secrets made the Duke's parties swing, though. Anything goes, just like the song. If you were ritzy and could keep your mouth shut, you were in.

Sure, the Duke tossed a swell party, even when the world was ending.

Lightning and then thunder. The walls shook with music and then with the rumble of the storm.

Esther staggered to her stocking feet, tossed her cigarette to the floor, and ran her fingers through Joe's hair. He tried to stop her from leaving but she left him there, on his knees and hard, wet with champagne, and she squeezed through a pair of dancers on her way to the tall windows at the far side of the old mansion's ballroom.

"It's ok, Joe, maybe I'll work on that tent pole later. Or maybe one of you boys can lend a hand."

Laughter from the heavy fellow dressed as cupid. Esther gave him a wink.

She would have given her hair a tousle as well, but she'd gotten a bob that left it short.

The wink was enough. Cupid laughed again and blew her a kiss.

So many people. This was the biggest bash yet, and for good reason, of course. It was Halloween and everyone's fortunes had died a quick death, so better to celebrate than to curl up in the corner and cry.

She needed a moment to gather herself.

Maybe I'll start playing with Joe after all, Esther thought as she stepped over the Bloomburgs while they grunted and humped on the elaborate Turkish rug that warmed the cypress hardwood floor.

I don't know. Joe's swell, but he's a small man in every way, and I can do with something more fun than that. He'd be the appetizer but Sheriff Irving, he'll be the main course if he agrees to play nice. Nothing weird.

That Sheriff liked to do things differently when he partied and Esther didn't know if she had what it would take.

She gave the Sheriff a quick glance.

Sheriff Irving was bound by a slender rope and wore nothing but a flapper's dress. The light from the table lamp near his head was amber, and it revealed the bright red ball in his mouth.

His eyes were wide open, and she couldn't tell if he was in pain or pleasure. The thick salt and pepper hair of his chest poked out of the top of the dress and it was slick with sweat. The little vein on the side of his temple pulsed.

No, Esther thought, *not sure if I can handle the Sheriff tonight.*

She grabbed a soft red blanket from the back of a sofa and tiptoed over to him.

"What if nobody finds you till tomorrow, baby? Our little secret," she said and covered the Sheriff with the blanket.

He tried to kick a bit, but the bondage was good and tight.

She blew the flame out of the lamp for good measure.

The Sheriff was well hidden.

Esther laughed and left him there. *I'll let him simmer for an hour or two, then I'll ride in to save the day,* she thought with a grin.

Save the day. That's rich.

Her grin faded and become her standard facial armor, the look of a woman who was proud that she didn't care.

Can't even save myself from myself. Some hero.

There was a colorful bird perched in a tall, ornate cage. Esther stood in front of the bird and made little whistling sounds with her dark red lips.

Hi, feathers. It's like looking in a mirror, you and me. Pretty as can be, locked up, wings clipped, marked as property, shit all around.

She slammed her hand against the cage and the bird

rustled and squawked.

"That was mean, feathers," Esther said under her breath, "but it's a mean world. We all need to get used to somebody smacking us around, right?"

Her fingers then gently traced the metal of the cage, and she made cooing sounds.

Someday we're both flying out of our cage, right feathers? Someday we'll find that place where birds like us can be together.

Esther walked on through the movement, smells, and sounds of the party. So many things to see and do.

"Excusez- moi," she said as she stumbled into two men dressed as mice who danced and held each other close, even though the swing of the music was fast. They were the Robersons, a pair of brothers from New York who owned most of the groves near Haines City. Or at least they did in theory.

Maybe the bank owns those groves now, she thought. *How long does it take for that kind of shit to hit the fan?*

"You poor house mice," she said as she passed, "better hightail it out of here if the bank cat shows up."

The younger brother flipped her the bird and the mice brothers continued to shine their buttons.

Esther spun in a circle to the music, her head dizzy from drinks and smoke. She glimpsed Charlie Boswell's blonde wife on her knees in front of the old rover who owned the rail stations in Bacopa County. Her head bobbed up and down like a kewpie doll from the carnival. The old rover, Purvis Mitchell, looked like he was going to pop his cork any second.

Swell. There's one less for me. That's fine, she thought. *Purvis isn't a pleasant ride. Too bony and he smells like boiled peanuts.*

Four or five of the guests were in a writhing tangle by the coat closet, lit by lightning flash and low electric lights. They looked like an octopus devouring its own tentacles. One of them was making sounds a goat would if it stepped on the third rail.

Wait. What's with that kid?

The Duke's son, only five, was a shadow in the corner. He wore blue pajamas and his eyes were slits.

Not sure if junior should be here, she thought. *Haven't seen the Duke yet, and mama is dead some three years now. Isn't there some sort of maid that's supposed to watch him?*

"Hey, kid. Scram. Go to bed. This is a grown-up party."

He stared back at her and didn't say a word. He just slid back into the darkness until he disappeared.

Well, I tried to be good. Esther laughed and walked on. *We're all going to hell, anyway. Send me to the chair now and be done with it. I mean, some say the Duke offed his wife with some kind of pest poison, so there are plenty of damned souls roaming the halls tonight.*

Still, the damned and the doomed had good taste. There were objects of art from all over the world, shadows and amber light, smoke and lots of it.

It's the end of the world, baby, Esther's husband told

her that morning, so let's party and burn the damned place to the ground.

There were so many pretty things and so much money worth nothing more than kindling.

Sure, and maybe after this party and after the burn, this little bird can find a way out of the cage and fly away with her flock, Esther thought.

The windows were at least twenty feet tall and just as wide. This time of night, you couldn't see the lake unless the moon was full. But lightning flashes popped on and off, and in them Esther could see the vast black, the green of the long lawn that sloped down from the mansion to the water, the cypress trees and their Spanish moss that hung like an old widow's hair.

Esther looked out to the storm and wiped sweat from her eyes.

She felt a hand on her back.

When the voice came, it was deep, and the English accent made her squirm with delight.

"Halloween night is when the dead dance, my dear."

She turned and looked up into the steel-blue eyes of The Duke of the Cotswolds, Sir Reginald Williams. His breath was gin and tobacco. When he smiled, he reminded Esther of a watermelon slice.

"Swell party, Duke. But that storm. That's a humdinger, and it's coming this way."

"Oh, the storm came two days ago, Esther. Now we're just feeling the thunder."

Esther wanted to roll her eyes and say, "That's rich,

9

Shakespeare," but she thought better of it and just watched the lake. The Duke sounded a little different tonight. Maybe drunk, maybe high on that fine cocaine the boys from Louisiana always carried.

Well, he just lost all the money in the world, like the rest of us, so maybe he's just dying inside, she thought.

There was movement to the right, and it caught Esther's attention.

A girl with a mop and a bucket. She was young, not much more than a kid, pretty, dressed in some sort of uniform, and she started cleaning an area of the floor where there had been a bit too much fun and a puddle shone in the lightning light.

"Alma, you startled us." The Duke's voice was low and his words slurred when he spoke.

"I'm sorry, sir," said the girl. *Her hillbilly accent is wonderful,* thought Esther. *Like some kinda doll or angel. An angel doll.*

"Hurry and do the nasty chore before one of these rounders takes you off into the parlor for a kiss or a tumble."

She cleaned and left without another wasted motion. Esther paid little attention. She watched the lightning.

All the pretty birds get cages, don't they, Alma? All the pretty birds get those wings trimmed down so nice and tight. Even birds with sweet southern accents. Especially those. And then they're left to fend for themselves.

The storm was closer now. The thunder, when it crashed, was louder than the band.

"Alma came from Appalachia to work the groves, and I stole her from such drudgery. I imagine she sometimes pines for the days of those old Kentucky hills. She's game, though, more often than not. Silence is complicity, or so they say, am I right?"

"Sure. You throw the best parties, your majesty."

Esther smiled when she said it.

"I'm no royal, my dear. Far from it. Here's a little secret. My title is nonsense. There's no such thing as Duke of the Cotswolds. It's my little affectation. But thank you. I pride myself on my little soirees."

"From what I've heard, Dukie, your soiree ain't so little."

He laughed and kissed her neck. Esther wasn't sure if she felt good or bad about it. The old Duke might just be a killer. Imagine what his wife must have felt as the pesticide ate into her guts. If that's what happened.

Doesn't matter, she thought.

Her hand went to his crotch.

Choice made.

"Let's dance, your majesty. Let's dance like the world's on fire."

Sir Reginald Williams fumbled with his trousers as Esther presented herself over the plump velvet chair by the window. She felt his fingers as they worked around her flapper dress and panties, felt him as he entered and did his thing with as much vigor as the old man could muster.

Esther got little out of his grunting and flopping.

Disappointing, Sir Duke. A big dud.

Esther just watched the storm and made phony sounds like she was having the time of her life.

When it was done, the Duke kissed her back without a word and shuffled away into the party. Esther adjusted and tidied herself.

She thought about the maid the Duke called Alma.

Poor kid. Nowhere to run, especially now.

Esther made a little sign of the cross and shrugged. She was hungry, and it felt like a good time to grab some grub from that ritzy banquet table.

She had trouble making her way through the crowd that was gathered around the feast. Looked like everyone at the party had come to that spot. Esther pushed and slid and shoved her way to the front of the mob.

"Sweet sarsaparilla," she said.

The center of the banquet table was no longer a pile of beef and crab. It glittered and shone now in the light of the lamps and the lightning, a mound of gold bars, jewelry, and even cash.

A king's ransom. At the center of the pile of treasure, there was a strange object.

Esther wasn't sure what she was seeing at first, then it became apparent.

It was a golden column as high as a man's leg, with great golden wings that sprouted from either side. Mounted at the top of the column was a citrus fruit the size of a watermelon.

The orange was golden, and it was jeweled with diamonds, each as big as a fingernail.

Wouldn't that get me to Paris? Just a little piece of that beauty would let me fly away free. Me. In Paris. Or London. New friends and a swinging new time. A new life. Wouldn't that be the dream?

The band stopped. The party was quiet. Even the woman who sounded like an electrified goat was silent.

Esther noticed that the kid was there. He stared at the golden treasure with his little squinty eyes. His face was blank.

Sir Reginald jumped onto the table. He held a Thompson Machine Gun in his left hand and his right hand stroked the gleaming surface of the metallic orange.

He looked down at his strange treasure and smiled, then fired the gun, and the plaster fell like dandruff as the .45 caliber slugs peppered the ceiling.

"Here's to a Halloween like none since the dawn of time. Has anyone here lost everything they hold dear? Come, come, don't be shy about our shame."

Cheers and laughter.

"I suspect that the combined wealth of losses in this room would give Midas pause. There will be no tomorrow for us, this much is certain. Without the banks there will be no citrus and without the citrus there will be no rail, no merchant, no whore who survives what's yet to come."

The cheers tried to start, but fell apart into silence.

"We will be a town of ghosts, sunshine friends. The forgotten spirits of our dreams and desires will gnaw at the bones of this place. There will be a rot, a decay, and though the groves might return, we never will."

"So, before us, my treasures. And the great golden globe, the risen and departed dream of our once limitless futures, now gone to blight."

Esther looked at the faces of the once wealthy and proud around her. *They're not sure how to take old Duke,* she thought with a smile. *What a right bastard.*

Then she really saw the scene, really let the moment soak in. The man who had been the richest son of a bitch in town, standing like a god on a banquet table of treasure with a gun in one hand and a golden orange in the other.

Every bird in this room is broke by morning except for the Duke here. He's got that pirate treasure and I bet he ain't willing to share. Them that have, keeps what they have, that's the way it always is, right? The kings and the birds in their little cages waiting to get fed and there ain't enough seed to go around.

The shape of the globe atop the bejeweled column reminded Esther of a millionaire's dream of a hard-on and she giggled.

Sir Reginald heard her, turned his head, and winked at Esther.

"A toast."

The gathered crowd raised their mugs, their glasses, their bottles, their smokes.

"Drink today and drink all sorrow. You shall perhaps not do tomorrow. Best while you have it, use your breath. There is no drinking after death. The anchors up, the sails are set, and off we glide."

The party cheered once more and clapped their hands together in a sound almost as loud as the thunder.

In a dark corner under a red blanket, Sheriff Irving heard the noise and wondered what he was missing.

"Say hello to the future, sunshine friends," said Sir Reggie.

He leveled his gat at his guests and panned it around, letting it linger for a moment on each smiling face.

Esther was still hungry. The gold was a treat, but she'd rather have a steak. She reached into her purse and pulled out a cigarette. She lit and dragged and the smoke felt good coming out of her lungs just as Sir Reginald Williams of the Cotswolds opened fire with his Tommy Gun and one of the .45 slugs hit those same lungs and nothing felt good about that, nothing at all.

The thunder, the screams, the cello roar of the machine gun hurt her ears as she choked out her final breath.

Esther looked up, darkness coming, her breathing flooded with her own fluids, and stared into the eyes of the little boy in the blue pajamas.

Angels get real wings, she thought, *so we're all going to get to fly. All of us angels, flying to Paris, maybe. Flying to heaven somewhere.*

The housekeeper, Alma, stood next to the kid with

her arm over his shoulders. She was crying. The kid, though, he just stared back at Esther with those damned squinty eyes.

We're going to get to fly away, now, kid. It's going to be beautiful, so stop with the hate and grab your wings.

Esther's eyes drifted to the Winged Golden Orange and its many pretty diamonds as the sound of gunfire and screams went on and on. The gold was the last thing Esther Jones saw before she took wing into the darkness.

The kid who would come to be known by the name Irv Irving watched as the ghosts flew out from the dead and found their home in the walls and cypress floorboards of that great old mansion by the lake.

When the killing was done, Sir Reginald went to the boy and knelt in front of the child. The old man's face was freckled with blood specks. The knife in his hand was dark and wet.

Alma stood in the darkness of a corner and trembled.

"Some party, yes, son?"

Nothing.

"Oh, Irv, they're better off. Imagine a place where your every dream comes true and you dance and play all the day. Imagine a place beyond the pain and the loss. Beaches and flowers and the sun is always shining. A sunshine place for sunshine friends. They're in that better place."

The old man smiled.

"No hard feelings, son, but I'm going to run now, because the police will be on their way and I'll either hang or be put away in an institution for the rest of my days. But just you watch. I'll give them a merry chase."

Sir Reginald Williams, the Duke of the Cotswolds, stripped naked and scampered off without another word. The Duke's old fella smacked against his thighs with little whap whap sounds as he gamboled away, through the entry door and into the storm beyond.

Alma dropped to her knees and screamed. There was thunder, the dripping of fluids, and then a rustling sound from the corner of the room.

The Duke's son, the boy who would soon become Irv Irving, went to the rustling sound that came from a large mound covered by a blanket. His small, pale fingers pulled the blanket away and revealed a man with a red ball in his mouth. The man was tied up in an unusual series of knots, and his eyes were wide with terror.

Irv Williams went about the work of untying the bonds that held Sheriff Irving as the rain fell and lightning made sounds like whip cracks on skin.

2

Winter Paradise, Florida, March, 1946.

Irv Irving, formerly Irv Williams, the son of the late great and insane self-proclaimed Duke of the Cotswolds, was fresh from the European Front and ready to conquer the world.

In his mind, Irv Irving had a solid pitch, and he had his solid pitch down cold.

He stood on the broad inlaid mahogany table that centered the conference room in the East Wing of the Williams Mansion on the shores of beautiful Lake May. This, of course, was the same table where Sir Reggie had stood while slaughtering over twenty people, but the bloodstains had been scrubbed away and the sound of gunfire was just another ghost.

Around the table six serious looking men who wore serious looking suits and sported serious bolo ties to show that they were Southern by the Grace of God. There were a couple of impressive mustaches, a pair of honest to goodness monocles, and one fellow who had hair the color of wire that flowed down to his thin shoulders like a ginger waterfall. The room smelled of last night's gin and lavender soap.

Irv cleared his throat and began his pitch.

"All of Florida in one place. Men, women, and children from around the world will come here to see the entirety of our state's glorious beauty in a single day. Think of it, sunshine friends. Beaches, oranges, alligators, Seminoles, swamps full of adventure and beautiful girls in bathing suits. Park your car and leave your worries at the door."

The six serious men stared at him as if he'd just dropped his pants and started diddling his baby maker.

"Let me repeat," Irv began.

The man with the red hair held up his hand. "Please don't, Irv. We heard you the first time."

The six men laughed.

Irv Irving did not laugh. He was a big man, tall and wide, with hands made strong from working the groves even though he had money and didn't need to labor. Irv was tan against his all-white suit and he stood with confidence gained from wealth, work, and his time in the war.

Irv Irving let the laughter settle.

He stared down at the six without moving a muscle.

"Maybe you'll listen to my father," he said in a low

voice.

Sheriff Winnie Irving eased into the room. He was round and red and the sweat stains on his uniform made him look like he was wearing camouflage.

Sheriff Irving looked nervous enough to lay eggs.

"The blight's killing us, boys. You know that. Killing us," said the Sheriff.

One of the impressive mustaches turned to Sheriff Irving and the Sheriff's eyes went right to the floor.

"Winnie," he said, "we're busy men. If your boy wants to run away to the damned circus or build a carnival, have at it, build away, but don't look to us for investment. My God."

The other mustache spoke then. "Blights happen. Hurricanes happen. Frost happens. Citrus survives. Citrus thrives."

"Well," said the Sheriff, "what if it doesn't? I mean, this up and down rollercoaster of those things you just mentioned. Damn, it's a hard ride, men. Irv's plan is for something that's stable. I'm not a real citrus man and Irv doesn't want to be in the business either, guys. I think he's got a good little plan here."

The young girl in the pretty yellow dress ran into the meeting then, chasing a bouncing rubber ball. She laughed as she ran and couldn't have been over three years old.

The serious men turned and stared at the little girl as she scrambled under the magnificent mahogany table to retrieve the ball.

The only sound then was that of her laughter until Irv Irving muttered, "What the hell" in a voice low and harsh.

Alma, the housekeeper, ran into the room then and her face was flush, her eyes wide with terror. The housekeeper's long dark hair was tied up in a knot and there was some gray showing here and there. The blue dress was crisp. Her hands, red and raw from work, were reaching for the child as she ran.

"No, Rosie, not here. Quickly now," said Alma.

The little girl stopped laughing then. She held her red rubber ball and stood staring at the serious men, Irv Irving, and the Sheriff. Her dark eyes grew wide. Fear began to creep into those eyes, and the mouth dropped open.

Alma had her arm around the girl in an instant and pulled her back toward the door.

"Alma," said Irv Irving.

She stopped and turned, her head low and eyes on the oak floor. "Yes, sir. I'm so sorry, sir."

Irv Irving stepped down from the table and walked to the woman and the young girl. "Your daughter is not allowed in this room while I am meeting with these important men. Rose, you know that, don't you?"

The little girl nodded the affirmative. Her lips trembled.

Alma stepped in front of Rose and spoke with that thick Kentucky accent. "Yes, sir. I'm so sorry, sir. It won't happen again."

Irving towered over the woman, and she seemed small. The little girl tried to disappear behind her mama's skirt.

Irv grabbed Alma by the face and forced her to look up at him. There were wrinkles and tears around her eyes. "Do we have an understanding or do we not have an understanding, Alma?"

Alma nodded yes.

The fingers pushed hard into her cheeks as tears fell.

"Take Rose away, Alma."

Alma tried to say something, but the big fingers had her mouth in a grip that wouldn't allow a word.

Then Irv released her, and Alma hustled her daughter out of the room.

There was silence for a moment, then a few low laughs. One of the white suits made a thrusting motion with his index finger into his other closed hand. "That baby girl one of yours, Irv? You've been up to the devil's business."

There was more laughter then. The ginger waterfall got the discussion back on track with a definitive "Citrus is stable."

"Oh, that's bullshit you just tell yourselves to feel safe," said Irv Irving. He paced, his voicing growing louder, booming. "Blight hits, we lose. Takes a while to come back. Then bam, frost, we lose again. Up and down, gentlemen, never stable. What I propose doesn't get blight, doesn't hurt from frost. Hell, if we build it well enough, the damned hurricanes can't touch it this far inland."

"You don't know your ass from a hole in the ground, son. No offense."

"I know this is going to work, with or without you. No offense."

"A carnival. You're proposing a golldarned carnival. Winnie, talk some sense into him."

Irv Irving took a deep breath and looked around the room. He'd played in here as a kid.

He'd seen a thing or two in this room.

"It's not his call. Sheriff Irving is my adoptive father, but Sir Reginald Williams left this ten-thousand-acre grove to his only blood relative. That's me. His son. My name is on the deed, not Sheriff Irving's, so Winnie won't be talking sense to anybody."

"They should have called the will and testament void. The man was a lunatic," said the monocle.

"Well, they didn't void it, my friend, so you'll tread lightly," said Irv Irving, and his voice went low and wasn't much more than a snarl. Irv stared at the man with the monocle and there was violence in that stare.

"Calm down, young man," murmured the ginger waterfall under his breath.

"I'll do it without you and you can come crawling to me later."

"What's your little carnival called, Irv?" The monocle threw the question out with a laugh, and the others joined.

"FloridaWorld," Irv said, but low so nobody could

hear.

Then he stopped and turned, and when he spoke, his voice was thunder.

"FloridaWorld," he said, and this time, everyone in the room could hear him.

Irv Irving walked out of the conference room and crossed through the ballroom on his way to the door. He didn't hear the ghosts, but he felt them. He always felt the ghosts of 1929 when he came back through the ballroom. He always heard the screams and the gunfire and he always smelled the weird death smells and heard the curses and gasps of the dying.

He was five years old again.

Irv watched his father roam the ballroom to finish off the moaning survivors with a knife, then run screaming into the storm. He was above the scene now, watching himself from on high as he pulled the red blanket from Sheriff Winnie Irving and untied the bondage rope. He saw himself remove the red ball gag from the Sheriff's mouth and heard the man who would become his new father howl in horror at what he saw.

Irv saw these things and heard these things and smelled them too every time he walked into the ballroom.

And he didn't mind.

The ghosts and memories comforted him, even when the bullets were flying at the Battle of Hurtgen Forest. They gave him solace when the nightmares and doubts came in the night and jabbed their icy fingers into his heart. They gave him encouragement when he took his time with Alma Campos on the old oak floor, despite her protests.

I mean, where else is she going to go? Some romping is a small price to pay for safety and security in this wonderful house.

Homes in Florida rarely had a basement. The Williams Mansion did because it sat on a man-made mound of soil, and the basement is where Irv Irving went next. Only his father and Alma knew of the basement or of what Irv kept there, hidden in the dark.

He used a metal cigarette lighter to guide him to the antique iron safe that was as tall as Irv and twice as wide.

Twist, turn, click, click, click.

Irv opened the safe and held his breath as he looked at the mound of jewels, jewelry, gold bars, and other glittery items. The Golden Orange was there too, atop a shaft of silver and crusted with diamonds, but he had no intention of selling it. There was no need. The other items would fund his dream.

The great Golden Orange was sacred and he would hold it so for all of his days.

Such wonders I've known in my life and such wonders still to come.

Yes, this was a wonderful house, and the ghosts assured him that things could never get worse than that night in 1929. It was the Atomic Age, an age of limitless possibilities.

The future was bright and soon Irv Irving would

welcome so many new sunshine friends to the wonders of FloridaWorld.

3

Wisconsin Dells, Wisconsin, June, 1971

"We bought this boat to fit in with the neighbors, not to kill our boy," his Mom said and she sounded angry. Mom was scary when she was angry.

Eric Walters was seven years old, had just learned to swim, and was coughing up lake water so hard that he thought he was going to puke.

"Watch your head," his dad yelled, just before tossing the ski handle from the boat. The heavy wooden thing landed with a splash inches from Eric's head.

"Let's try it again, Eric. Remember, don't pull on the handle. Just hold on, tuck your knees up to your chest, and let the boat do the work," Dad said.

It was a warm afternoon on the river, and there were no clouds in the bright blue sky. There were plenty of other boats sharing the Wisconsin River that day because it was the weekend, it was early summer, and family time on the water was just what people did here in the Dells.

The water was cold even though the day was warm, and Eric shivered as he reached over and grabbed the handle. He was floating thanks to the big orange vest and the wooden skis on his feet that dangled and clattered in the water. He pulled the ski rope between his legs and held the handle tight with both hands.

Water sloshed in his ears and Eric hoped that it wouldn't be another ear infection. Those hurt something fierce. He coughed again and more river water came up.

"Do as Dad says, Eric, but if you want to stop you let me know," his Mom shouted from the back of their new boat.

Well, the boat wasn't new, exactly, but it was new to the Walters family. Eric loved the boat and he loved the idea of waterskiing because the neighbors all seemed to enjoy getting out on the lake and skiing around. Then there were those Life magazines Dad bought with articles about a place called FloridaWorld where everyone was friendly and smiling and there was a show on the water with daredevils and ballerinas, and speedboats, and even clowns. Eric imagined that it was even better than the *Tommy Bartlett's Thrill Show* that helped to make the Wisconsin Dells so famous. His family had moved to the Dells last summer, just in time for them to see that show. Eric enjoyed it, especially

Aqua the Clown, but in his imagination the FloridaWorld water show was wilder, faster, and more amazing than anything Wisconsin could offer up. And there were alligators!

Their little town had their own amateur waterski club called the Aqua Pixies. It wasn't a big show but it seemed like a fun way to meet new friends. Eric's dad seemed to think they'd fit in better with their neighbors if they joined the team. Now they had a new/used boat and were learning to ski. Eric didn't mind at all.

"Not gonna stop. I can do it," Eric shouted to his Mom. He watched as she shook her head and sat down in the back of their boat. She wore one of the orange life vests over her pink bathing suit. Dad sat in the driver's seat with a pipe in his mouth. The back of his bald head was a dark cue ball against the blue sky.

His Dad raised his hand in the air and gave Eric a thumbs up. "Ready?"

Eric coughed and shouted, "Ready!"

He pulled his feet to his chest, and the skis made more clattering sounds as they twisted around in the water. Eric heard the boat motor roar, and the rope played out fast in front of him.

Don't pull up on the handle. Lean back. Let the boat do the work, he thought.

The rope went tight and Eric felt the sudden, powerful pull of the boat. He dragged through the water for the briefest of moments, his thighs burned, and then he was up, the two skis just in front of him gliding across the surface.

I'm skiing!

The victory was short-lived. Eric pulled up on the handle, his body went forward, and the next thing he knew he was face down in the water again with the wind knocked out of him. It was a horrible feeling. He rolled over and tried to breathe but nothing happened. Eric didn't hear the boat come around and barely felt his Dad's hands reach down and pull him up and out of the river.

Eric's breath came back with a gasp as he lay on his back on the deck of their new/used boat. Water sloshed in his ears and he wanted to cry but fought back the urge. His Mom and Dad knelt on the deck with him.

His Mom was smiling. "You did it! For a second there, you were waterskiing!"

"Told you not to pull up on the handle," his Dad said, the pipe clenched tight between his teeth. Eric's Mom gave his Dad a dirty look and slapped him on the shoulder.

"I thought we were out here to have fun," she said. Dad laughed.

"He'll have more fun if he gets up on those skis," he said. Dad leaned in close to Eric and jabbed a finger into his chest.

"You can do this, son."

Eric coughed up some river water and smiled.

"I know, Dad. Let's try it again."

Before the end of that day, Eric Walters figured out

the physics of the thing and skied the waters of the Wisconsin River behind his families new/used boat. Warm wind on his face, the clear river moving so fast beneath him, his Mom and Dad cheering him on. In his mind he was dodging alligators and performing in the big thrill show at FloridaWorld. Then, after a few more ski runs, they pulled up along shore for a picnic. Mom laid out the spread under the shade of the towering green maples, a feast of bologna sandwiches and potato chips, while Eric and his Dad scoured the banks of the river for Indian arrowheads.

"The Menominee tribe was here for a long time, Eric. You keep looking, you're bound to find some things they left behind."

"What happened to them? Are they still around?"

"Not so much, son." Eric thought that meeting a real Indian would be cool, although they were usually the bad guys on the western shows they watched. Of course, people like his Mom and Dad were usually the bad guys too, or just maids and bellhops.

How swell would it be if I found an arrowhead? Eric dragged his hands through the mud, picking through the rocks and pebbles, searching for something cool.

When Eric went to bed that night, he sure as heck had a Menominee arrowhead next to his pillow. He stared at the pages of Life magazine by the amber light of his bedside lamp, the story of FloridaWorld coming to him in words and images on the slick pages. Beautiful girls on waterskis, real alligators, fresh oranges, and a place where everyone was friendly with everyone else, no matter what they looked like or where they came from. They were all "sunshine friends" at FloridaWorld.

After a while, when it got really late, Mom and Dad kissed his forehead, told him they loved him, and shut down the lights.

Eric Walters was exhausted from the day on the river. Sleep came fast, and the dreams were good.

4

Winter Paradise, Florida, January, 1972.

"Paulina, you wait here. Mommy will be right back."

Florida can get cold. Don't believe someone who tells you differently. Sometimes, in the heart of January or February, the temperature drops, but the humidity lingers, and it's the cold that seeps into your bones and hurts you.

It was cold that night. The heater in the car was broken and there wasn't enough gas to run the engine for long anyway, so Rose Campos, daughter of Alma, tucked Paulina in blankets and dirty clothes to keep her warm.

The car sat in the darkness away from the streetlamp on the dirt road that ran miles into the heart of the orange grove. This is where the workers lived during the season in shacks that held as many as could fit.

There were times during the year when the air was rich with the smell of orange blossoms. Paulina loved that smell. Tonight, though, the trees weren't blooming and the dark grove was just a wall of dark shapes that seemed to stretch forever.

There was a party in one of the houses. The music was loud and there was laughter and shouting. Paulina didn't like the sound, so she covered her ears with the blankets and held her plush monkey Mr. Jingles close. She snapped on her little flashlight and read her *Pinocchio* picture book.

Paulina lost track of time, but her mama was gone for a long while. When she returned, she moved into the car so fast that it startled Paulina. Paulina could see the fog of her mama's breath in the darkness and dim light of the dashboard.

Mama smelled like smoke and there were other smells too that Paulina did not recognize.

"Sorry I was so long, baby, but we can go now. I got my medicine so we can go."

Mama's hands were shaking. Paulina thought she must be cold. She then dropped the keys and cursed under her breath. There were some voices in the darkness. Paulina thought they sounded like men, and they were walking toward the car.

"Sorry, baby," said Rose. The keys found their way into the ignition this time. The four-cylinder engine ticked and shuddered, and they pulled along down the dirt road toward the distant lights of Winter Paradise.

Paulina poked her head out of the blankets enough to look out the car's foggy window at the universe of stars. There were so many stars tonight. The sky was clear and deep blue and it looked like heaven had opened up above them as they went. Paulina wrote her name in the fogged glass.

Paulina did not understand why they no longer lived in the grand mansion on the lake with Granny Alma and Uncle Irv. That was such a wonderful place, and it sat in the heart of FloridaWorld, where there was such happiness and fun. She did not understand why they had left such a dream place and such a kind old man. Uncle Irv sometimes gave her ice cream cones and he would sometimes even play hide and seek in that grand mansion.

She wanted to live in the mansion on the lake at FloridaWorld, not in the car, but this was the way things had been for a few days. Mama had argued with Uncle Irv so loud that it scared Paulina and that was the last time they'd been to the big mansion on the lake. Paulina didn't ask her mother about it because she didn't want to make Mama sad.

Anyway, the car was comfortable and as big as the little room they'd had in the mansion when Mama worked there. It didn't have a bathroom, though, and that was bad, especially when it was cold like tonight. Paulina missed Granny Alma too, but she was sure that they would go back to at least visit soon. Granny Alma always had sweet treats and would read Paulina the most wonderful stories about the blue people of Kentucky who flew from France in a balloon and talking bears who danced a jig.

They stopped in the darkness of a parking lot along Lemon Pip Lane. There were no street lamps here, no other cars, and Rose pulled the car into a tight space behind a dumpster where it was well hidden. Rose killed the engine but kept the battery running for a bit so that she could listen to the radio. Not too long, though, because the battery would die and they would need a jump in the morning, and that always made Mama nervous.

Paulina knew then that this was where they would sleep tonight.

Her flashlight was dim, so there would be no more reading. Paulina felt sleepy anyway, so she held Mr. Jingles and closed her eyes. She felt her mama's warm hand on her cheek.

"Night night, sweetheart. Mama loves you to the moon and back."

Paulina giggled and said, "I love you to Pluto and back."

Rose sang a song to her daughter then, a song she'd learned from her mother and came from the distant green hollows of Kentucky. The low ballad was both a prayer and a love song, full of dark imagery and simple dreams.

When the song was done, Rose touched her daughter's cheek again and then Paulina heard the springs of the car's front seat squeak as Mama settled in. A moment passed, and then Paulina heard a rustling. Mama would be taking the bent Fresca can from underneath the seat and throwing some cigarette ash onto the holes that were poked in the aluminum. There was the click of a lighter and a light glow from the flame.

Paulina heard her mama take a deep breath from the can.

It was warm enough under the blankets. Paulina drifted to sleep as her mama burned the little pink rocks in the front seat of their home slash car.

Paulina was cold when she awoke. The morning sun wasn't quite up yet, but there was enough golden light so that Paulina felt comfortable climbing up to check on her mama.

The world spun then because something was wrong and neither Mr. Jingles nor Paulina knew what to do next.

Rose was pale and still and her eyes were open as if she were still looking at the stars over the orange groves of Bacopa County. There was no cloud of fog from her breath. There were no stars, only a dumpster, and what had once been Rose Campos stared at nothing at all.

5

Winter Paradise, Florida
Christmas Eve, 1992

It might have been a small hotel room in any small hotel in any place in the world. This was a place of death, though, a place of goodbyes and ghosts and peace.

There was a little Christmas tree atop a table in the corner. The lights from the tree and in the hospice room were dim so that the old shell of a thing that had once been Alma the housekeeper seemed to be nothing more than another fold in the sheets. There was little left of the strong and proud Kentucky girl who had seen terrible things on Halloween night, 1929, at that mansion on Lake May. Her life had been long and stubborn. She worked until she could work no more, and she fought the illness and the age until the battle could not be won.

Paulina sat in the hospice's quiet room and held Alma's hand. She thought that her grandmother's hand felt like a tiny, featherless bird, a chick fresh from the egg, twitching and frail. So frail for such a strong old woman, the woman who had raised her when Mama had passed.

Alma spoke, and her words came hard. Each one pushed out with all the breath the old woman could afford to give.

"The Old Man hurt me inside. He hurt your Mama, too. Many times," said Alma, "Your Mama. I couldn't protect her. I was weak, and I reckon I'll go to hell for it."

The granddaughter's heart raced, and she thought that her head would explode. What was her grandmother saying?

"But we kept him from you. That was our deal with the Old Man. That was the deal."

"What do you mean?"

"You know what I mean, child. You stay away from him now. Stay away from that Old Man. The deal will be done once I'm dead and you stay away from him. We can't protect you anymore."

What?

Alma tried to pray then, but there was less of her than ever and the words were rambles of spit and cough.

"I'm a gonna burn in hell, and I'm so afraid, child."

Alma pulled Paulina close and prayed into her ear. The words were a madness of Jesus and giant alligators the size of whales, of murder, deceit, gold, and diamonds. The granddaughter sobbed because in that moment she knew Granny Alma's mind was gone and this tower of strength she loved so much now gibbered of fantasies and loss.

When the last words had been spoken, the old eyes focused on something above Paulina's head, and Alma was welcomed into the company of spirits.

Paulina sat in the silence and amber light. It would have been lovely if she had felt the spirit of her grandmother pass into the heavens.

Well, that would have been nice, but that didn't happen. Paulina did not feel peace in that moment. She did not feel the gentle spirit of her grandmother ascend into the infinite.

She felt ghosts though. And horror.

There was the ghost of her dead mother, the ghost of the secret just shared on her granny's deathbed, the rising horror that became rage and the spirit of everything she once thought was true falling apart into nothingness.

Of course. It made sense. A horrible, terrible sense.

No, there was no peace in that room, in that moment.

Mama and Granny Alma could not protect her anymore.

Paulina held the frail bird skeleton of her dead grandmother's hand and thought of days playing on the mansion floor, of toys and games and the great gardens beyond the white walls of the place, of the beautiful lake and the storms that would come and go on summer days. She thought of chasing dust moats in the shafts of light that came through those great tall windows. She thought of a theme park as her backyard and of the Old Man who treated her to an ice cream cone from time to time when she'd been good and quiet and hidden. She thought of Uncle Irv Irving, the kind Old Man who called her his sunshine friend and kept a Valkyrie as his companion and spoke to the ghosts who would come during the night dressed in fancy clothing. She thought of Uncle Irv, of her mother dead in a cold car next to a dumpster, of her granny sweeping and cleaning and working so hard to make it all work, to give them a chance, of the pride and strength of this dead woman and now of the things done to keep her safe.

Paulina thought of these things and more.

In the days that followed there was the tending of business, as one does, but Granny Alma had little of consequence and so there wasn't much to tend. Paulina did not return to the mansion on the lake and Uncle Irv did not appear at the funeral. This was not a surprise, as the Old Man was bound to his bed with age and illness, but it was a bitter relief. Paulina did not receive a call or note from him.

That was fine. That was quite fine.

#

The funeral done, Paulina stared into the broken bathroom mirror of the single wide she'd claimed as her own on the dirt road just beyond the old orange grove. The night was hot, even now in winter, and sweat ran down her back. The power was on again, as her most recent paycheck had been enough to do the trick. Next month, who knows? She didn't dare run the window mounted air conditioner, though, and a single bulb was all that let her see the lines and angles and sweat of her face.

The crying was done. Her skin was numb. Paulina looked hard into her own eyes, but she wasn't sure what she was looking for, so it just became a staring contest with the ghost in the glass.

A mosquito landed on her neck and sucked. She didn't move to kill it.

Nobody left to protect me, she thought.

Her Bacopa County Police Department Beretta 92 service weapon rested atop the porcelain of the toilet to her right. Thick muscles under brown skin, a front tooth chipped by a fight with a drunk, a scar on her forehead from a ski handle, a tattoo of a knife on her left forearm from her time in the Army, a tattoo of a rose on her wrist.

Paulina broke the staring contest and tried to smile but nothing came. Instead, she spit into the sink.

The mosquito flew away, fat with blood.

Nobody left to protect me? There's nobody to protect you, old man.

6

Winter Paradise, Florida
January 15th, 1993

The ghosts of Williams Mansion on the shores of Lake May were accustomed to violence. This was a home built in blood and horror, so the ghosts knew the songs and rhythms of the place. Their voices went on, their footsteps echoed, their mists showed themselves in the corner of your eye or in the cobweb breath of nothingness that would caress your neck at night. The spirits of the place went on about their business and so did the great grand world around them, so on that cold night there was no surprise that violence came once more.

Paulina was well trained by the U.S. Army and Bacopa County Law Enforcement to use a gun but that wouldn't be slow and painful enough. This night she carried a box cutter, a small blowtorch, and a blue nylon rope.

She would take her time with the Old Man, and he would pay his debts piece by piece.

There was no security in the old mansion. No alarm system, no guards. After all, the mansion sat on the shores of Lake May in the middle of the secure grounds of a gleaming wonderland called FloridaWorld, like the fabled realm of Asgard at the end of the Rainbow Bridge. The mansion was secure because everything around it was secure.

Paulina knew the mansion and everything around it as well as anyone so she had no trouble breaking into the place at two in the morning with her tools of choice.

There were no lights, but she knew the place well enough that she could make her way through the darkness of the entrance lobby and then beyond, into the grand ballroom, with no trouble.

A sound.

She froze in place. A hazy blur of white moved in the corner of her field of vision.

A rustle, what sounded like a word or two.

There were echoes of the past in the mansion.

She was not afraid, because these were old ghosts, and they had suffered as much as anyone. They wouldn't harm her. They were just there, conversations recorded into the wood floor and the plaster walls, laughter in the paint, a footstep locked in the memory of the concrete blocks that repeats like a vinyl record stuck in a groove.

She went up the steps with no wasted motion, every step deliberate and silent. The Old Man's bedroom was off to the left, past the conference room turned museum and the game room where the spirit sound of billiards being struck still echoed.

The Valkyrie came to her then. Or, at least that's what appeared to descend out of the gloom and block her path. The strange figure was tall and wide in the darkness, arms open as if to take Alma's granddaughter into an embrace. The figure was a large, muscular woman dressed in a costume that gave her the appearance of something from an opera about dragons and vikings. She had wings like a great eagle and wore a helmet and metallic chest plate that gleamed even in the darkness. The snake around her neck was thick and long and Paulina knew its name was Jormungand because she'd seen it many times before.

The woman dressed as a Valkyrie spoke in a warm, deep voice.

"I can't let you do this, Paulina. Besides, you don't want to do this, not now, not when real justice is so close. Real justice and real treasures, Paulie."

Paulina looked up into the blackness where the face of the Valkyrie must have been.

How old are you, Hilda? It's so hard to tell because of the costume and makeup. Or, thought Paulina, *have you always been here, standing guard over the old bastard? And you let it all happen, didn't you? You didn't stop him.*

"You never said a word. You never stopped him. Stay out of my way, you bitch."

The Valkyrie named Hilda burped, erupting with the scent of collards and bourbon.

"So, now you know what's true and what isn't and it's time for us to have the talk, Paulie. Let's go downstairs. Quietly. Don't wake him."

"Why should I listen to you?"

Hilda dropped her muscular arms and reached out to touch Paulina on the cheek. The hand was rough on her skin and the metal bracelets around Hilda's wrist jangled softly.

"I trusted you," said Paulina.

"I protected you, even if you won't believe me. I really did protect you. There was a night when he was terribly drunk. I stopped him, Paulina, at a cost," Hilda said and she lifted her chin. She pointed at a long scar along her neck.

Paulina swatted away Hilda's hand. The slap of skin on skin was shocking in the silent darkness of the mansion.

"I know what you want and I don't blame you but there's a better way, Paulie. The treasures of Valhalla await if we're patient and wise. There's a long game we can play here. You'll get yours, he'll get his, and more. Let's talk."

Paulina was strong, and she was certain that she could drop Hilda in three moves and continue with her mission. There might be some noise from those three

FloridaWorld

moves, though, and that might ruin everything. The snake was big enough to be a problem as well.

She listened. She would deal with Hilda the Valkyrie downstairs where it would be quiet and quick.

The Valkyrie weaved quite a story.

As Hilda spoke, Paulina saw so many memories twisted in different ways and heard so many voices from paths of the past and choices not made. Rage took her heart in a grip and squeezed until Paulina thought she might cry but she didn't. She listened as the Valkyrie told her the secrets of the place.

Upstairs, Irv Irving slept the sleep of the guiltless and dreamt of winged victories while Paulina Campos and Hilda the Valkyrie set their sights on murder, revenge, and all the treasures of Valhalla.

7

Winter Paradise, Florida
Thursday Night, March 1st 1993

PBR was the first.

There was a corpse under a dock on beautiful Lake May. Only three people knew about it, and one of them was the corpse, the late Pub Boat Roger, so he didn't really count. The other two were the ones responsible for the death of Pub Boat Roger and since one of them also called 911, there would soon be quite a few people who knew that a dead man with a citrus fruit jammed in his mouth and hogtied in waterski rope was tucked away under that dock.

A fat old alligator was also well aware that PBR was ripening in those clear waters because, as gators will, she was saving the corpse for dinner once the flesh had softened up.

But gators don't spill the beans when it comes to murder, as far as we know.

Lake May was still and silver under the waxing moon, her shores just a suggestion in the night, her waters calm following the afternoon storms. Now the air was thick, the breeze a whisper, and the two Bacopa County Sheriff's Deputies on the old wooden dock were wet with sweat.

"Who gave the tip?"

"Just a call to 911. No name."

Deputy Paulina Campos could barely hear her partner's voice through the orchestra of mosquitos and night bugs. The dock was overwhelmed by reeds and cypress trees, a dark finger reaching out from a swampy stretch of shoreline with canals, creeks, and tributaries that extended for miles into the woods.

"Caller said there was a body in the water near the dock at the north end of the lake off of Jackson Road. That's all."

Of course, Campos knew the area well. But her partner, Joe Seaton, was from Orlando. He was new, and Campos was pretty sure that he was scared. She was scared too, but for many reasons.

There was a spot where the water was shallow beneath an old boat dock.

They used their flashlights.

"Watch for gators," said Campos. "Shine for the eyes."

Seaton threw the beam of his flashlight out into the

blackness of the lake.

Dozens of little red dots gleamed back.

"Holy shit," said Seaton.

"You're not at Disney World anymore."

Campos dropped to her stomach, leaned over the edge of the dock, and trained her flashlight under the old wooden planks.

He's supposed to be here, thought Campos. *She said you would be here, Roger.*

Bullrushes and spider webs. Cockroaches scurried from the light. Campos leaned further down and brushed aside some weeds. *Show yourself.*

And then, there he was.

A corpse wrapped in ski rope with an orange in its mouth stared back with white eggs for eyes. PBR floated face up in the water only inches from Campos.

Something huge moved in the darkness.

Paulina felt her stomach lurch. She didn't expect the sound.

Fuck.

The slither became a splash, and her flashlight beam caught a wall of dark green leathery skin.

Campos rolled over and up just as the big gator wallowed out from its hiding spot.

Her partner couldn't even scream, he just backed away down the dock, clawing at his weapon.

"Fucking gator," said Paulina as she stood and brushed off her uniform.

She saw Seaton with his weapon out.

"Stand down," Paulina said. "We have a Signal 7. Caller wasn't wrong. There's a body."

Seaton stood at the edge of the dock and locked down at the dark water. "Was it the alligator?" he asked, "Damn, what a way to go."

"No. I think the gator just found a ready-made meal. Stick your head down there and look."

Deputy Seaton shook his head no.

"Don't be a wimp. The gator's gone. See?"

It must have been ten feet long, at the least, and it created a wake as it swam off into the moonlight gloom.

Deputy Seaton took a breath and leaned over the edge of the dock. He aimed his flashlight into the darkness. After a moment he stood back up and turned to Deputy Campos. His eyes were wide.

"Is that an orange in his mouth?"

"Yes. And that blue rope? That's nylon waterski rope."

It seemed as if something came to Deputy Campos then, and her mouth dropped open. She was a poor actor, but it was dark so that mattered little. She ran back to the edge and looked down again.

The face stared back at her. It bobbed up and down in the clear water, the white sand like a blanket underneath. The skin was bloodless, and the face was puffy, but the corpse hadn't been there long at all. Paulina took a long moment to stare into the eyes of the dead man.

They accused, those eyes.

Paulina bit the inside of her cheek so hard that blood came. She was dizzy then and realized that she hadn't taken time to breathe. She rolled back up and came to her knees.

"I know him."

"What?"

"That's Pub Boat Roger. PBR. I know him. He's a boat driver in the FloridaWorld ski show. Was. He was a boat driver."

These were not lies, Paulina told herself. Her hand went to her radio.

Of course I know him.

"This is Campos. We have a Signal 7, Signal 5. Our 10-20 is the dock on Jackson Road. Repeat, Signal 7 Signal 5 out at the dock on Jackson Road. Standing by. 10-48."

The sirens and detectives couldn't be here soon enough for Campos.

Get away from here.

She had processing duty at the County Jail in the morning and that was only six hours away. She walked to the end of the dock and looked out over Lake May.

Sorry, Roger. She said she was quick about it. You probably didn't feel a thing.

There was a shooting star then, and it burned in many colors. Paulina imagined it was just a piece of the Rainbow Bridge to Asgard and the fireworks were a celebration of the first step on a voyage that would lead the righteous warrior to Valhalla and all her treasures.

Then she thought of Pub Boat Roger.

You were a decent guy and now you're under a dock with eyes like eggs and an orange in your mouth.

The granddaughter of Alma the housekeeper dropped to her knees and threw up all over the dock.

No way out now. I could have stopped it but I didn't and now there's no fucking way out.

8

Winter Paradise, Florida
    Friday Morning, March 2nd 1993

That song by *Right Said Fred*, about being too sexy for this and too sexy for that, was still in his head. It was the last piece of music Eric Walters heard from the jukebox at the bar as they dragged him to the squad car.

Damned catchy, but he hated that song.

They didn't let you smoke just anywhere anymore, not even inside the Bacopa County Jail, but that was fine because Eric was trying hard to quit. Marlboro reds got him through a few things when he was in Iraq, but they were expensive and that was money that could be used for beer.

Three smokes a day. That was reasonable.

Of course, he had to get the hell out of jail first.

It was a simple procedure. The zip tie cuffs weren't

off yet, and he still wore the orange jumpsuit, but the deputy had the paperwork out to sign, and his things were in a bin near his hip.

The room was gray cinderblock and steel. The air smelled like the ten thousand smokes that had been smoked here back in the day when it had been fine - hell, encouraged - to light up once every five minutes. He was just another guy going through the process, another sausage coming out of the blender.

Three other men stood behind Eric, a row of orange popsicles ready to hit the street. The one closest to him smelled like roadkill on a hot summer day and had hair like a thick smear of tar.

The deputy held out the clipboard and the attached papers to sign. Eric didn't have a cop fetish, but she caught his attention. She was attractive, in a "way too tired and over this and I might kill you" kind of way. Eric took the clipboard with his two hands and fumbled with the pen, as the cuffs made it awkward. Black bangs only partially concealed a scar along her forehead. Her dark eyes glanced up at him then back down at her paperwork.

"Hurry up," said the man who smelled like a dead raccoon on the side of the road.

"Yes, boss," Eric said under his breath.

The tendons in his hands popped out like piano wire, and the pen seemed small in his fingers as he signed.

"We don't need to see you again, Mr. Walters. Deal?"

Eric thought she sounded like that actress from *The*

Bob Newhart Show, but with a southern accent. It was sexy as hell.

He noted her name tag and used it.

"First time, last time, Deputy Paulina Campos. Stupid mistake. Call me Eric."

He handed the clipboard back to her, and she slid the bin full of his things closer while she reviewed his signatures.

"You're on a rocket ride to success, Mr. Walters."

"In a slump, ma'am."

"I checked your story. Archeology Major at Cal Berkeley but dropped out. Dinosaur bones aren't your thing?"

"That's paleontology. It's different. No dinosaurs."

"Why did you quit school?"

"Family finances went sideways and backwards after my folks died."

The roadkill man itched his scalp with great vigor and yawned.

"Then you were a Navy SEAL. Served in Desert Storm. OTH discharge just a few weeks ago. So you got kicked out with less than honors."

"Are we done?"

"Dropped out and then kicked out. And here you are."

"Here I am."

Paulina looked up at Eric and then back down to the paperwork. He noticed her strong, tanned hands. There were small scars around the knuckles and a tiny tattoo of a rose below her wrist.

"Shiner's lucky you didn't kill him."

"Who?"

"Mike Thomas. Shiner. The guy you two hit the other night."

"Two hit?"

"You hit him, and he hit the floor."

"Is he okay?"

"He's fine, from what I hear. He didn't press charges, so you're free to go find some new way to screw up your life."

Harsh but earned. Eric was relieved. His memory of the fight was fuzzy with whiskey and anger.

Roadkill farted, a real rattler, and waved his hands in the air in a gesture that meant either "get on with it" or "Please step aside, I've shit myself."

"Settle down, Charlie. I haven't slept and I'm not in the mood," she said with a yawn.

"I got places to be," said Roadkill Charlie.

The deputy rolled her eyes then looked back to Eric.

"You're from Wisconsin. Why are you in Bacopa County?"

Eric said nothing. He held out the cuffs. She smiled and cut the zip ties with a pair of pliers.

He stretched and rubbed his own thick shoulders. It felt good to have a little freedom of movement. His left elbow got a little too close to roadkill, and the old stinker had to take a step back.

"I'm going to FloridaWorld."

Paulina Campos smirked.

"Tickets to Disney too expensive?"

"They still have a waterski show, right? At FloridaWorld?"

"They do."

"I'm going to try out for the show. I can ski a little bit. Drive boats too. I'm going to get a job at the show."

The slight smile on Deputy Campos's face disappeared. She closed her eyes and saw the dead face of a man with an orange stuffed in his mouth.

"Do you think this incident might be a problem?" Eric asked. "I mean, do you think this might screw up my chance to get my foot in the door at the ski show?"

Deputy Campos didn't respond immediately, and when she did, her voice was so low that Eric had trouble hearing.

"No charges, no problem. You should be fine, if you can actually ski or drive a boat. Pretty sure there's an opening."

"Hey, maybe we can grab a coffee some morning," Eric said with more than a little hope in his voice. The deputy didn't acknowledge the pass.

He started rummaging through the bin. The shirt he'd been wearing when he finished the fight at the Grill wasn't spattered with blood anymore. Paulina Campos opened her eyes again, with effort, and scribbled information onto the paperwork.

They clean these things? Who knew?

Jeans, belt, underwear, socks, shoes, wallet, pack of

smokes, cheap plastic lighter, Oakleys, a little cash, and car keys. Check.

"Shiner's an asshole when he's drunk, so he probably deserved what you gave him, but he's a friend, so we'll take a raincheck on that coffee," said Paulina, her voice loud and confident again.

Eric unzipped the front of his orange jumpsuit.

"Slow down. Take your gear to the dressing room and change in there."

"Sorry," he said, "just eager to get some fresh air."

"No more fights. Stay out of trouble."

Eric picked up the bin and walked to the changing room. "My mistake. Won't happen again. And I'll count on that coffee."

"Oh, for fuck's sake, this ain't the Dating Game," said Roadkill Charlie.

Deputy Campos jerked her thumb at the dull gray changing room door. "Change."

"I'm trying. That's why I came here to lovely Bacopa County, the Citrus Capital of the World."

The deputy looked up at him. Eric felt his stomach flip a bit. Her dark hair was back in a tail, her uniform wasn't flattering, and her skin was slick with sweat. There were bags under her eyes that spoke to no sleep and plenty of stress. The scar on her forehead was white against her brown skin.

She was pretty and tough and she scared him more than just a little.

"Look, I'm sorry. Seriously. And I'm really here to try

out at FloridaWorld. Checking on a cash job in the interim," Eric said, "just something to get a paycheck so I stay out of trouble. Recycling place out near Lake May is looking for help. They had a sign up at the laundromat."

"Mid-Florida Recycling?" she asked.

"Yes. Why?"

She made a sound somewhere between a laugh, a sigh, and a yawn. "You'll see. Get your gear on and hit the road, Mr. Walters. Next. Your turn, Charlie."

Roadkill Charlie bowed with great elegance and slow clapped as he stepped forward.

#

Florida weather gets a bad rap but there are times, few to be sure, when the sky is a clear, cool blue, the wind is light, the air is crisp, and you would swear there could be no better place to be on the face of the planet.

Eric did not step into such a day.

It was hot for the time of year, thick, and there was no breeze, not even a bit.

Felt like Iraq.

His car waited for him, a dark blue 1979 Pontiac Firebird with a rebuilt four speed and an undercarriage so rusted from the salts of Wisconsin winter roads it was one big, red, mass.

His dad helped him rebuild the engine and clutch back when Eric was leaving for college. That was just before Mom and Dad passed and everything changed. A lifetime ago.

Eric was twenty yards from the Firebird when he heard the crunch of footsteps on gravel behind him.

"Excuse me, Mr. Walters," said an old man who looked like a boiled egg propped up by a pair of toothpicks. He had thick glasses, no hair, and was dressed in what Eric understood as "doctor casual." Khaki pants and a white lab coat. He reminded Eric of that psychiatrist in *Halloween*. His accent was so southern that Eric had trouble understanding him for a moment.

Eric turned and looked at the old man, but said nothing. He was tired and hot and done.

"You are Eric Walters, yes?"

Eric nodded affirmative.

"I am Dr. Claude Bluford."

"Right," said Eric.

"Do you have a moment?"

"What's this about?"

The doctor hesitated, and when he spoke, he lowered his voice. "I understand you are a man who finds things."

Eric felt a moment of genuine surprise.

"Excuse me?"

"It's so hot. Maybe we can discuss this over a cold drink?"

"No. This is fine."

"Well," said the doctor, "I review most cases that are booked through the Bacopa County Jail system as part of my duties and your resume intrigued me, so I did some quick research on you, Mr. Walters. I have friends in the Navy."

Eric interrupted him.

"Hold up. What are your duties?"

The doctor smiled. His teeth were brown nubs. "I am on the staff at the Bacopa County Mental Wellness Center. That's our new name. Much better than sanitarium, I think. More dignified."

"Sanitarium. You're a psychologist? I'm done." Eric walked away, and Dr. Bluford grabbed him by his arm.

Eric stared down at the doctor and he released the arm as if he'd been whipped.

"Sorry. I'm sorry. This is important, Mr. Walters. Can we at least move to the shade?" The man's head was wet with sweat.

"No," Eric said, "we can't."

"There's a great deal of money involved, potentially. Does that interest you?"

Does that interest me? I'm broke and living in my car until I can get a paycheck of some kind, Eric thought, *absolutely that interests me. But what a weird morning.*

"Go on."

"It's quite legal, for the most part, I think. But you are a man who finds things, yes?"

Eric's mouth tasted awful and all he could think about was getting away from this man and brushing his teeth. "Look, Claude, make it quick," he said.

"It's hot."

"Yes. Go on."

"The shade would be nice."

"You're losing me."

"Right."

The doctor took a deep breath then and when he spoke, his words came fast.

"Through my work with patients and their families at the sani...at our wellness center...I come to know many things, Mr. Walters. Some of those things are good and some are terrible, and I am sworn to secrecy in all cases. Recently, something came to my attention that was both terrible and, shall we say, lucrative? I am an older man, as you can see, sir, and I'm quite ready to retire from all this, but Bacopa County doesn't pay well and I've built up some debts - through no fault of anyone but me, to be fair. So the possibility of coming into a great deal of wealth was intriguing. But I'm an older man, as I've said, and no man of action, that's to be sure. These are the hands of a man who doesn't venture much, Mr. Walters. So I've been sitting on this information for too long. It's eating at me, Mr. Walters. And then, well, you entered the room. A man who finds things."

Dr. Bluford turned beet red and strained for a deep breath. The monologue had exhausted him.

Eric thought for a moment. At first he'd been worried that this was some sort of medical scam, then he thought that the man might be hitting on him, and now he wasn't sure.

"Look, Doc," he said, "I need some sleep. I'm not

going anywhere, at least for a while, so maybe you've got a card or something?"

The old man fumbled in his coat pocket and retrieved a battered business card. He handed it to Eric.

"Great. So here's the deal. I get some sleep and a shower somewhere and I'll be in touch. Cool?"

The doctor smiled again. "Of course. Just know that there's a time limit on this, Mr. Walters."

"How long?"

"Maybe a couple of months. Perhaps a few weeks or even days. The time limit isn't defined, but it is quite certain. A man is dying, sir. We need to have our discussion well before he expires."

"Wait. Is this about something that could help save this guy?"

"No, sir. This is about what he will leave behind."

Eric thought about that for a moment, then turned on his heel to leave Dr. Bluford sweating in the parking lot.

"Mr. Walters?"

Eric didn't turn around, but he stopped.

"What?"

"Why are you here?"

Eric turned then. "FloridaWorld. I'm here to try to get a job at the ski show. Do you know anyone who could help me out?"

Dr. Bluford smiled.

"I'm afraid my recommendation would not carry much weight, sir. It might actually be a hinderance to your cause. I'm sorry."

"Worth asking." Eric walked to his car then, and it had never looked so good.

I've gotta get away from that nut job.

The metal of his car door handle almost burned his hand when he touched it. The white pleather seats were dirty, and he thanked God that he wasn't wearing shorts because that would have been a ball-scalding nightmare.

What the actual fuck was that all about? I haven't been in town two days and I've been in a fight, been to jail, and been stalked by a creepy dude who speaks in riddles. I mean, what the actual fuck?

He took a glance into the backseat to make sure that the rest of his gear was still there. Yep. A blanket, a pillow, a pile of paperbacks, some odds and ends. Like a room at the Ritz.

Windows down. Smoke lit quick from the knobby little lighter with the hot orange ring on the dashboard. He glanced at the business card, then tucked it into the glove-box.

"Only three smokes today," he swore to himself, pretty sure he couldn't make that little wish come true.

Key in the ignition. Clutch down, gassed, engine roared, sputtered, then roared again. He checked himself in the rearview.

I guess the other guy didn't get much of a shot on me, he thought.

Just a scrape. Stubble, bloodshot eyes, but no real damage. One hand on the shifter, one hand on the wheel. Knuckles? A little scratched up, but nothing bad.

What the hell had the fight even been about? He couldn't remember, and it didn't matter now.

Fear of a Black Planet was in the cassette player. Eric wanted a CD player, but it was low on the list of necessities at this point, so he punched the play button and cranked it up.

Reverse, slow back out, then into first gear the second as he made his way through the lot toward FloridaWorld Drive.

The breeze felt wonderful on his face. The AC in the car could blow hot air if you were into that sort of thing, so Eric left it off.

Winter Paradise was more like his home in Wisconsin Dells than he'd ever imagined. So many lakes. Everywhere you went there was water, big lakes, little ponds, lakes everywhere. The lakes in the Dells didn't have dinosaurs in them, so there was a difference there, but man what lakes. Roadside motels, hotels, tourist traps? Check. They flashed past as Eric drove, most built back in the '50s when this place was destination number one for tourists, back before Walt built his mouse temple out by Orlando. There was Fudge-O-Rama, offering fudge of all kinds, even the exotic "goat fudge" that seemed to be a big enough deal to take up most of the street sign. There was Willy's World of Boots, Galaxy of Citrus, restaurants, bars, and little shacks that might once have been something for the whole family, but now were tattoo parlors and skin joints.

You could see what had once been something pure, something shining, something that could attract the world to Bacopa County. That spirit was still there, but the mouse had it by the throat and was strangling it more every day.

Eric had been in Bacopa County for a couple of days and he could already see it, could feel the slow decay everywhere you looked.

This place must have been something, that's for sure, back in the day.

He jammed his smoke out in the little metal ashtray.

The sign at the laundromat said "Mid-Florida Recycling - Now Hiring Laborers."

Anything to put some quick cash in his wallet would do.

"Well, let's give it a try," he said as he pulled into the gravel lot and *B Side Wins Again* blasted through the Alpines.

After all, apparently I'm a man who finds things. Let's see if I can find a way to make some money.

#

It was a tall and open warehouse of aluminum and steel that stretched the length of a football field. There were no fans inside, so the air was still. The smell was the smell of backwash beer in countless cans that had been sitting in the Florida sun for days or more, the pungent reek of moldy newspapers bundled into bunches, and the sharp stink of the diesel fuel that powered the bailer where things were crushed and packaged to be taken away.

Eric walked inside the main office, a little hut partitioned off to one side of the great warehouse. The owner of Mid-Florida Recycling was a bulldog on two legs, with sweaty skin and a scalp of close cropped silver nails.

"Excuse me, sir," said Eric, "I saw your ad. Are you still hiring?"

Two red eyes shifted from the "Club" magazine to Eric, gave him a quick look up and down, then returned to his soft core porn.

"Pays cash. Twenty bucks a day at the end of each shift. We open up at seven in the morning and close at five. No weed or liquor while you're working the bailer. Can you count out cash?"

"Yes sir. I've run a till."

"You just got a promotion. Congratulations. Twenty-two bucks a day. Go tell Bobby to show you the ropes and he'll get you started."

That was that.

Bobby was a giant but a kind one and he walked Eric around the layout. Simple work. People would show up at the front dock and drop off anything from old car batteries to bundles of magazines. All walks of life. Expensive trucks loaded down with bags of beer cans would pull in and so would homeless old men pushing Publix carts with little black garbage bags of a dozen or so cans. All the same. Eric would weigh the trash and pay out cash straight from the till. Once there was a big enough load of aluminum or paper, they'd fire up the bailer and slice open the bags or bundles, and dump it in to be crushed into nice big cubes.

Eric had never seen so many roaches. That first garbage bag he sliced open with a box cutter spilled out dozens of beer and pop cans and then erupted into a frenzy of inch long dark brown palmetto bugs that skittered and tried to take flight. It was horrific, but Eric needed the money, so he just kept cutting bags and shaking the bugs from his clothes.

The place was hot. It smelled awful and Eric was soon soaked with the juice from countless rancid cans. There were a handful of other workers. Bobby was the chief. An old man who was built like a bowling ball and never said a word worked the bailer more often than not.

Eric was carrying a bundle of old magazines to the paper pile when there was the sound of a heavy engine and heavy tires. The forklift came to a hard stop next to him, and Eric looked up at the driver.

"Ah, damn," he said as a flood of memory hit him.

A wiry little guy with a swollen eye sat in the driver's seat of the forklift. A cigarette dangled from his mouth.

"You back for another ass kicking, champ?" asked the wiry little man through a cloud of smoke.

He slammed his hand on the wheel of the forklift. A horn blew.

"Hey fellas," shouted the little guy, "this is the poor bastard I beat the hell out of the other night!"

Eric had a fuzzy memory of holding the forklift driver

by the neck and trying to avoid flailing fists.

Well, of all things, he thought, this day is an absolute rollercoaster.

"Hey, I'm sorry about all that," Eric said.

The wiry little guy laughed.

"I had it coming. I get lippy when I've been into the Cuervo. Only reason I didn't go to jail with you is I know people and you don't. Name's Shiner. Kind of like what you gave me."

"I'm Eric. Thanks for not pressing charges."

"Do I look like a bitch to you?"

"Thanks anyway. I don't remember much."

"Neither do I, so we'll call it even. No hard feelings, Mike Tyson." And with that, Shiner Thomas went back to handling the forklift and Eric went back to scattering bugs and slicing bags.

Lunch break was a half hour at noon. Bobby dropped a bag of sandwiches onto a table and men gathered around.

"Boss man always pays for lunch. He's got a deal with the Jiffy Mart down the road. Sandwich, chips, and a Coke," Bobby said for Eric's benefit. "Get yourself some."

Eric's hands were thick with rancid backwash, but he was hungry, so he grabbed a wrapped Cuban and dug in. Shiner Thomas ran over from the forklift and sat with the others.

"I'd eat the asshole out of a dead raccoon, fellas, step back," he said. Shiner smiled at Eric and extended his hand. "Don't hit me."

Eric shook his hand.

"No promises."

The men began telling rude jokes and giving each other a hard time, as men often do. The food and drink were gone in an instant, but there was time left on their break, so playing cards came out. Eric declined.

"I'll need a payday before I'm good to play," he said.

"Where you from, man?"

Eric wanted a cigarette, so he lit up his number two for the day. "Wisconsin."

"No shit," said Shiner. "I know some people from Wisconsin. Bunch of jack offs, each of them. Packers suck," he said with deadly seriousness.

Eric didn't take the bait. The little guy was a bundle of energy, a hot wire quick with a joke and an insult and a smoke. Couldn't weigh more than a buck ten and probably not much older than Eric.

Harmless.

"Jack offs. Sounds about right. But our new quarterback is the real deal, sparky," said Eric, also deadly serious.

"What the hell are you doing in Bacopa County? You kill somebody? Selling crack? Baby diddler?"

Eric didn't mention FloridaWorld or the waterski show because he felt that it would have sounded silly. He could have said "I grew up wanting to be a skier or a boat driver at FloridaWorld and I'm running out of time, running out of chances, running out of everything. So, I'm here because my parents are gone, my career is dead, and I'm chasing a stupid dream."

He could have said that, but he didn't.

"Need to make some cash short-term to pay for gas and food and a place to stay. I've got something else I want to do while I'm in Bacopa County. Personal business," Eric said.

"Never mind that shit. Nobody cares. Did you hear about the two nuns in the strip club?"

Shiner proceeded to hold court with a series of jokes, each one filthier and more offensive than the next. By the time the break was done, the men were all laughing so hard that there were tears in their eyes.

The day was long, and the work was hard, but it was simple and Eric fell into the rhythm of things. A boombox on the cash counter was tuned to a local AM station that played R&B and amateurish local commercials, and Eric soon found himself feeling better than he had in some time.

The shadows grew long inside the warehouse. The bulldog man came out and pulled a rope across the entry to the place. Closed for the day. The men lined up and the bulldog man handed out their cash for the day.

Eric walked outside to a setting sun and a light breeze that felt good after the stale air of the warehouse. Bobby slapped Eric on the back as he walked off.

"Smoke?"

It was Shiner. The little guy offered Eric a cigarette. Eric waved it off with a smile.

"I'm trying to quit. I'm on a three a day plan. Thanks, though."

"Coward," said Shiner as he lit up. "God hates a quitter. You need a place to crash?"

"Well, I was going to see if I could find a cheap motel room. Been sleeping in the car, but it's damned hot and a room with a shower would be nice."

Shiner saw Eric's Firebird parked in the lot. He whistled. "Nice ride. You hauling Coors to Tex-Arkana?"

"Funny. She's seen better days," Eric said.

"Haven't we all. Look, let's grab a case of beer and you can crash on my couch until you get a few more paychecks in your wallet."

"That's nice, man, but I don't want to impose."

"Screw that. Serious talk, though, before you say yes because you'd hear it from somebody eventually," said Shiner, and he looked hard into Eric's eyes as he spoke. "I'm gay as Christmas. No shit, not kidding, that's just who I am. Not one for the ladies. Playing ball for the other team. So, if you have issues with it, then I can't help you. Believe me, I'm a fucking unicorn here in Bacopa County, but for some reason, I haven't been run out of town yet. Must be my charming personality. Anyway, you'd find out from the guys at work, so I'm just being upfront. You still cool?"

Eric shrugged.

"I'm cool. Doesn't matter to me. I'll take you up on that offer, too. Tired of sleeping in the car."

"Cool, cool. You'll need to drive, though. I've been riding the bus since my DUI."

Eric thought about it for a hot second.

"Sure. Beer sounds good, too. Thanks."

#

The house was little more than a shack, but what a view. A million-dollar view.

Shiner Thomas's place was a one-bedroom shotgun shack on the shores of Lake Michelle. The Firebird's tires crunched the pale Myakka soil driveway that led through the pine trees down to the little white house with the tin roof and tiny screened in back porch. There were no streetlights, so when Eric shut off the ignition it was like somebody put a bag over his head for a moment and then there was a blue glow from the moon and stars. The air smelled of lake water and pine, crickets played leg violins, and there were little chirps that he'd learned were frogs.

Shiner carried the case of Budweiser under his arm like a football and made his way to the aluminum and screen front door. Eric brought the bag of ice and an open beer.

"Mi casa es su casa, my friend. It ain't fancy, but the futon folds out and you're more than welcome to hang as long as you need," Shiner said.

"Thanks, man. I appreciate it. I'll be out of your hair as soon as I get some cash."

"No worries."

The inside of Shiner's mansion was surprisingly tidy.

The little guy kept things clean. The futon, an overstuffed chair, a small television on a stack of milk crates. A kitchen area big enough for one. A little hallway that led to the bathroom and the single bedroom in the back. Another metal and screen door led out to the back porch. Shiner led the way there, snapping on a couple of lights as he went.

"You can throw the ice and beer in that cooler. I gotta drain the zipper weasel."

Shiner scrambled off to the bathroom. Eric filled the cooler and sat in one of the two lawn chairs that faced out to the lake, beer in hand. Shiner was back in no time. He sat in the other chair and cracked a beer and a fart.

"Great location," Eric said.

"Thanks. Not bad. Lake Michelle is one of the smaller ones on the chain, but it's wicked quiet. Nobody comes back here. There are a few houses like this around the shore. Shotgun shacks from back when this was all citrus industry. These were the worker houses. Some of the guys will drop the boat in now and then and we'll take a ski run."

"Citrus isn't a thing anymore?"

"Real estate. In ten years, there'll be mansions all along this lake and every lake in the chain. You go to Winn Dixie and the only oranges you'll get are from Mexico."

"What happened?"

Shiner sparked up a tightly rolled joint and took a

deep hit. He offered, but Eric waved him off.

"If I need to get tested for a job, I need to be clean. Thanks, though. Rain check," said Eric.

Shiner shrugged. "Disney happened, that's what happened. Orlando blew up, Tampa blew up, then there was SeaWorld and Universal. Now it's all about real estate. I figure FloridaWorld has just a couple of years left before they need to sell. Nobody comes out here to Bacopa County anymore."

Eric considered it for a moment.

"Well, sounds like you can sell this place for a fortune," he said.

Shiner laughed. "It's a rental. The old bastard who owns the place will kick me to the curb once the offers get high enough."

"Let's hope that doesn't happen too soon," Eric said.

"Amen, brother. If I ever won the lottery, I'd buy this old shack and fix it up nice. Guys like me don't win the lottery, though. No such luck."

They drank their beers and watched the dark waters of Lake Michelle for a moment.

"This might seem like a weird question," said Eric, "but do you know any of the skiers from FloridaWorld?"

Shiner raised his eyebrows.

The little man reached into the cooler and pulled out another cold one. Popped the top and handed it to Eric.

"Maybe. Why do you ask?"

"That's why I'm here. I'd like to ski at the show. I was

a skier, back in the day, with my family in Wisconsin. Always loved it."

It seemed as if Eric was going to continue, but he didn't. He just stared off, focusing on nothing.

Shiner let the silence reign for a minute then took another toke. His cheeks bulged like one of those green tree frogs Eric had seen clinging to the walls at the processing plant.

"Small world. I ski at FloridaWorld on Saturdays and Sundays. I suck, so I'm usually doing the clown act," Shiner said with a gasp through a cloud of weed smoke.

Eric looked at Shiner as if he'd just grown another head.

"You're a skier?"

"Hard to believe, I know," Shiner said, "but most of this town has had some connection to FloridaWorld so I was just doing my patriotic duty. Still, like I said, I suck."

"If you ski professionally at FloridaWorld, I doubt that you suck," Eric said, and sipped his beer.

"Well, compared to most of the guys. I'm better than some weekend Wally, though. And clown isn't as easy as you think. Especially with our new show theme. That's a whole other shit storm, there."

They sat for a moment. Shiner farted again without apology or fanfare. He drank deeply of his beer.

"Some people say there's no such thing as destiny or coincidence. Just random things that sometimes intersect in ways that make you scratch your head. I'm in that camp, especially at the moment, because it's been a really weird day," said Eric.

"Dude. Are we going deep? I can go deep. The SS Minnow set sail on the three-hour tour the day after the Kennedy assassination. You can see the flag in the harbor at half-mast in the opening of the show. Here's something deep to chew on. The Skipper got that boat shipwrecked on purpose. Someone on the island is the killer."

"What?"

"I thought we were going deep. Ginger shot JFK. She was a tool for Castro."

"That's where you're wrong. It was the Howells. Why do you think they packed so many clothes?"

"Good point."

"Look, what I was talking about before you went off on a tangent is coincidence. The random nature of things. Is everything just coincidence or is there some cosmic plan? I want to try out for a job with the FloridaWorld ski show. Now it turns out that I'm talking to a skier. Makes you wonder."

"Brother, like I said, you can't swing a cat in Bacopa County without hitting somebody who had something to do with that show over the years. I ain't special. I can put in a good word, though. Introduce you to the show manager."

"Thank you."

"Better get in now before they shut the fucking place down. It's on the skids. What makes you want to work there?"

Eric took a deep pull on his beer.

"A dream since I was a kid, reading about it, watching stories about this magical place called FloridaWorld on tv," he said, "and I'm at a point and a place where maybe I should go all in on dreams. Nothing else has worked."

"What's your thing? Barefoot? Jump? Doubles?"

"I can barefoot but I'm really into driving. Drove my Mom and Dad around back in the day, drove for our little ski team in Wisconsin when I was just a kid. Got real familiar with fast boats in the Navy."

Shiner started humming the song by Village People, then stopped and said, "I'm scheduled at FloridaWorld tomorrow, but not at the ski show. Tuesdays I'm a piss monkey. Can you be up and ready to go by seven? I could use a ride."

Eric nodded affirmative. Did Shiner say something about being a piss monkey?

"Wait," said Shiner, "something you said just registered. You're a military guy?"

Eric nodded yes.

"Navy SEAL."

"Those are the bad asses that go in and do crazy stealth shit like sneaking into palaces and knifing heads of state or making out with beautiful princesses while their daddy, the Sheik of Turdistan, fingers a donkey in the next room. Am I right?"

"Not even close."

Shiner whistled and farted again. "I'm lucky you didn't kill me."

"Yes, you are."

"So you drove a boat in battle? You water-skied in Operation Desert Storm? No shit? Bad ass."

Eric didn't quite know how to respond. "Well, no. Not at all. Different kind of boats."

"Oh. Right."

"That would have been something, though. Barefooting onto the beach at Al Mishab," Eric said with a smile.

"Would have rocked the casbah. Well, if you can drive a boat, we might have something for you. Don't mean to sound callous, but there's an opening, that's for sure. One of our drivers was killed. Murdered. It was all over the news."

"I heard about it," Eric said.

"Awful stuff. I loved PBR like a brother. Still, we have an opening for a driver now."

"That's cold."

"Just keeping it real. No promises, but walk around the park tomorrow and see what you think. Might be right up your alley."

"Park? Just so we're clear you're talking about -"

"FloridaWorld."

9

Friday Night

Eric knew the tall man in the corner was going to hurt him, but he also knew that he was in a dream, and all he had to do was scream and he would wake himself up. He just had to scream, but he couldn't find enough breath. He couldn't open his mouth and force the sound out of his throat.

The tall figure was a shimmer, a horror, and all he had to do was scream because none of this was real.

He was going to die in his dream.

He fought to breathe, his heart pounding and his terror growing by the moment.

That man in the corner was shimmering faster. Eric didn't want to see his face because in that white shimmer, he might see something more horrible than he could imagine.

In the white shimmer, there was a face struggling to escape and when it escaped, it would swallow Eric whole. That face in the shimmer was his father, his mother, the boy in Kuwait with the colorful backpack. It would be that spider in Khafji the size of his head. It would be the isolation, the drift in the darkness after the shit went down, his men were gone, and he was in that boat alone.

If he saw that face, and it was coming, it was almost here, he would never wake up.

He made a sound, a cry, then another, louder, then he screamed, but he couldn't wake up.

Eric was awake and yet not, just in that drift, nothing around him for miles, for years, nothing except the shimmering man in the corner who contained so many things that would hurt him.

He screamed as loud as he could and that's when Shiner slapped him hard across the face.

"Dude," Shiner said, "wake up! It's a dream! Dude!"

Eric shoved the little man hard in the chest and sat up in bed. He was soaked with sweat and his heart was racing. His throat was raw.

Shiner almost fell, but staggered up and stepped back from Eric.

"It's a dream, man," he said again. "Holy shit."

Eric looked around the small living room. It was still dark. The taste of stale beer was in his mouth. He didn't know at first where he was and then it all came back to him.

"Sorry," he said, his voice quiet. "That's embarrassing. Thanks for waking me up."

"Must have been some nightmare. You didn't piss the futon, did you?" he said.

Eric wiped the sweat from his face. The dream was fading, as they all did. The terrors were getting worse, and Eric didn't know what to do about it.

"Didn't piss. Yeah, some nightmare." Eric said. "I get 'em sometimes. Sorry to freak you out."

Shiner found his cigarettes on the little kitchen table and fired up a Marlboro Light. Eric raised his hand.

"You got a smoke I can bum?"

Shiner tossed the pack to Eric.

This wouldn't count against his three a day plan. Night terror smokes were exempt.

His hands shook, and he had trouble lighting the smoke.

"What was it about?"

Eric's faced glowed from the lighter and then the ember of the cigarette.

"I can't remember. Something was trying to kill me. I couldn't breathe. Just a dream. I never remember them when they're bad like this."

"Does that happen a lot?"

Eric smiled.

"More lately. Started when I was overseas. Made me real popular with my squad."

"I bet. Hey, no worries, my brother. We all have our demons. I'll see you in the morning." Shiner walked off into the darkness to his bedroom.

Eric sat on the foldout futon and he could see the lake beyond the yard and silver under the moon. His head hurt, his heart was still pounding, and the cigarette smoke was rough on his throat.

There was a time when he would have called his parents just to talk things through and settle himself down. He stared at the old rotary phone on the kitchen wall and for a moment, he thought he was going to cry.

He could call the old number, but they wouldn't answer because they were dead. The bank took the house and certainly the family phone was part of the deal, along with everything else.

"Jesus, get a grip," he said to himself.

He listened and imagined the voice of his father. His dad, in particular, had a way of talking Eric down from whatever ledge he found himself on. He could say a few words, slowly and with great deliberation, and Eric would feel like things were slipping back into place, into a good place, or at least a manageable place.

He missed the voices of his parents.

He missed the belief that everything was fine.

He missed feeling connected to anything.

His heartbeat slowed a little, but Eric still felt a strange sense of separation. Everything around him seemed just out of reach, as if he was an astronaut on a spacewalk and someone had cut the line that connected him to his ship. Now he was just floating in space, floating alone in a universe of cold, black, nothingness.

Floating alone until he died.
No more sleep tonight.

10

Saturday

"Just drop me at the Jiffy, my brother," Shiner said through a cigarette clenched in his teeth. The air was cool, coming in through the open windows of the Firebird as they made their way down Lemon Pip Lane.

Eric pulled into the Jiffy Store parking lot. Shiner was digging through his fanny pack.

"Got something for you. A little something for the effort," he said. He pulled a paper ticket out of the pack and dropped it into the change bin behind the stick shift.

"Don't you need a ride the rest of the way?"

Shiner hopped out of the car as he spoke. He had a lot of energy for this early in the morning. "Not really. FloridaWorld is walking distance from here and I want to pick up some food for lunch later. This place makes some amazing burritos. And I like to flirt with the guy behind the counter. Makes him nervous as hell. Super awkward."

Eric picked up the ticket and gave it a glance. "What's this?"

"Free pass to FloridaWorld. I'll meet you at the first ski show of the day, then introduce you to some folks. Get your foot in the door. Adios, dude." Shiner jetted off into the Jiffy Store.

Eric pulled out of the lot and spotted a McDonald's just a few blocks down the road. He shifted into third and made his way down the blacktop four lane that bisected the strip malls and fast-food huts where a family living hand to mouth on a theme park paycheck could shop and eat and still have enough left over for a trip to Blockbuster. The chain stores and dime a dozen local shops thrived because of FloridaWorld and they would die alongside her.

Now we're in the nasty nineties and this corner of FloridaWorld Drive, Lemon Pip Lane, and Tangelo Boulevard is where the bourgeoisie drive past for greener pastures, he thought.

He pulled into the parking lot and found a spot near the entrance. The car made a satisfying thud as he slammed the door and locked up.

The air was thick and hot, the sky gray without clouds. He'd ditched the jeans for cargo shorts and the Oakleys dangled from his neck on a pair of straps. There were cigarette butts, scraps of trash, and some "action fresh" condoms like fat wet worms by his black L.A. Gears in the crabgrass and sand spurs of the parking lot.

He tried to imagine the place where he stood on the hot summer morning if he could hop in a DeLorean and go back to a time when all around were the green of orange groves, the white of the buds, the impossibly beautiful scent of the bloom.

He remembered sitting in the boathouse on his family's place on the lake in Wisconsin, reading magazines about distant Florida, about the sun and the dolphins and the beautiful people and beautiful things. There had been a magazine, a colorful shiny thing called "Water Follies" that showcased the pros and the amateurs of his chosen sport. Ads for boats and ropes and skis held provocatively by women in bikinis and guys in short shorts.

But most of all, there had been articles about this place.

Writers soiled themselves gushing about the glories of what Irv Irving, the Godfather of Water Spectacles, had created out of whole cloth on this massive lake in Central Florida. Before Walt became the Godhead, there had been Irv Irving and his paradise by the inland sea where thousands came to see the bronze and beautiful skiers dare the jump ramp, dart about in mini-boats, perform the elegant adagio of the liquid stage, and barefoot across the dark, calm waters.

These were the dreams Eric had dreamt of this place, the impossible destination called FloridaWorld.

Eric wondered if memories lingered in inanimate things, if spirits or echoes from other times could be recorded into the roads and shops and land all around. If so, what would these streets think of life in the latter stages of the 20th century? What would be on the minds of the tourist ghosts from days gone by who might haunt the tattoo parlor, the Blockbuster, and the adult book shop.

Eric imagined the spirit of a father roaming the aisles of a porn shop that was once a FloridaWorld souvenir shop, trying to find a toy alligator for his son, confused by the skin magazines and exotic marital enhancements. Or, the ephemeral but still sexy aspiring show skier from the golden age of FloridaWorld, unable to make sense of the empty stores, the faded signs, and the sometimes quiet streets.

He piloted his car through the fading old town and felt an urge to smoke. He buried the urge with thoughts of food. According to Shiner, the park entrance was just down the road, but the gates wouldn't open until nine in the morning.

A piss monkey? Shiner said he was going to be a piss monkey today. Can't wrap my head around that, thought Eric, *but I'm intrigued.*

He had time to kill, so Eric entered the McDonald's and soon sat with a coffee, an egg sandwich, a copy of the "Winter Paradise Daily Juicer" that was free for the taking on an empty table, and his thoughts.

His massive stash of cash was now down to nineteen

bucks and change. Things would be lean for a couple of days.

The local paper was lean, too. The lead story was about the poor bastard found underneath the boat dock, tenderizing in the murk. The driver from the ski show. There were quotes from friends and colleagues, glowing endorsements of the man's character. The paper even quoted a Deputy Pauline Campos that was a short and to the point statement. "Jammed under a boat dock with an orange stuffed in his mouth. Bad way to go. He was a friend. We'll find who did it."

No wonder the deputy seemed exhausted when she was signing me out. She's had a rough couple of days, thought Eric.

The big metal and glass front door slammed open.

The kid who ran into the Mickey D's was wearing bright blue gym shorts and a white polo shirt to go with his K-Swiss tennis shoes. He came into the place on a wave of Drakkar Noir.

There was nobody else at the counter, so the kid walked right up to the little elderly woman in the red and yellow uniform and jammed his finger in her chest.

"I want all your biscuits, right now. Hand 'em over, Lilly," he said.

Eric tensed. The kid wore a backpack and immediately every part of Eric felt like he was plugged into a socket. Backpacks were not always a good thing, not at all. He'd seen backpacks do horrible things in Iraq and even though he was thousands of miles away, he was back there in an instant when he stared at that aggressive kid and his backpack.

The kid reached into his backpack then and pulled out the biggest rubber penis Eric had ever seen. And he'd seen a few.

The kid flipped a switch at the base of the penile shaft, and the shocking phallus vibrated.

"I said all the biscuits now, Lilly, or say hello to my little friend!" the kid shouted as he shoved the vibrating member into the cashier's face.

"Mother of God!" screamed the cashier. She was elderly and Eric assumed it had been some time since she'd been confronted with such a tally whacker.

The restaurant manager came around the corner then. His eyes were wide and his face was as red as his apron. He held an order of hash browns in one hand and a cup of coffee in the other.

"Oh, for the love of -" he started to say, but he was interrupted by a tall, muscular man in tight spandex who burst through the other side doors. His flowing cape was made of gold fabric, and so was the lucha libre mask that covered most of his face. Bright white teeth shined through a wide smile. The man reminded Eric of a pro wrestler from one of those regional wrestling shows he had watched as a kid.

"Courage, dear citizen! Commander Freedom is here to save the day!"

Eric looked at his coffee and wondered who slipped him the purple microdot because this had to be a hallucination.

The kid with the rubber penis looked startled, melodramatically so, like something from a cartoon.

"Curses! Foiled again! You'll never capture me, you caped clown!"

Dildo boy screamed and dashed toward the door.

Commander Freedom pointed heroically, legs akimbo, and shouted the inevitable: "After that arch criminal!"

He ran, but the manager reached out and snagged the shiny gold cape. This stopped Commander Freedom in his tracks.

"Gary," said the manager, "you can't go around shoving dildos at our employees. Especially Lilly Rosenbaum; she's a widow, for Christ's sake. Come on, man."

Commander Freedom saluted the manager and walked in the most super heroic manner out the door, arms pumping, long strides, and chin held awkwardly high. His Cool Water scent was graced with more than a touch of weed.

The manager put his arm around the cashier. She was near tears.

"It was so huge, Arnie, and it was wriggling in the most unholy way." She looked as if she'd just stared into the maw of hell.

"It was a horror, Lilly. Why don't you go take five in the break room?"

Lilly made a moaning sound and clutched at her

throat as she wandered off.

Eric sipped his coffee and watched as Commander Freedom and his arch nemesis ran out of the McDonalds and across the street.

They did so quite dramatically, stopping upon occasion to throw mock blows at each other.

"Sorry about that, sir," the manager said. The man was at Eric's table, visibly embarrassed.

"No problem. Lucky for us, Commander Freedom showed up," Eric said.

The manager didn't laugh. "They're good kids. Once in a while they smoke the whacky weed and get up to no good, that's all. Locals. They ski over at FloridaWorld. Commander Freedom is on the pro waterski tour. When he's not, you know, being a goofball."

"They're water-skiers?"

The manager tilted his head slightly, surprised.

"Why, yes they are, sir. Rowdy, but with good hearts."

"I grew up in Wisconsin by a lake. We had a really small amateur ski team. They were like family. And most of us were rowdy."

The manager smiled. "Those boys are shook up, I bet, letting off steam after what happened to old PBR," the manager said, and his eyes drifted to the newspaper headline.

"I'm sorry. You knew him?"

"Everybody around here knows PBR. Dumb as a skillet, but wouldn't hurt a soul. Must have gotten mixed up in drugs. Lots of that around here, nowadays."

The manager leaned over and lowered his voice.

"If I had to put money on it, I'd say those migrants down in the groves had something to do with it. Gang vengeance, like in Mexico."

He looked around, as if frightened of being overheard. "Anyway, can I buy you another cup of coffee? For the disturbance?"

"Sure."

The second cup was better than the first. Probably a fresh batch.

A patrol car passed outside the window at one point and Eric wondered if that sexy deputy Campos was on duty. The coffee would have tasted even better with her sitting in the booth by his side.

That ship has sailed, he thought. *Won't see her again unless I get into another brawl.*

The breakfast was a hit to his finances, but the food gave him some energy. And the entertainment had been fine.

Eric pulled Shiner's theme park ticket out of his pocket and gave it a look. He considered how much he could make by selling it to some tourist.

No. I'm doing this. Worst that could happen is they say no.

"Hey, handsome," said the whisper-thin woman in the yellow and red uniform, "we have a thing here where, if you want to stay, you need to pay. After an hour, we'd rather you move on. You've had to sit through the sideshow with the plastic ding dong, so we'll cut you some slack. But rules is rules, all and still. Please and thank you."

Eric smiled and put aside the newspaper.

"No problem," he said.

The server leaned in and pointed at the newspaper. When she spoke again, her voice was low.

"That poor boat driver. The one who was murdered. I think it was one of those skier pranks that went too far. Now it's a coverup. A conspiracy."

She touched her finger to her lips and nodded knowingly to Eric.

"You never know."

"Ain't that the truth, sweetie," she said and returned to the other customers.

Eric drained the last of his coffee.

Time to go to Florida World, he thought.

#

Eric saw the place as he crested a little rise just past the last row of cars in the parking lot. Green grass and lush landscaping softened the edges of the asphalt and concealed the security fence.

It's kind of beautiful, he thought.

The park was nestled away from the overdeveloped chaos of the main road and the instant Eric saw it, he felt transported back to the 1960s. The clean, retro lines, the bold fonts and the bright colors, the hues you might see on a citrus postcard from back when man was flying to the moon.

The place, the park, looked optimistic, if a place can be such a thing.

The sun was citrus yellow and hovered just over the top of the large orange, blue, and white "FloridaWorld" sign that straddled the path, held aloft by massive white and blue columns. The sun touched everything with a wonderful golden morning glow. A wide path meandered along the foliage and toward a row of ticket booths. Eric could smell orange blossoms as he walked, and the scent was rich and pleasant.

Citrus trees in bloom lined parts of the pathway. Nice touch. He hadn't seen many orange groves on his drive up from the port.

There were already quite a few people making their way toward the entrance to the park. Seniors dressed in light linens were passed by running kids and excited families. A stocky woman in a *Lynyrd Skynyrd* t-shirt practically stiff-armed Eric as she rushed toward the ticket turnstiles, followed by a thin man with an epic mullet whose flip-flops made slapping noises as he walked.

He presented his free ticket to the young woman behind the screen, and she smiled and waved him on. The bill of fare indicated that a single ticket into this place would have kept Eric in cigarettes and beer for a month.

The entrance plaza, the area before the turnstiles that let you into the park, was a space half the size of a football field. Pavers had been laid to create the shape of an orange. Or a lemon. He couldn't tell.

A building to his left was built to resemble an enormous shark. Restrooms. Next to that, a tiny kiosk shaped like a citrus fruit selling all manner of upgrades. Across the plaza, there was a stand selling soft drinks and hot dogs.

There came, then, a voice. It was warm and grandfatherly. *If this isn't the voice of the legendary Irv Irving, then it's some guy doing a decent impression,* Eric thought.

Eric knew that voice.

"It's a blessed morning, sunshine friends," said the voice of Irv Irving. "We ask that you now please take off your hats and place your hand over your heart for the singing of our national anthem."

There were easily a hundred or so people already standing in the plaza now and they all obeyed the voice. Baseball caps came off, hands were lifted, eyes shifted here and there, looking for an American flag to focus on.

Oh. There are the stars and bars. Right below the "FloridaWorld" flag on the flagpole by the pisser.

Eric started calculating while Lee Greenwood crooned the anthem. *Let's say there are a hundred people here right this minute, each paying for a ticket and parking certainly wasn't free. Hundreds more will be pouring through those gates today. Maybe thousands more. That's real money,* he thought.

The song ended, some wag shouted, "Play ball!" and heads were covered once more.

"Thank you, sunshine friends. FloridaWorld is now open. Come surf your way through a magical day."

Eric had a moment, then. The running of the bulls? Kid's stuff compared to the mad dash for the turnstiles. Families, couples, creepy single men with big cameras, everyone raced to the turnstiles like Irv himself was going to be there bigger than life and handing out jello shots.

Then came the stilt-walkers.

There were three of them.

One was a lizard of some sort, the next was an orange blossom, and the last was inexplicably an Egyptian Pharaoh, complete with Staff of Ra. It would make more sense if Eric knew that the costume was a leftover from the temporary "Curse of the Camel's Toe" exhibit, now used at the park opening every morning in place of the original "Southern Belle costume" because the "Belle" dress was soiled beyond redemption during a debauched after-hours park party.

Eric hoped that the stilt-walkers didn't have megaphones, but of course, they did and they pitched the various amusements available in the park that day. They seemed to concentrate on items available for purchase, oddly enough.

Eric no longer smelled orange blossoms. Now he smelled popcorn, sunscreen, and body odor.

"Can I help make your day shine, sunshine friend?"

Eric nearly jumped out of his skin.

The lizard stilt-walker was bent over and right in his face. The kid didn't look old enough to shave and his smile was a rictus of teeth in a variety of positions, none of them straight.

"I'm good, thanks," said Eric.

"Grab a park map. They're free of charge until 9:02 and you've got seconds to spare," said the stilt-walking lizard kid. His breath was the minty scent of chewing tobacco.

What? No wonder there was a stampede to get into this place, Eric thought as he walked to the kiosk that held park maps.

A loud buzzer sounded the moment after he grabbed his copy. A man in a blue and orange outfit appeared out of nowhere and stood bodyguard over the kiosk. He had a change belt around his waist and his expression said, "these fuckers are no longer free. Hand over your cash or I will cut you."

"How much? Just out of curiosity."

The man didn't look at Eric as he answered. He was focused on his maps.

"Ten bucks. Buy three or more and save ten percent. That's the family map for a day plan. New this year and recommended."

"Why 9:02? That's specific."

The map man looked Eric up and down as if he were inspecting an alien species. "9:02 in the AM April 15th of the year 1952 is when FloridaWorld opened her doors for the first time. That's historical, young man. Important numbers."

"Roger that," Eric said.

Eric stepped through the turnstiles with a loud thunk and a stiff blow to his hip from the metal bar. He moved out of the traffic flow to look at the map.

Oh, I get it, he thought. *This really is Florida World. As in all of Florida, in one place.*

That was the idea. See all of Florida in a day.

Eric tried to imagine some bright morning in 1946 and a young Irv Irving pitching the concept to potential investors.

That must have been some pitch meeting.

#

The map was crammed with so much information that it was almost impossible to decipher and navigate. There was a cartoonish sketch of the park's layout with different attractions highlighted, a list of restaurants and shops, different ads for special appearances and shows.

Eric scanned the performance times. The waterski show had two performances, one at noon and the other at four. Time to kill before the first, where he was supposed to meet up with Shiner. He gave up trying to make a plan and just started walking along the main path. It was designed to look like a small town from the 1940s with little gift shops and snack huts. Kids ran in and out of the candy store, the soda shop, and a magic shop where you could buy all manner of trickery.

The central square was a lovingly tended

horticultural piece, a topiary of a huge alligator surrounded by beds of flowers. The gator was easily twenty feet long and was posed as if rising up to strike. Eric approached and noticed a small bronze plaque below the thing, embedded in the garden.

"Monstro - The Titan of the Swamps. Rest In Peace."

Hmm. Must have been some gator.

Eric meandered down the pathway for a minute or so, peaking into storefront windows at the colorful gifts and snacks.

There was an old-fashioned theater marquee on the facade of a tall building to his left.

"See the Story of FloridaWorld!"

Sure, thought Eric, and he walked inside.

The theater was dark, cool, and small. It smelled of disinfectant spray rather than popcorn and reminded him of an adult theater that he'd visited when he was in college. The floor was even sticky, although in here Eric was fairly confident that the goo was just dried soda pop.

There were several other people in the theater with him, and it wasn't long before the lights dimmed and the screen grew bright.

The film began with a sweeping helicopter shot of orange groves. The color was pushed hard in that unreal, hyper vivid technicolor way. The orange was too orange, the greens so lush you could almost reach out and touch them. The image had a thick grain, though, and many scratches. This print had been run through the projector sprockets more than a couple of times.

That voice again. Deep and confident with a sweet Southern drawl.

"This is Florida," said the voice, "the Sunshine State as seen through the sharp eyes of history. A magical world of citrus, of beaches, of beauty."

Images on the screen reflected the dialogue. The white sands below a sign that proclaimed "Daytona - The World's Most Famous Beach!" Tanned legs attached to beautiful people frolicking in the too blue surf.

"Imagine if you could see all of this state's many glories in one single, impossible day. What a world that would be, my friends, if such fantasies were indeed possible. Well, imagine no more... welcome to FloridaWorld."

There were quick shots then of golfers, surfers, deep-sea anglers reeling in marlin, race car drivers on white sand beaches, astronauts giving the thumbs up as they ascended into the capsule of a great rocket.

"It began with a vision. A dream."

There he is, thought Eric. The old man himself, Irv Irving, was standing in front of a Florida state flag and a flag of the confederacy. Between that and Irv's blinding white three-piece country squire ensemble, Eric couldn't help but think about the KKK.

"Hello, sunshine friends, I'm Irv Irving. My dream started small, you see. Everyone around these parts said I was plum loco. I'd invite folks for tractor tours of my citrus groves, and, at the end of the ride, they could sip a juice and visit my turtle farm."

He held up a squirming cooter, smiled, and spoke into its little green face. "The biggest turtle farm in the world. Isn't that right, Mercury?"

Irv Irving waited a moment for a response that never came, then placed the thing back down again into a plastic terrarium.

"Soon, though, I had an idea. War was over, the boys were coming home, and America needed a show. Not just my cooters. Something bigger. Something grand. I was inspired, you see, by two things. The USO Shows I'd enjoyed on my tour of the European Theater."

Footage then of Jack Benny and Bob Hope entertaining the troops. Dancing girls, swing bands, cheering soldiers.

"And I was intrigued by a sport I'd seen practiced along the shores of my beloved Lake May."

Black and white footage of water-skiers came then. Athletic young men and women being towed by cherry outboards along calm waters, through Cypress Tree canals, over jump ramps and even in daring flat kites that soared over the lake.

"Could such a thing, waterskiing, be a show? Well, we soon found out. And what a show it was, and remains to this day. Our Aqua Circus. The longest running entertainment spectacle the world has ever known."

The montage transitioned into vibrant color footage of the FloridaWorld waterski show in its heyday and glory. The stands were full, so full that the crowds were spilled out over the emerald-green lawn to the side. Costumes so bedazzled and brilliant that the entire thing seemed like some Broadway musical brought out onto the water. Every man an Adonis and every woman a Venus. Then came celebrities who had graced this ski show stage. There was Sammy Davis Jr. Esther Williams. Johnny Weissmuller. Eartha Kitt. The Creature From the Black Lagoon. By God, there was Elvis himself, and he was shredding the lake on two long skis.

This was the golden dream of a place that Eric remembered from those magazines and television specials. It was extraordinary.

"Now, nobody's perfect, not even old Irv Irving. I've had my share of boners."

Eric snorted. A mother with two children turned and gave him a scolding look.

"Take this, for example."

There was black and white footage of a dolphin show. Leaping dolphins, laughing children, animal trainers in short skirts with a fish in one hand and a hoop in the other.

Then there were serious men in white coats taking away something large, wrapped in a tarp, lying deathly still on a long stretcher.

"Never could figure out how to keep the darned things alive. We'll let Marineland corner that market, I reckon," Irv said with a self-deprecating laugh.

"Then there was this tragic day in 1978. Sky Follies."

Soaring kites and enormous balloons shaped like citrus fruit filled the sky above the ski stadium. Then, chaos from the old footage as the performers holding the kites and balloons were yanked into the air. Some plummeted into the lake, some hung on, drifting off into the sun as the camera fell to the ground. One unfortunate dangling from a colossal lime appeared to drop directly onto a cast member dressed as a seahorse.

It was the Hindenburg footage, but with grapefruit balloons and kites shaped like fish.

"That was my biggest boner."

Eric snorted a laugh again and again the mother shot him a dirty look.

Footage of a funeral.

"Bad mess, that. But I think after your blessed visit today you'll be able to say, Irv Irving...you did swell. You can even pay your respects to the lost at our Sky Follies Memorial Bubble Fountain near the Tangerine Tilt-A-Whirl. There, the bubbles never stop blowing in memory of those swept away by what scientists today call a microburst."

Irv looked sad for a beat, then lifted his chin back up with a grin. "That wraps up our little promenade down memory lane."

A poorly animated pelican swooped into the shot and landed on Irv's shoulder.

Scale's a little off, thought Eric. *Either that's a tiny pelican or Irv's a giant.*

The pelican squawked at Irv and the old man smiled,

laughed, and winked at the bird. "Oh, that's right, Pete. These folks are getting restless with me rambling on and on. Go on now, go fishing, my friend. Catch a whopper!"

The pelican flapped away. Irv turned to the camera as it pushed into a closeup.

"I'm sure you're eager to see what we've done with the place. Who's ready to visit the sunshine state, tip to tip and coast to coast? Welcome, sunshine friends, to FloridaWorld!"

A song began then as the Space Shuttle lifted off and then the credits started to roll.

Eric thought the "FloridaWorld" anthem sounded like a bluegrass band covering a Beach Boys track while stoned on ditch weed as the "Up With People" kids sang about grapefruits and NASA.

The lights came up and Eric stepped back out into the morning sun and hit the park's main pathway, which led to a crossroads with a tall way faring sign in the middle.

To the left was "Daytona Sands," the "Everglade Critter Jamboree," and "Tallahassee Commons."

To the right, "Space Trek - On Ice!" and "The Monkey King of Splashy Springs!"

Eric hooked right.

If I were a piss monkey, I suspect I'd be in Splashy Springs.

There was music playing wherever you went. It was just loud enough to be annoying, and it blared out of cheap metal speakers hidden in shrubs and hanging from trees. Eric soon determined that the music changed depending on where in FloridaWorld you were at that moment. As he approached the theater, shaped like a rocket ship, where he would experience the glories of "Space Trek - On Ice!" the music was all theremin and Moog.

This place must have been something thirty years ago, he thought.

Paint was faded and chipped here and there. You could see where some patch jobs had been done to walls and pathways, but not in a way that was complimentary, more like the lowest bidder had slopped some cement down and called it good.

Plants and trees covered some of the old and ugly. Somebody was clever and planted plenty of bamboo to conceal things that couldn't be fixed on the cheap.

Still, the surrounding crowd was excited and he couldn't help but feel a bit like a kid again.

He was too early for the first performance of "Space Trek - On Ice." He stopped for a moment in front of the billboard marquee at the exterior of the weird retro theater.

There were photos of the cast. The names were there too and the cast all seemed to be of Eastern European descent. They were dressed in spacesuits and posing in a variety of ice-skating ways, smiles as big as the moon. One of them, the bad guy Eric suspected, was a green alien with enormous pointed ears. He was pointing a ray gun at some hapless space maiden in a silver bikini.

The copy for the show was intriguing.

"Boldly celebrate the 25th anniversary of our ice skating spectacular. This far-out tribute to our heroic NASA space program will thrill you, surprise you, and perhaps even arouse your interest in science! Join our Gold Medal team of Soviet refugees as you explore weird new worlds, find love on Uranus, and battle the evil of Professor Blight's Minions of Mayhem! Strobe lights will cause seizures. This is a warning. Thank you."

Eric made a note that this spectacle was not to be missed.

Just past the ice skating theater, the horticultural styles changed, as did the music.

Eric heard jungle drums and ominous native chanting. The trees were taller, there was more bamboo, the pathway narrowed and felt claustrophobic.

A wooden sign overhead declared, "Enter the Realm of the Monkey King."

The queue line of heavy rope and bamboo weaved around and back again through the tropical vegetation. The crowd wasn't overwhelming, so Eric moved quickly and soon came to a man-made river with small cargo boats that resembled miniature versions of the sort of thing Bogart captained in "The African Queen."

A teenager in an ill-fitting safari costume spoke into a microphone.

"Please face forward and step quickly into your safari vessels."

Eric hopped into one of the replica steam boats, the kid hit a button on the wall, and his boat lurched into action.

The vegetation on either side of the lazy river became thick then, even growing overhead to create a tunnel effect. There was a strong smell of chlorine.

Speakers were concealed in the landscaping and amid rock work as the boat ran along the lazy river. They creaked and cricketed like the cones hadn't been replaced in years.

First came the tribal drums. Then the sound of wild animals howling. Lions, birds, and an ominous native chant.

The lazy river opened up a little and revealed some signage, a wooden billboard that explained how all manner of ape was brought to a film shoot on an island near Splashy Springs back in the 1940s. Rather than transport the monkeys back to the zoo, the producers of "Tarzan and the Sinkhole of Dismay" simply let the apes roam free. There they remain to this day, breeding and flinging poo at those brave enough to pull their boats up to the shore.

That's when something wet hit Eric's cheek.

Hell no.

There was a bloodcurdling shriek, a blur of motion overhead, a rustle of bamboo.

Well, there's a piss monkey.

There were ropes and bridges built into the canopy over the lazy river. The guests in the little boats ahead of and behind Eric screamed and shouted because, above them on a rope bridge, was somebody in a gorilla suit with a water pistol.

That ape was squirting everyone he saw.

Eric wiped the water from his cheek just as another shot caught him in the eye.

Son of a bitch.

More monkeys appeared then, each of them hooting and gibbering and squirting tourists. The gorilla suits were identical, low-grade black and brown fur costumes with plastic faces.

Shiner found his calling, thought Eric.

The flow of water increased then from a gentle stream. The boat picked up speed and bobbed in the quickening river. Chlorinated water splashed over the bow and Eric was soaked from the waist down.

The boats moved down the river now and there were shouts, screams, and the occasional profane comment aimed at the offending primates.

The boat took a hard turn to the starboard side. A fiberglass tiger roared out of the ferns and Eric jumped.

A tiger? In Africa? Or Monkey Island? Or whatever the hell this is?

A hard turn to the port this time and a tyrannosaurus rex towered over the river, one thick concrete molded leg on either side of the water.

Dinosaurs. Sure. Why not?

A young woman charged out of the jungle and shrieked. She wore a barely visible fur bikini and jabbed at Eric and the other guests with a wooden spear. The savage cave woman grunted and mugged as she menaced the guests.

I guess she's a little something for the dads in the audience.

The boat drifted on through the choppy river, then slowed down as the river calmed. A large sign overhead warned, "Beware the Reptiles of Brunhilde!" A massive rubber snake had been wrapped around the signposts. The rubber was falling apart in the chlorinated atmosphere so that it appeared to Eric that the poor creature was suffering from some terrible malady.

The background music took a turn to the Teutonic.

Eric recognized the track as something by Wagner.

Rounding a bend, the tropical decor gave way to a series of reptile displays. Jewel tanks featuring various snakes and lizards. A tarantula. A bat.

There was a scream from the boat ahead and then laughter. Eric soon realized that the river was going through a wide alligator exhibit.

There were dozens of the creatures, some of them bigger than the boats, and the only thing that seemed to separate the shrieking guests from the gators was a little concrete ledge on either side of the waterway.

The alligators were well fed, fat, and happy. They moved little more than the T-Rex statue. Eric didn't think they'd pose a threat even if he jumped in the water holding a dead chicken.

More signage. "Meet Monstro - The World's Biggest

Gator!"

Yes, there's that damned big lizard again. He's a whopper for sure. Like a whale.

Monstro must have been twenty feet long, and he was as thick as a compact car. Unlike his topiary doppelgänger near the front of the park, the enormous creature on display here was dead, stuffed, and positioned on a stone platform under some signage. There were some facts and figures about the old thing. Apparently, he was already a massive adult alligator when he was captured and brought to FloridaWorld. His age was estimated at over a hundred years when Monstro went to gator heaven in 1983.

Impressive job by whoever did the taxidermy work on this thing. It's huge. Belly looks swollen, like it swallowed a Volkswagen. Would hate to have run into that thing back in the day.

Then the volume of the music rose as they approached a platform where a large woman was standing. At first glance, Eric thought she was wrapped in rope, but it became apparent that this tall, muscular woman was draped in living snakes. A sign next to her boasted we were witness to "Brunhilde - Mistress of the Serpentarium!"

The woman moved slightly and slowly as the boat passed, dancing to an imaginary tune only she could hear.

She did not look at the guests. Hilda just stared straight ahead as if her thoughts were a million miles away.

That woman has probably seen a million faces come through here, staring at her and pointing as she just stands there covered in snakes. Does she even know that we're here? I think I would lose my mind, thought Eric.

Now the lazy river slowed and brought the boats to a stop.

The end of the ride.

Another teenage employee in a baggy safari suit hit buttons and helped guests out of their boats. Now and then he would speak into his microphone and encourage everyone to "watch your step as you exit the ride."

Eric was confused. *Wasn't there supposed to be a Monkey King?*

A voiceover came on then.

"Beware, tourists! Your journey is not done! Behold, should you dare, the majesty, the glory, of the mighty Monkey King!"

The path led Eric and the guests to a shrine and at the shrine sat the biggest, fattest, hairiest ape of them all. The thing wore a golden crown and held a scepter.

Well, there you go, thought Eric.

"He was a king in his world, but now, he exists only for your cheap amusement," said a recorded voice.

There was a thunder crash.

"Be warned! His hands can crush coconuts!"

Eric was impressed that somebody could be in such a huge, furry ape suit in this dense Florida heat.

I hope they pay that guy extra.

The guests pointed and stared at the actor in the ape suit for a moment and the beast seemed to pay them no attention. Then, with practiced dramatic effect, the Monkey King reach under his backside and removed what appeared to be a handful of thick chocolate pudding.

Eric felt his mouth drop.

A man next to Eric gasped.

"Ruth, that filthy ape is going to sling his poop," said the man.

He wasn't wrong.

The big ape reared back and chucked the pudding.

Eric flinched, the crowd screamed, and one woman fell to the ground in fright and horror.

There was a sound like mud hitting a window. Because that's kind of what happened.

The brown pudding spattered the clear plexiglass between the Monkey King and the guests.

The other monkeys arrived then and began spraying the crowd with their water pistols.

Applause. Laughter. A couple of profanities.

Eric and the crowd moved on and, undoubtedly, some poor employee ran out with a squeegee and wiped away the faux poo to prepare for the next group to pulse into the Monkey King's realm.

They exited through the gift shop. Eric would learn that day that you always exit through the gift shop. There were plastic apes, ape puzzles, ape blankets, stuffed apes, squirt guns, and plastic monkey poop. If you were hungry, you could order a "Monkey Weiner in a Dino-Bun" with a cup of "Monkey Juice" to wet your whistle.

Shiner's got himself some gig here, thought Eric. *Some gig.*

Eric visited "The Wicked Pirates of Olde St. Augustine" after his Monkey King encounter.

A section of the park had been constructed out of coquina and heavy timber to give it a Spanish fort vibe. The attraction was a walk-through, a meandering journey through a dark building lit by fake candles and populated by wax figures dressed as Spanish conquistadors inflicting horrific agonies on other wax figures that were hardly dressed at all.

After that came a quick stop at a weird little exhibit called "Magical Chemicals - Better Citrus Through Chemistry!" A brightly lit room held displays that touted the wonders of DDT and let you into a gift shop where you could stock up on a variety of citrus fruit products, all purified by the cleansing touch of said marvelous chemical.

It was eleven thirty.

He spotted a directional sign for the waterski show.

Eric smiled.

#

The path that led to the waterski stadium opened up into a broad promenade that meandered through towering trees and colorful gardens. Spanish moss draped the thick branches above. Bees swooped and hovered in the canvas of flowers.

The pathway rose as it led to the ski show area.

Eric glimpsed a colossal roof structure through the trees.

Was that the top of the stadium?

He saw her then, Lake May, a broad vista of dark blue and green that extended far to the left and right. The opposite shore was just a thin line of white sand and cypress trees on the horizon.

The flowers smelled good, and the breeze was kind enough to cool the sweat on his skin. He noticed that there was no music here. Was that a choice, or was the system down in this part of the park? Either way, Eric enjoyed the quiet.

Eric felt his stomach tighten. Nerves? He felt as if he was going to meet a blind date that he'd been hearing about for years, a beautiful, brilliant, perfect blind date who would take one look at him and shut the door in his face.

In my experience, big expectations always lead to a bigger kick in the teeth, he thought.

The pathway opened up and revealed the waterski show stadium. The structure was massive, an open amphitheater built right on the shore, positioned so that the lake was the stage and the sky was the backdrop.

Eric guessed that the place could hold as many as two thousand guests, maybe more. There weren't traditional seats - too hard to deal with in open weather conditions, he imagined, rather there were long wooden benches fashioned of cypress.

He walked along the backside of the stadium and noticed a bronze plaque on one of the enormous concrete columns at the base of the place. Eric considered it for a moment.

"The Irv Irving Aqua Theater. Established April 15th, 1952. The birthplace of show skiing and home to the world's longest running aquatic entertainment spectacular."

The tension in his stomach ramped up even more. *There's no way in hell these people will hire me. I don't belong here.*

There was a little snack hut along the path. He smelled hot dogs. The nervous tension he felt gave way just a little bit to hunger, but Eric wasn't cash liquid enough to pay five bucks for a hot dog and coke.

He dropped a dollar on a bag of chips.

"How much is a cup of water?"

The woman behind the counter was old enough to be Eric's grandmother. Her skin was tanned the color of chocolate and her hair, whipped up and sprayed into a conical tower, was dyed a shocking shade of orange.

She looks like an orange ice cream cone.

She smiled and poured him a cup. He noticed the vibrant green of her eye shadow and wondered whether the citrus look was her choice or if it was direction from FloridaWorld. Either way, it was a stunner.

"On the house, sweetie," she said, "I hope you enjoy

the show. Is it your first time?" Her voice was like orange blossom honey.

"Yes, and thank you," said Eric.

"You'll love it. Some folks are all bent out of shape and lodging complaints, but they just don't have a sense of humor, that's all. I like the original Ski Haw better, if I'm being honest, but this one's just fine."

"I'm looking forward to it," Eric said.

"Keep an eye out for Hitler. You never know when that Nazi son of a bitch is going to show up," she said with a wink.

What?

"That's sound advice, ma'am," was all he could think to say.

Eric sipped his water as he walked toward the stadium seating.

Hitler?

#

Eric looked out over the water from his seat in the lower center of the stadium.

No. This isn't a stadium, thought Eric. *This is a theater.*

It was designed so that the lake became the stage. Sure, there was a small stage area at the center, on the shore, but your eyes couldn't help but be drawn to the beauty of the water and sky beyond. There was something magical about the concept, something lunatic and beautiful. Theatrics performed on a stage of water, powered by speedboats, with the sky as your proscenium.

There were several hundred guests in the theater now and more were arriving by the second. Some carried bags of popcorn, some carried beers, some had their cameras at the ready. A sunburned family of five, each wearing a "Monstro" alligator t-shirt, shuffled their way to center seats five rows from stage. An elderly couple bounded down the wide steps like school kids, holding hands as if they were on a first date.

To the left of the house, on the shore, there was a sprawling theatrical set designed to look like a fisherman's shack. It was dressed with colorful buoys and crab traps, and there was a miniature version of a red brick lighthouse erected above the area. Above this fishing shack set was a billboard with "Ponce Inlet Florida" written in colorful font.

To the house right side, there was a much more elaborate set, and it made Eric's jaw drop open.

What am I looking at? Eric thought. *Is that a bunker? Like at D-Day?*

Well, yes. Wood was painted to resemble large blocks of gray stone. Trompe l'oeil technique was used to create the illusion that the bunker and the other elements were bigger than they were and carried depth. Cannons poked out of slots in the wood, there was something that looked like barbed wire wrapped around posts in the sand, and above the thing flew a large Nazi flag and a banner that declared "Berlin" in militaristic san serif.

What the hell?

Eric looked around at the gathering crowd and wondered if he was the only one who thought this was inappropriate. After all, Bacopa County was deep south and a notch in the Bible belt. But the crowd was mixed, not just a sea of white faces.

Well, he thought, *let's see what happens. I mean, I guess it worked for Hogan's Heroes. Sort of.*

There was what appeared to be a man-made island perhaps a hundred yards offshore and positioned so that it became something of a backdrop to the space. On the island was a massive billboard that represented, as near as Eric could tell, the theme of the show.

Cartoon renderings of hillbillies were engaged in fisticuffs with cartoon Nazis. Word balloons declared "Take that, you Nazi rat!" and "War Movie Cliches!"

At the center of the billboard was the title of the show, writ large in Comic Sans.

"Ski Haw Meets the Nazis."

I'm not sure if this day can get any stranger.

Between the island set and the carpeted center stage area were two jump ramps. These were impressive aluminum ramps set at a steep angle so skiers could ride over them and perform all manner of acrobatics. The two ramps faced in opposite directions on the water, about fifty yards apart. Eric considered they might be as much as sixteen feet wide and six feet high.

There were little fountains of water dancing from the top lip of the ramp.

His ski club growing up in Wisconsin had used

something similar, he recalled, to keep the surface of the ramp slick. He'd never been much of a jumper as a kid, but he'd enjoyed watching his friends take turns riding over the old ramp.

Dad tried to learn to jump but crashed every time. Always came up laughing, Eric thought, remembering the fun they'd had back then as a family, those days in Wisconsin when the water was cool and the air was warm.

Banjo music began then.

There was a young man with an impressive mullet and a banjo, and he stood on a tiny circular stage to the left of the stadium. The banjo man was dressed in a three-piece suit of broad stripes, a bowler hat, and a bright red bowtie, like a Scott Joplin fever dream, and he sang into a microphone that hung from a coat hanger around his neck.

"Good day, sunshine friends! Is everybody having a good time at FloridaWorld?" the banjo player asked, sweeping his arms around to indicate the entire audience.

There was a smattering of replies and some applause.

The banjo player was having none of it.

"Is this thing on? Hello? I said, are you ready to have some fun today?"

The crowd cheered as if on command.

"That's what I like to hear," he said, "I'm Banjo Bob, The Traveling One Man Ragtime Band and Kazoo Master. Our show begins in just a few moments, but first here are a few songs that will bring a smile to your face and sunshine to your heart."

Banjo Bob picked out "Dixie" on his instrument.

To Eric, the racist overtones of the song coupled with the slightly out of tune banjo made him feel like he was listening to two feral cats in a bag fighting over a chicken wing.

Eric tuned out Banjo Bob and stared out at Lake May.

It was a stunning venue, and the weather was perfect. A clear blue sky, a light breeze, and sunlight so pure that the entire scene seemed to be a 1960s era postcard come to life. Ski boats, MasterCrafts, idled around the lake. They were older models, faded by the sun and showing their age, but they probably still had plenty of power under the hood.

Sure, there had been some strange and disturbing moments, but right then, in that moment, FloridaWorld was the place that had lived in his adolescent imagination.

Just beautiful. Like the cover of one of those old magazines Mom kept on the living room table.

There was movement to his side. A little man sat down next to Eric. It was Shiner, sweaty and out of breath, cigarette dangling from his lip.

"What's up, cheese head? I saw you down there. That was me squirting you in the puss. How'd you like the piss monkeys?"

"That was something."

"Damn straight. Pay's almost as good as Mid-Florida Recycling. I'm practically a movie star."

"You should sign autographs."

Shiner laughed.

"Smoke?" he offered.

Eric declined.

#

Banjo Bob took a bow, then another, then another, to dwindling applause. Even the audience seemed tired of his shtick. With a smile and a wave, he dashed off, stage right, and Eric noticed a boat coming in fast from the far western side of the lake. From what he could see, it was a ski boat of some sort but tricked up to look like it was a military vessel. The paint was gray and black and red. Prop guns were mounted on the side rails.

What drew Eric's attention was the swastika on the bow. There was an audible gasp from the audience and a smattering of boos.

He took a sip of his water and for the next thirty minutes Eric Walters experienced what he could only imagine was a surreal dream, something that resulted from the mosquito bites, the lack of a decent meal, and maybe the echoes of some head trauma suffered in the war.

There was a plot that introduced the villains, led by the head nasty, old Adolph himself, and a gaggle of hillbilly heroes who had been drafted by Uncle Sam to battle the Nazis. It was as if some drunken scribe had shuffled papers between a script for the Beverly

Hillbillies and Hogan's Heroes and called it a day.

The story? A daring hillbilly fishing boat off the coast of Florida went to war against a naval Nazi invasion that would have, if our heroes failed, put FloridaWorld under the thumb of Der Fuehrer himself.

No wonder there's a controversy about this show, thought Eric.

The plot wasn't the thing, though, and that's where the disconnect began for him, the disconnect between the show's bizarre theme and its essence as a display of waterski skill.

Eric was mesmerized by what he saw on the water. He dismissed the buffoonish comedy and the complete lack of self-awareness and just focused on what mattered. He focused on Lake May, because there was something magical happening on her waters.

There was an extraordinary dance between boats, a nautical choreography that was timed to the split-second and created a flow of energy and visual focus that he'd never seen before. The athletes, the water-skiers, performed the most wonderful stunts while being towed by the powerful ski boats.

There were gorgeous women who seemed to dance and pirouette on a wooden board while skimming across the surface of the water at speeds that would get you pulled over in a school zone. Then there were men who flew at even faster speeds over the jump ramps, sometimes spinning in complete circles, sometimes performing backflips, sometimes combining the two into an acrobatic move Eric couldn't wrap his head around.

Light years beyond my friends and my dad crashing and flailing over the jump ramp back home, he thought.

The horrible nonsense about Nazis, the silly moment when skiers chased a shrieking Hitler with pie launchers, all of that just disappeared and Eric felt he was seeing something from a dream, something that he had imagined when he was a child growing up on the lake with his Mom and Dad.

Our local ski team was never like this, he thought. *We had fun, we made friends, we learned to ski. But this. This is...incredible.*

For Eric Walters, everything around disappeared in that moment and he watched a dream come to life on the waters of Lake May, a dream of a Florida that might once have been, of a golden place where golden people did impossible things against a backdrop of sunshine and palm trees.

Tip of the hat to old Irv Irving. He was onto something, and it might just be a ghost of what it was, and this show plot is horrific, but man, when it came to waterskiing, he was onto something.

The clockwork precision of the action on the water, the boats, the skiers, the speed of it all, was hard for Eric to track. The sun on his face began to feel too warm. The potato chips sat heavy in his stomach.

I don't have a chance in hell of getting a job here.

\#

After the show was done, Shiner led Eric down the steps to the front pathway of the theater and then cut hard right. They walked under the cannons of the Nazi bunker and passed through a little walkway out into a wide space that was hidden from guests by tall cypress trees.

"Boat dock and staging area," said Shiner.

The floor was a green carpet over concrete and wood planks, helpful to the shoeless skiers running about. There were skis and ropes scattered about, and beyond that was a series of boat lifts.

Eric counted five separate lifts, each designed for the show's ski boats and covered by a metal roof.

A speaker hung overhead, blared the music from the theater that played as guests exited. Eric thought it sounded like the soundtrack to an old silent film, something with Charlie Chaplin or Harold Lloyd.

They impressed him with the post-show activity. It seemed almost as choreographed as the action on the water.

Athletic men and women in bathing suits ran here and there engaged in various post show duties. Ropes were being coiled, skis were being retrieved and reset for the next show, costumes were being gathered and carried away, presumably to dry.

The skiers were a well-organized machine, or at least, that's what it seemed.

The skinny man who had been the show announcer wasn't helping with the show strike and set up. He'd already stripped down to a speedo and was lying on a beach towel near the water, catching some sun. There was a book cracked open over his face.

Shiner pointed to a beefy man in a festive speedo and bright yellow tank top.

"Come on," he said as he led Eric over to the man, who looked up and smiled when he saw them.

"Well, look what the cat dragged in," said the beefy man. He was tan and thick with short cropped silver hair, athletic in a beer and hamburger kind of way. The lemon yellow tank top and tiny bathing trunks suggested to Eric that this was a man who did not give a damn what others thought of his fashion choices.

"Kent Westheimer, you son of a bitch. You doin' alright? Helluva thing about PBR," Shiner said.

Kent took a drag from his cigarette. "As well as can be expected, what with the news. I mean, who would kill that man? He was a teddy bear."

Shiner frowned. "It's crazy. I can't wrap my head around it," he said.

"Damn, Shiner, everybody loved Roger."

"He was a legend."

Kent leaned in and his voice went low. "They say his body was violated with an orange. What kind of a world are we living in?"

Shiner pulled out a pack of Marlboro lights and offered Eric a smoke. Eric declined. Shiner lit up.

"I thought Roger was clean, too, but do you think this had something to do with coke? Maybe he was back in the business."

Kent was quiet for a moment. "He was clean, as far as I know. But, sure. That's the only thing that makes any kind of sense. A deal gone bad."

"I'm surprised you guys didn't do some sort of tribute during the show," said Shiner.

"We thought about it, but old man Irving would lose his shit if we did something like that," Kent said.

"Sure, but how long had PBR been at the park? He was a fixture."

"Twenty years this summer. He was due to get his name carved on the big jump ski. No, the old man doesn't go for that sort of thing. He thinks it breaks the spell of the show theme. Doesn't think the audience would care."

Shiner snorted. "Break the spell more than Nazis?"

Kent shook his head. "Brother, you're not kidding. We're taking a beating in the press. I told those creative types that it was a bad idea. Did you read some of the letters to the paper? We had a synagogue protesting outside of the park, for God's sake," said Kent.

"It's not like we let Hitler win."

"Right? We beat the hell out of that son of a bitch. He's the damned clown. They're the bad guys. Still, this theme was a swing and a miss."

"Oh shit, sorry," said Shiner. "Kent, this is my pal Eric Walters. The guy whose ass I kicked the other night."

"Holy donkey balls, he's huge. You're lucky to be alive, Shiner."

"Nah, he got me on a bad night. Eric's from the Dells and he's a top-notch skier and driver."

Eric reached out to shake Kent's hand.

"Not sure if I'd say I was top-notch, but it's nice to meet you," said Eric.

Kent's grip was strong, and the skin on his hand was tougher than leather.

"Pleasure. The Dells are beautiful. Still doing the show up there?"

"Yeah, still there, as far as I know. I've been away for a few years."

Kent smiled, scratched his bristly silver hair, and shook his head.

"Well, sorry you had to sit through that mess today," said Kent. "Like I was saying, this new show theme is a dud. We're in the middle of trying to change it right now, but we can't do anything until we've got the new show ready. Takes time, ya know."

"Sure." said Eric. "Our amateur club back home didn't have any themes or stories or anything. Just skiing. Some of the other clubs would do theme shows, though. Seemed like fun."

"I hate it. The old shows here focused on the skiing. Now they bring in low-rent Hollywood writers and off-Broadway types to tell us what we're going to do and how we're going to do it. They say we need a story and characters and that sort of bullshit."

"For perceived entertainment value. Like the skiing isn't cool enough," said Shiner.

"We're doing the replacement theme ourselves, thank God. I'm working with the announcer, Johnny Fig, trying to come up with something decent. Not because Old Man Irving trusts us."

Shiner made a gesture with his fingers. Money.

"The well's run dry, so no more paydays for Hollywood hot shots. Just as well. They paid those sons of bitches my year's salary for two weeks' work and we got Hitler on waterskis. Jesus wept," said Kent.

"I told Kent we need to do a nudie ski show," said Shiner.

He seemed serious.

"The last thing Bacopa County needs to see is your hairy garden weasel winkin' at 'em. Look, it's nice to meet you, Eric, but I'm sure you fellas have something to do," said Kent.

Shiner waved him off. "No, we're here because you need a driver, and Eric's your man," he said.

"Christ on a fiddle stick, Shiner. PBR isn't even in the ground yet."

Eric held his hand up. "Sir, Shiner isn't speaking for me," he said, feeling about as uncomfortable as he'd felt in a long time. "I wasn't looking to swoop in here like a vulture looking for a job. I'm sorry for your loss."

Kent smiled at him through wide, nicotine-stained teeth. "It's okay, son," he said. "We're just going through some tough times, that's all. Look, why don't you guys meet us at The Tavern for a cold one after the last show? The whole team's going out tonight in honor of Roger. I'll buy you a beer and we can talk about getting you in here for a tryout."

"Thanks." said Eric. "That sounds amazing."

11

Saturday Night

Eric pulled the Firebird into the parking lot of The Tavern and dropped the volume on the stereo. It was his Dead Kennedy's tape, a kindness to Shiner, who wasn't into rap, but Eric liked punk just fine. He thought punk and rap had more in common than not, at least when you listen to what they were saying.

The night was thick with the threat of rain. Shiner sat next to him and the man's face was yellow in the dashboard light and the glow of the cigarette that dangled from the corner of his mouth.

"Park anywhere." Shiner said, "They don't tow after six.

It was a strip mall but a big one and The Tavern seemed to be the anchor. The place was massive, with a faux wood frame exterior that gave it an "old lodge in the woods" look. The titular neon sign was bright blue and red and you could see the glow of televisions through the wide windows.

Inside it was a soundtrack of smoke and voices and hair metal by bands like *Poison* and *Ratt*. It was packed. People were lined up two deep at the long bar that dominated the far side of the place. The upper level looked like the game room, with pool tables and darts, the sound of ceramic balls smacking together, and a haze of smoke that looked like a fog bank. The lower level of The Tavern was a big sports bar with televisions overhead and everywhere, plenty of tables, servers running pitchers of cold beer, and only slightly less smoke.

The Tigers were playing the Red Sox on most of the screens. Few were watching. Something from NASCAR held the attention of a few guys in ball caps toward the back of the room.

Just breathing in the air could count as Eric's third smoke of the day.

Shiner pointed to an enormous table. There were a dozen people standing and sitting, drinking, platters of wings on the table.

Eric recognized Kent, the ski show manager. The big man was wearing a FloridaWorld ball cap over his silver hair. He'd traded in his speedo and yellow tank top for some tight shorts and a polo shirt with the collar popped up.

The people at the table are skiers, thought Eric.

Definitely with the team.

They were all tanned and fit, dressed in everything from sponsored ski gear and t-shirts to cowboy hats and flannels. A woman who reminded Eric of the brunette from *"Charlies Angels"* was dressed for clubbing. She was deep in conversation with a guy in a *Van Halen* concert shirt and stone-washed button fly jeans. While their fashion choices ran the gamut, they were all obviously athletic, attractive, and bursting with energy.

Eric and Shiner made their way to the table and by the time they got there, everyone saw Eric's little wingman and let out a cheer.

They really like the guy. Well, he's certainly a personality. A life of the party type.

A few of the skiers noticed Eric and gave him a slight nod. Shiner began cracking jokes.

"Hey ladies, how do you get a nun pregnant? Dress her up like an altar boy."

There was some laughter, a few groans, and there was a beer in Shiner's hand as if by magic.

Kent stood up, adjusted his crotch, and shook Eric's hand.

"The boat driver. Good to see you. Eric, right?"

Eric smiled and nodded affirmative.

"Damn, son, you're empty. Mitch, beer me." Kent whistled and pointed at the pitcher. One of the skiers, a stocky young guy with a buzz cut, filled an empty mug and passed it along.

"Thanks," Eric said. He took a deep drink, and it was

about the best thing he'd had in a very long time.

"Sit," Kent said.

He poked a thick finger into the shoulder of the woman sitting next to him and jerked his thumb to say, "Move it." The woman was young, probably no more than twenty, and she rolled her eyes and slide down to another seat.

Eric tried to catch her attention and say "thanks" but she engaged in conversation with that end of the table.

Oh well.

Eric sat.

"The Dells, huh? Half the team has either skied there for a summer or they went up for Nationals to party. Love it there. Or loved it, past tense. I'm too old for that kind of crazy."

"Sure. Interesting place to grow up. Skiing in the summer and hunting in the winter. Always active."

"I bet. What brings you to Bacopa County?"

Eric smiled while his mind raced.

I'm a drop out, sir, and was just kicked out of the Navy. A real winner. You'll definitely want me on your team.

"Discharged from the military a few weeks ago out of the base near West Palm. Always a dream to try out for your show, so I drove north. I'm sure I've got no chance but need to give it a try at least."

A good compromise answer. Some truth, some things left unsaid.

"We'll see about all that. Army?"

"Navy. You? Military background?"

"Oh, hell no. Professional coward. But God bless you for doing what I wouldn't." Kent raised his mug and Eric felt obliged to drink along to the toast.

"Again, sorry to hear about your driver. Was there any news about what happened?"

Kent shrugged. "No. Probably won't be, either. Bacopa County Sheriff's not exactly on the cutting edge of police science. Bunch of dumb crackers who can't get hired as security at the mall."

Deputy Paulina Campos reared up out of the darkness, grabbed Kent by the ear, and pulled. The big man let out a high-pitched shriek.

"Crackers?" she asked.

Eric hadn't even seen her approach.

"Shit, sorry, Paulie, let go of my ear bone," said Kent. "I didn't know you were standing there. Bunch of crackers and one half-Mexican half-hillbilly wildcat. We good now?"

She complied with a slight smile.

"Never," she said.

Eric made a move to stand and offer her his chair, but she put her hand on his shoulder and forced him back down.

"Stay, big guy," she said.

Deputy Campos wore a cut up flannel shirt with jean shorts riding high, wide black belt, and hiker boots. Her long, dark hair was tied back. Not much makeup, if any. Eric thought it was a great look, but he felt she could make pretty much anything work. She was strong.

Looked like someone who could kick some ass and still look great doing it. He noticed her nails were cut short, no paint, all business. No ring.

"Deputy," he said.

"Staying out of trouble?"

Eric laughed.

"Yes, ma'am."

"You guys know each other?" asked Kent.

There was an awkward moment. Campos stared at Eric with a smile, as if waiting for him to explain.

"I spent the night at her place," Eric said.

Kent's mouth opened and dropped.

"The secret's out, I guess," said Paulina, "Mr. Walters and I got to know each other pretty well in a short period of time."

Kent sputtered and stammered for a moment as he searched for something to say. Eric let him off the hook.

"Deputy Campos was the one who processed my freedom after my fight with Shiner," he said. "Nothing to be proud of, but it happened."

Kent took a deep drink of his beer. "Well, if she's still talking to you, then you're okay," he said.

Paulina tightened her grip on Eric's shoulder for a moment, then wandered off to the other end of the table. Eric watched her go with a little regret and a great deal of curiosity.

"She grew up at the park," said Kent, "her Grandma and her mama worked at the mansion. Couldn't even swim when she started at the show."

"What? She's a skier?"

"Paulie hung out with some skiers in high school. Grew up in the mansion, even. She was strong, physically a beast, so we brought her in and taught her to roll ropes and do doubles. Then she learned to ski. Took to it real quick. Decent on the swivel but a great bare-footer and she can climb a pyramid like nobody's business. She's tougher than most of the guys on the team. Military, like you. Army, though."

"Really?"

"Got her degree in law enforcement as part of the deal. So now she skis a couple of days a week to make some cash. Bacopa County Sheriff's Department pay is for shit and she's just part time, so it's tough to make ends meet."

Eric took a moment to drink in the scene. The Tavern was loud, busy, but friendly. The smell of wings and beer was strong and wonderful. The skier table was growing by the moment and the team seemed to be treated like celebrities, but not in an arrogant or slick way, more of a friendly and respected way. He liked the environment and there was something about the ski team he liked, too.

Family. They seemed like a family. A band of brothers and sisters. There was an easy camaraderie among them, an openness. He'd gotten a taste of that in the service, but it was darker and more intense there and you knew going in that you might not survive the day. Worse, your brothers might not survive.

This was nice, at least at first glance.

"So," said Kent, "you're looking for a job. We need a pickup boat driver. Not much more than minimum wage to start, but it's the most fun you'll ever have at work."

"Pickup boat?" he asked.

"That's what we call the little outboard that picks up skis that are dropped during the show. You zip in, grab the skis, throw 'em in the boat, and get out of the way in time for the next act. It's an easy gig, and once you're in, we can put you through some tryouts to see where you go from there."

"I just started at Mid-Florida Recycling, but that's a cash job, so I should be able to make it all work," said Eric.

Kent smiled. His broad face was weathered from years in the sun and when he grinned, there were deep lines around his eyes.

"Sure. First things first, we'll get you in to drive the pub boat around a bit. Just a quick test to make sure you're not a complete fuck up. Then, we'll take it from there. You dive certified?"

"I was a SEAL."

"Right. I'm a dumb ass. Can you come by tomorrow morning, say, eight o'clock?"

"Yes, sir."

"I'll put your name at the Security Gate and they'll let you in. And don't worry, we don't drug test, so if you puff the whacky weed, you'll be fine. Just don't get that stuff around me. Makes me stupid."

Eric heard a pounding sound. It was Shiner. He stood on top of the table and was stamping his feet to get everyone to settle down.

He held his beer mug high.

"Here's to Pub Boat Roger."

The skiers raised their drinks, and the room became quiet except for the televisions and the sound of the pool table upstairs.

"You were a great friend and a great driver. You were family and we'll miss you, my brother."

He drank, and everyone followed his lead. The noise resumed, but this time it wasn't as raucous, just a low rumble of conversation and movement.

One of the skiers, a tall kid with muscles like ropes, picked Shiner up and brought him down from the table, then gave him a hug.

Hey, that's Commander Freedom, thought Eric. *Secret identity blown.*

Kent Westheimer excused himself and went over to the other side of the room to join others in conversation. Eric sat and sipped his beer. Paulina Campos drank alone at a small table in the corner.

He thought for a moment of sweeping in and joining her, but there was something about her, the way she stared off at nothing, disconnected from everything, that seemed to say "stay away" so Eric chose to stay put.

A boat driver in the FloridaWorld ski show.

Damn.

Now all I need to do is not fuck things up.

12

4:07 AM Sunday Morning

Marcus Traster had seen some strange things during the midnight shift at the Jiffy Mart on the corner of Highway 27 and Lemon Pip Lane.

The night the Valkyrie came down from Valhalla and shot Marcus dead was not the weirdest, but it was the most violent and it was the last.

His first night on the job, a redneck the size of a silverback gorilla walked into his store and grabbed as many cases of Bud Light as he could carry, then walked right out the door, never to be seen again.

It was such a nonchalant robbery that it didn't even register as one until Marcus had a moment to consider what had just happened.

There were the nice young men in crisp khakis and pressed white shirts who would play Centipede on the machine in the corner by the restroom until all hours and ask Marcus if he would like to be orally pleasured. Marcus always responded with a polite "No, thank you."

He wasn't one to judge such things, and he was tempted, but fear of being caught by his boss or his mom always stepped in the way of a good time.

One night, a biker walked into the store and asked if he could borrow one of the ballpoint pens in Marcus's Jiffy Mart shirt pocket. Marcus handed him a blue pen. The biker pulled the tube out of the pen and shoved it up his own nose until it could no longer be seen. The biker bowed, Marcus applauded. The pen was pulled back out from the biker's nasal cavity and reassembled. Marcus said "No, thank you," when offered the return of his pen. An hour later, he'd watched in mute astonishment as a couple of high school field trip chaperones in t-shirts and tighty whiteys tackled the biker in the parking lot and began to beat him with their fists. After Marcus called the police and the situation was sorted, it turned out that the biker had strolled into the motel next door to the Jiffy Mart and gone room to room, exposing himself to a high school girl's swim team in town for a tournament.

There were plenty of stories about Marcus's midnight shifts at the Jiffy Mart.

The night The Pickle Man came to call, for example, was on a different level of strange and for purposes of brevity will not be explored here. Marcus never told his friends or family the peculiar tale of The Pickle Man and since he was going to be dead in moments, he would never have that unique opportunity and the world of peculiar stories would be the less for this failure.

These things and more prepared Marcus well enough for the muscular angel who walked out of the dark mist of the parking lot and toward his store at 4:07 am that Sunday morning.

There was always a "last call" rush just after 3:00, when the bars kicked out the drunks and they staggered into his Jiffy Mart looking for smokes, condoms, toilet paper, and beer. The rush was done now, and the store was quiet except *"Hair of the Dog"* by "Nazareth" coming from the little radio Marcus kept under the counter next to the safe.

Marcus was reading a Team Aquanaut adventure paperback titled "Kill Mermaid, Kill!" and there was a tickle in his innards that presaged an impending bowel eruption.

Relieving himself would require locking up. That was a bit of a hassle, but he'd scarfed one of the Jiffy Mart hot dogs for dinner and it was buzzing in his belly like angry bees.

He glanced up from his book and saw the angel flash out of the darkness, her white robes blinding under the glare of the parking lot's sodium lights.

She was revealed by the light for just an instant, and then she was concealed in the night fog.

The angel was tall and thick. She had arms like a weight lifter and long hair that was tied in pig tails. There was a metal helmet on her head and her white wings were folded up like an eagle at rest. She wore long white gloves, thick metal bracelets, and a metallic chest plate.

There was something long and dark around her neck and chest that Marcus thought might be a big rubber snake.

Or at least, he hoped it was rubber.

Marcus thought it was odd to have a costume party in March, but Bacopa County was an odd place.

Wait. She was almost at the door, revealed again by the fluorescence, and it dawned on him that this wasn't an angel. This was a Valkyrie, like in the comic books with "Thor" and "The Defenders" and such.

That's badass, he thought. *A Valkyrie from Asgard, or Valhalla. With a giant snake. Sweet.*

"Bitchin' costume," he said as she entered his store.

Then it dawned on him.

"Hey, ain't you that crazy lady with the snakes over at FloridaWorld?"

Those were the last words of Marcus Traster because Hilda the Valkyrie walked up to the counter, lifted a handgun, and shot him in his left eye. Some of Marcus sprayed the Centipede machine before he fell dead to the floor, and some flew far enough to speckle the neon beer sign above the coolers.

Hilda turned on her heel and walked out of the store

and into the night, where a Bacopa County Sheriff's Department patrol car waited with the engine running.

She made sure that her snake was safely wrapped around her neck and chest, then sank into the passenger seat.

"Done," Hilda said.

Part-time Sheriff's Deputy Paulina Campos stared straight ahead, hands on the wheel, and stepped on the gas pedal. She was wearing her uniform now, not the flannel and shorts of The Tavern, but she still smelled of the bar's smoke.

Hilda liked the smell but thought it best not to say so.

"Next one's a woman with no family. She lives alone, but she has a dog, so we'll need to be careful," said Hilda. She handed Campos a sheet of paper with a woman's name and street address printed on it. Campos glanced at it as she drove, then set it aside.

"I don't know her," said Campos.

"Good. That's best."

"Tell me who else."

"No. One by one."

Paulina understood this kept control in Hilda's hands. She was on a need-to-know basis, and all she needed to know was one name at a time.

"One more after the next woman and we're done, Paulie. We go our separate ways."

"I hate this. I hate you."

"I know, Paulie. But you'll get what you want. We'll both get what we want. And don't worry. I won't hurt the doggie unless I must."

"Just stop talking."

The aging Ford Mustang SSP pulled out of the lot and onto Lemon Pip Lane. Its tail lights faded as it went and the old car carried Paulina and the Valkyrie away in the morning mist.

Mr. John Wiggins entered the Jiffy Mart twenty minutes later to pick up some instant coffee and a pack of smokes. He found Marcus dead behind the counter in a wide pool of blood that spread out like a dark red Rorschach blot.

There was a lurid paperback on the floor as well and a radio was playing *"Flirtin' with Disaster"* by "Molly Hatchet."

Mr. Wiggins screamed and screamed even as he dialed 911 from the black phone on the counter. The poor man would never be the same and the police would be frustrated by the complete lack of evidence in large part because somebody, probably the killer, had disabled the security cameras.

Marcus Traster was dead, Mr. Wiggins had nightmares for the rest of his life, and Bacopa County had its second murder in the space of a week.

Again, there were three witnesses and one of them didn't count anymore.

13

Sunday

Eric was astonished by Shiner's ability to function after so much beer the night before. The little guy was up and bouncing around the house at sunrise with a smoke in his mouth and a cup of coffee in his hands. The sky was dark orange, not a good sign for the day's weather, and a chorus of birds and insects hummed and clicked softly like static in the background. Eric pulled on his shorts and went out to where Shiner stood at the end of the little wooden dock.

Shiner offered Eric a cigarette, and the offer was accepted. They stood and smoked and looked at the stillness of the lake, the almost imperceptible rise of the sun, the shadows of Cypress trees becoming gold in the glow.

"Are you a piss monkey today?"

Shiner shook his head no. "I need to be at Mid-Florida by seven."

"I'll give you a ride on my way to the tryout."

"Muchas gracias. Eggs?"

"Sure."

#

The breeze felt good on Eric's face through the open windows of the Firebird. The sun was up now and the heat was on, but so were some clouds. There would be rain later. Probably storms. He drove from Mid-Florida Recycling out onto 27 and then down FloridaWorld Boulevard at just over the limit, a bellyful of eggs, and his second smoke of the day already on his lips. It was a cheat, but he was nervous and could justify the cheating.

There was an employee parking lot, a big one, not paved but green with grass and white with crushed shell sand. Eric didn't want to get towed, but he parked there anyway and left a handwritten note just under his windshield. "Job Interview Today."

He wore his khaki shorts, a dark blue polo, and a pair of sandals, his eyes shaded by a pair of Oakley sunglasses. Under the khakis was a pair of board shorts, just in case he needed to get in the water at some point. It had been a long time since he'd water-skied or driven a ski boat. The nerves were more present with each step toward the Employee Security Gate, a chain link and wood shack with enormous windows and an empty bulletin board nailed to the door.

The security guard behind the desk might have been born when the place was still an orange grove. His face was a maze of wrinkles and folds, like an old hound's scrotal sack.

"What's your business, boy?" asked the guard in a deep southern accent.

Eric let the "boy" slide. There were more important things to worry about, like getting the job.

"I'm Eric Walters. I'm here for a job interview at the ski show."

The guard made quite a show of checking the list of names on a clipboard at his elbow. He puffed as he performed, and the sharp whistle from his nose made Eric wince.

"Eric Walters," said Eric again, trying to be helpful.

"I heard you," the guard said without looking up. "Janitorial, you say?"

"Ski show."

The guard looked up then and considered Eric for a long moment.

"Hm." And he bent closer to the clipboard to resume scanning the names. "Nobody told me we were hiring new janitors."

Kent Westheimer charged into the shack smelling of beer and Old Spice. There was a growth of silver stubble on his broad, red face.

"Sweet Jesus, Quillis, he's here to meet me. Eric Walters. I called in the name yesterday, you racist old bastard."

Quillis, the guard, cursed under his breath, then waved them both through.

"Morning, Eric. Sorry about Quillis, there. We keep thinking we'll show up one day and he's either been fired or dropped dead of meanness, but no such luck yet. You get some rest? Not hungover, are you? Not still drunk?"

Eric laughed, the nerves fading a little.

"No sir. Only had a couple of beers last night. Wallet's light for more than that."

"Well, let's see what we can do about that."

#

Eric gunned the outboard and the sweet smell of Lake May, water hyacinths, and 50:1 mix hit him like a shot.

It was a 75 hp Mercury, and that wasn't much until you attached it to the back of a 16-foot fiberglass flat deck and then it was plenty to send you rocketing across the water like something the coyote would whip together in the ACME warehouse.

The show site was the sizable area of Lake May that rested in front of the ski stadium and served as the stage for the show. For the tryout, they'd scattered skis around the show site and were driving high-speed boat patterns to churn up the water.

The audition was for pickup boat driver, an essential but unheralded gig in the show. During a ski presentation, all manner of gear would get dropped in the water. Skis, costumes, you name it. Throughout the show, the pickup boat was responsible for jetting out into the show course and picking up everything that was floating out there. It had to happen fast, and it had to be thorough. They had to be fast, so they didn't get in the way of the other boats during the show. They had to be thorough because if they missed something floating in the water, it could be disastrous.

A forgotten ski floating in the show course could get run over by a boat. This meant a damaged ski and potentially damage to an extremely expensive ski boat. A barefoot skier could hit that floating, forgotten ski with his or her feet at 40 miles per hour and that would be a whole different, and dangerous, kind of damage.

The pub boat driver was often low man on the totem pole, but if they screwed up their mistakes had consequences.

Eric held the throttle of the Mercury outboard and surveyed the lake.

The show site was chaos. Kent was making sure of it.

The boats used in the show were old MasterCrafts with inboard engines. They were battered by countless shows and faded by the sun, but Kent and his team kept them running reasonably well despite the wear and tear.

Kent was driving one of the boats and an older man with a white handlebar mustache was piloting the other. This was Fergus, and based on the leathery brown skin and permanent sun squint, Eric suspected the man had been driving at the ski show since the dawn of time.

"Remember," said Kent, "pick up anything that floats and keep your head on a swivel. These boats don't come with brakes, so stay out of harm's way out there."

With that, Kent and Fergus were away from the dock in their boats and throttle down, doing figure eights on top of figure eights, creating a washing machine of choppy water that would make finding and retrieving the ski gear a difficult task.

Just in case Eric wasn't nervous enough, Paulina Campos sat on the edge of the dock with her strong dark legs crossed, a cup of coffee in one hand and a Pop Tart in the other.

Sunglasses obscured her eyes, but Eric was sure that she was watching him.

Great. No pressure.

Eric twisted the throttle of his outboard motor and pulled away from the dock.

Eyes open. Head on a swivel.

Jump skis floated twenty yards to port, revealed, then concealed in the chop.

Eric put the little boat on edge, went too hard, and nearly tipped.

Water poured over the transom.

He throttled back, gunned it again. The outboard coughed and then throttled back just soon enough to coast in next to the skis without pushing much of a wake.

He grabbed one jumper on the fly, dropped it onto the deck, and ran over the other ski with a grinding crunch. He winced and hoped that this wouldn't come out of his pocket. Eric came around hard to port and saw the ski floating upside down with a trench carved in the wood.

Shit.

He grabbed the ski and tossed it into the boat.

A MasterCraft flew past him at what felt like 300 miles per hour. The other roared behind him. He was covered in spray and his boat bobbed up and down on the surface like a cork waiting for a bass to strike.

This is difficult. Eric felt his stomach tighten.

He watched the water for the telltale white and blue of the ropes that had been strewn around the lake as part of the test. Ropes were never dropped intentionally in the show, but things happened sometimes. If you weren't paying attention and ran over some ropes, your prop would stop and you'd be dead in the water.

There and there. But there's something else, too.

He skipped the pickup for the ropes but swung wide to avoid chopping them up or tangling with his prop. A pair of skis to his starboard. He slowed down even less this time and had them in the boat in seconds.

That's better, he thought.

A swivel ski floated in the distance, the tall binder clearly visible, like a little shark fin, and he plowed through the wakes from the MasterCraft to retrieve it.

The boats flew by him again, port and aft, the wakes rolling in now. He wasn't sure what size engines those ski boats had, but they roared like dinosaurs.

Eric noticed his pulse rate then. He was shaking. His breathing was fast and his vision got blurry on the edges.

Damn.

SEAL training kicked in. He focused on the task, focused on his breath, focused on bringing his racing heart under control.

Piloted boats in worse spots than this, he thought. *At least nobody is shooting at me here.*

His breathing was under control, but his hands were shaking.

But I want this, he thought, and his panic kicked in hard again. *I really want this. Just slow down. Take a second. Slow down.*

Eric looked around to see check the locations of the other boats. One was fifty yards off to his right, the other close to shore and even farther away.

He throttled back and sat for a moment, gathering himself.

Eric counted backwards from ten. *There's no rush,* he told himself, *this isn't being timed, just show that you can drive the damned boat. Breathe. Chill.*

He heard those dinosaur engines roar, and they were getting closer.

Oh, no. Shouldn't have stopped in the show course. Where were those damned ropes?

He wanted to look back at the dock. Was she watching him? Of course she was. That was the point. Would he be able to see the disappointment, or worse yet, the mockery on her face? Had the Deputy already walked off for more coffee and a better show?

Get a grip.

The two MasterCraft were getting close now, so Eric gunned the throttle again, his heart now beating at a more manageable clip, and scanned for gear.

The water was rough, the skis were all over the place, and dodging the ropes was a challenge, but Eric gained confidence with each pickup, with every throttle down and throttle up moment.

Know where the other boats are. Keep your head on a swivel. Be quick on the throttle. Don't be stupid.

This was bad, but it could have gone worse. Nobody died.

I've got this.

The boat shuddered and there was a harsh sound from the motor just before it stalled.

Shit.

Water spilled over the rail from the waves. Eric scrambled to check the motor.

A nylon rope was wrapped around the prop.

I ran over a rope. All that and I still fucked up.

And that's when he looked up to see one of the MasterCraft coming right for him at a high rate of speed.

Eric had a split second to determine his options, and there weren't many.

He dropped to the deck and pulled up into a fetal position, head in his arms.

Kent was a good driver. He hard spun the wheel of the MasterCraft and the boat spun out just before slamming into the side of Eric's pickup boat. A wall of water was kicked up by the power turn and Eric's boat flipped.

Eric hit the water and started swimming to get clear of his boat. His head hit a ski and he was dazed for a moment, but stroked hard and made his way to the surface.

He treaded water, surrounded by all the gear that had only moments before been safely on the deck of his pickup boat.

Kent idled up next to him. The beefy old ski manager looked down at Eric with a combination of concern and anger in his eyes.

"You hurt?"

Eric shook his head "no" and didn't say anything.

"Well, that's good. Let's get you to the dock. Can you make it onboard?"

Eric swam to the ski platform at the back of the boat and lifted himself into the MasterCraft. Kent jumped on the radio and instructed Fergus, the other driver, to clear the show course and bring his boat back in. He turned his boat around and they made their way to the dock at just over an idle.

Fergus and Kent pulled their ski boats into the lifts with practiced ease. The two older men came to Eric on the wide expanse of the dock staging area.

He sat with his head in his hands. Paulina stood next to him, her arms folded across her chest. Her dark sunglasses still covered her eyes and her mouth was a straight-line.

Eric heard Kent's voice, but his eyes were shut tight. "You sure you're ok, kid?"

One of Eric's thumbs went up, but he kept his head buried.

"You can't stop and gather your wits in the show course during a show," Ken said. "Somebody'll get killed and it'll probably be you."

"Yes, sir," Eric said without looking up.

"Eric, look at me."

Eric raised his head up and stared up at Kent.

"Listen, you had a major screw up out there, but mostly you looked like you knew what you were doing. Good driving, quick, picked up what we dropped."

"He ran over a fucking rope and almost got you both killed," said Fergus.

Kent's thick face turned purple.

"Well, it wasn't my idea to throw the damned ropes out there. That's not something a pick up boat driver usually has to deal with, Fergus. You were just making it tougher than it needed to be on the kid. We should not have thrown the damned ropes out there."

Eric felt like he was going to throw up.

"I'm not a kid and Fergus is right. I ran over the rope and I knew better. Knew it was out there."

"He ain't got the stuff, Kent. Maybe someday, but you can't put him in the show," Fergus said through a cloud of cigarette smoke.

"Hey, Eric, you know your way around an outboard well enough," Kent said, trying to sound positive, "and you were doing aces until that mistake."

"I piloted something similar to that boat in the Navy."

That was true, and it wasn't true at all, really. Eric wanted to say, *"the difference, of course, is that I wasn't going to get shot by snipers while I was driving around. The sun was out, nothing smelled bad, and nothing was blowing up, but I still panicked. I just ran over some ropes that I knew were there. Stupid mistake there and somebody could get killed. Stupid mistake here and I almost got killed. Stupid."*

He wanted to say those things, but he figured that might further poison whatever chances remained of getting hired, so he bit his tongue.

"And it looks like you know how to roll ropes. Let's take a second. Look at me."

Deep breath. Eric looked up at Kent. Fergus paced along the dock and puffed his smoke like a madman. Paulina unfolded her arms and moved her shades down to the brim of her nose. She caught Eric's attention, winked, and forced a slight smile.

Kent smiled too. "That was a near miss. It happens. Wally's right, you aren't driving next show, that's for sure. You grew up around a ski show in Wisconsin, right?"

"Mom and Dad made me join one of the amateur clubs up in Wisconsin for a couple of summers. Aqua-Pixies."

Fergus spit onto the outdoor carpet.

"Aqua-Pixies? That explains a lot. Those fuckers."

Eric laughed despite himself. *What now? He doesn't like Pixies?*

Paulina turned on her heel and walked away. "I'm out," she said as she went.

Fergus walked over to Eric and motioned for him to stand.

Are we about to throw hands? What a fucking day, thought Eric as he stood on shaky legs.

Fergus jammed a big brown nicotine and grease-stained finger into Eric's chest. His enormous mustache bristled like a silver weasel.

"I was an Eau Claire Waterbat. You shits stole the state championship back in '68 and never once apologized. You brought in three jumpers from right here at FloridaWorld. They were pros, not amateurs. That's a goddamned disqualification and you know it. Screw the Aqua-Pixies and the horse they rode in on."

Fergus stared at Eric as if daring him to present a counterargument.

"I was four years old in 1968."

Fergus grunted and stormed off on thick, bowed legs.

Kent Westheimer held his hand up to Eric for a high five. Eric reached up and slapped the man's open palm.

"That was some decent driving, young man, up until the part where you almost died."

"Thanks, Kent."

"You want to be part of the team, we'll need to do some work. Can't offer you the job today."

"Yes, sir. Understood."

"But would you be interested in shadowing for a couple of shows? I'll pay you a few bucks on the side. Gives Fergus time to calm down and gives you a chance to prove yourself before we offer you anything."

Time stopped then. Time stopped, and Eric could smell that wonderful lake and gas scent, the sunscreen and Cypress. He felt the warm breeze and the heat of the sun.

I can do this.

He was with his Mom and Dad again and they were Aqua-Pixies and that was so cool that it hurt, but in a good way.

"No promises, Eric. Cool?"

"Yes, sir. If you'll give me a chance, I think I'd like that. I'll do whatever you need."

Kent slapped him on the shoulder.

"There you go. I'll introduce you around. First though, let's go get that pick up boat flipped back over. We'll have to trade out that motor, too. Probably full of water."

"I'll pay for any damages," said Eric. Kent waved him off.

"No worries, son," Kent said, "shit happens. Nobody died, and that's what matters."

Shit happens alright, thought Eric, *and it usually seems to happen to me.*

#

The first show wouldn't start for another two hours,

but the skiers were already arriving at the stadium.

Eric marveled at the almost universal physical perfection as they wandered through the dock area and into the stadium. Every single one of them was lean muscle, swagger, and cigarette smoke. A guy with curly black hair and a fanny pack gave Eric a wave as he went by. A stunning blonde woman in high and tight shorts smiled and Eric smiled back. They all wore what appeared to be "the uniform": a white polo shirt, red shorts, and white K-Swiss tennis shoes.

That would have been a bad look on most body types, but not this ripped parade of Bacopa County's finest.

Kent led Eric from the warm Florida sun of the boat docks and staging area into the coolness of the long tunnel that ran the length of the stadium's base.

The place was perfectly designed for the purpose of staging waterski shows. Beneath the enormous steel and concrete amphitheater, there was a hidden world of offices, locker rooms, and equipment facilities. The tunnel of the venue was like a great spine with ceilings twelve feet high and carpet runners along the wide floor. Exposed mechanical, electrical, and plumbing could be seen in the tall ceiling tucked away just underneath rows of fluorescent light panels. There were metal shop fans along the tunnel that kept the air moving and somewhat cool.

Paulina Campos walked by carrying a pair of fiberglass jump skis.

"Paulie," said Kent, "show Eric around and make sure he's at the morning meeting. I've gotta go drop the kids off at the pool."

"He's hired?"

Kent shrugged. "Unofficially. He can ride, shadow the drivers, get the lay of the land. We'll slip him some bucks on the side until we can make it official."

"Since when did you have a heart?"

"Getting old. So, can you show Eric around?"

"I'd rather not."

"Great. Thanks, Paulie."

Kent didn't pay any attention to Paulina's less-than-enthusiastic complaint. Instead, he rushed off down the tunnel and made a hard turn into the men's locker room.

Paulina set the jumpers against the wall. "Come on. I'll give you the tour."

The air in the tunnel was humid and smelled of sweat, sunscreen, and age. Through that, Eric could also smell the fresh shower smell of Campos. She smelled good.

She led Eric further down the tunnel. A tall man in board shorts and nothing else stood at a large cork board and wrote on a piece of paper that was pinned to the cork. There wasn't an ounce of discernible fat on him.

"Eric Walters, this Gary Peppers, our men's captain. Carol Champlain is our women's captain and you'll meet her in our morning meeting. They're Kent's number twos."

"Commander Freedom," said Eric as he extended his hand. Gary returned the handshake with a smile.

"You were there. At Mickey D's! I remember you! That was awesome. Welcome to the team. Kent said you're from the Dells. I grew up in Adam's Friendship."

"Thanks, yeah, not officially on the team, yet. Just shadowing. And I never skied at Bartlett's or anything, but I grew up in Wisconsin."

"Go Pack."

"Go Pack."

"You think the Magic Man gets his job back this season?"

"Not a chance. The kid from Mississippi is the real deal."

"The guy from the Falcons? Not a chance. I hear he's dumb as a post."

Gary went back to scribbling on the paper.

"When you come in each morning check this board for your dock duties," said Campos. "See that sheet Gary's working on? It has your name, schedule, and what you're responsible for each day. Morning dock is important. That's basically setting up for the first show."

"Seems like quite a bit of work. More complex, I mean, than I thought a ski show would be," said Eric.

"This place has been doing ski shows for over forty years, so we have it down to a science. Still, mistakes happen, as you of all people know."

"Noted."

"If we're lucky, nobody gets hurt."

"Are there many injuries?"

Paulina pointed at her knee. There was a scar like a crescent moon around her kneecap, the skin there was much lighter than the rest of her leg.

"Had that done two years ago when I blew out my knee practicing ride overs. It's back to a hundred percent. Most people here have had something at some point. And you ski through a lot of bumps and bruises."

"Anything worse?"

Paulina was quiet for a long moment. When she spoke, Eric thought that her voice sounded more distant, less connected.

"Sometimes, yes."

"I'm sorry," said Eric.

"Don't be. It's life. It's to be dealt with and we move on."

Paulina continued the tour and when words came, they were short, quick, and to the point. There was the motor room, where the drivers and mechanics would be found wrenching in clouds of cigarette smoke. Beyond was a large equipment room. Eric peeked his head inside. There was every imaginable waterski gadget hanging from racks or lined up against the white concrete block walls. Combo skis, slaloms, jumpers, swivel skis, kneeboards, shoe skis, and even circular ski discs. Ropes of every color hung from the walls as well.

The next room was smaller but also dedicated to the ski equipment.

"This is rope and ski," said Paulina. "We take care of all of our gear here and that'll be a big part of your job if you actually get hired. Mounting bindings, making pyramid ropes, you name it. We don't send the stuff out for repair. That's all done in house."

There were framed photographs on the walls of the tunnel and work rooms. Most were from the glory days of FloridaWorld. Skiers with buzz cuts and tight Jantzen shorts skimmed across the water, leaving spray like diamonds in the sun. The photos were remarkable, thought Eric, and positioned the skiers as celebrities. Any of the images could have been on the cover of a magazine back in the day, beckoning tourists to visit the sunshine state and experience the sexy wonders. There were award plaques too, dating back dozens of years, a litany of people who had left a mark on the place. Best jumper, best swivel skier, best driver, best this and best that.

Eric didn't recognize any of the names, of course, but it impressed him that FloridaWorld seemed to care so much about their heritage, their history.

It was touching and sad at the same time.

Such a history, now dying on the vine along with the rest of this old park.

There was a spacious break room with plastic chairs and tables, a snack machine, a soda machine, and a microwave. There was no carpet here, just the cold concrete floor.

Eric noticed a trend.

Everything was designed for a wet environment. Chairs were plastic because they needed to handle wet skier butts, the hall was carpeted so that the skiers could run during the show without slipping, there weren't a lot of fabrics because the tunnel was an open space, constantly exposed to the Florida humidity.

Kent caught up with Paulina and Eric in the tunnel.

"I'll take it from here. Thanks, Paulie," said Kent.

"Yeah, thanks," said Eric. Paulina gave a half smile and walked away, taking the good clean shower smell with her.

"And this is the meeting room." Kent led Eric into a sizeable space with plenty of plastic chairs, a desk, and a whiteboard. There was an old Sony television on a wall mount in the corner. Beneath it was a VCR. "This is where we start our day." Kent checked the clock on the wall. "And that's in a half hour. Shit. I still need to get you up to meet the boss. Let's go."

"The boss?"

"The old man. Irv Irving. Come on, kid, let's take a trip to crazy town."

#

Kent and Eric walked up the long driveway that led to the Williams Mansion, now billed as *Tallahassee Commons, Where Memories Become Memories.*

There were no tourists yet at the mansion. The park was just opening, and the tours hadn't begun. The rising sun made the white of the old mansion almost too much to take. It was so bright that it almost vibrated as you looked at it, the white veined with creepers and touches of old cedar and cypress here and there. There was a flagpole in the courtyard, and it flew the stars and bars of the confederate rebellion. Eric wondered how many men, women, and children died building the mansion and then how many dainty garden parties she'd held in her day. She was a glorious old place in a racist and violent way and she stood guard over the lush emerald lawn and tastefully designed topiaries of deer, birds, and children. A row of orange trees lined the path to the mansion, and they were just blooming. Their smell was clean and wonderful and brought Eric back to that place in his mind of Florida vacations as a kid, of road trips and motels and beaches.

The tall oaken doors were wide open and beyond, in the coolness of cypress floor, tile, and marble, there was a reception desk of ornate carved wood, and beyond that a split staircase that led up to the next level. It reminded Eric of the front entrance of the house from The Munsters, the old tv show. There was nobody at the desk. Kent smacked the little bell on the desk and the ring echoed through the place in harsh metal rattles.

Eric didn't expect a Valkyrie to descend from the heavens, but that's what happened. Well, not really the heavens, but the way she came with such power and grace down the stairs from above, it had a semblance of the supernatural about it. She was tall and muscular, built like a bodybuilder, with long hair in pigtails, a metallic helmet with a pointy tip, and a stern but attractive face. There were no wrinkles on that face, as far as Eric could tell, but the lines of her bone structure were so severe that she seemed both ageless and ancient.

Her white robe flowed around her with the breeze and there were white wings on her back that were folded like an eagle's wings at rest. For a moment, Eric wasn't sure if the wings were real or part of the costume. They were covered in the most beautiful white, silver, and black feathers.

The snake woman from the ride. That's Brunhilde, thought Eric.

There was a thick snake around her neck. Eric thought it was a python, a fat one, probably longer than he was tall. It must have weighed thirty pounds at least, and she didn't seem to notice the weight.

Sometimes this whole thing seems like a weird fantasy of what I imagined FloridaWorld to be, thought Eric, *like I'm in a coma somewhere in Iraq and my mind is piecing together the strangest things to keep me alive.*

The Valkyrie came to rest at the reception desk. She was several inches taller than he or Kent and Eric was pretty sure that this woman could kick his ass in a fight. She smelled of cigarettes and something else that he couldn't place at first.

This is real. I'm not in a coma. It's just really strange.

"You're Brunhild," said Eric. "From the Monkey Kingdom."

"Call me Hilda," she said to Eric and her voice was deep and sensual. "Good morning, Kent. Who is this?"

Collard greens. She smells like cigarettes and collard greens.

Kent cleared his throat. He sounded nervous when he spoke.

"Morning, Hilda. I'm proposing to bring this man onboard to fill PBR's spot. Need to run it by the big guy."

Hilda's eyes rested on Eric.

"Yes. It was a shame about Roger. The young man you called PBR is with the angels now, in Valhalla."

"Yes, ma'am."

Hilda stared at Eric. He couldn't tell if she was interested or not, but the gaze lingered.

"What's your name?"

"Eric Walters."

Hilda looked him up and down as if he were a piece of rare beef. Her tongue briefly met her lips. Eric felt uncomfortable.

"Welcome to Tallahassee Commons. The Williams Plantation House. I am Hilda, Mr. Irving's assistant. Mr. Irving will meet you now."

With that, the Valkyrie, Hilda, turned and made her way back up the wide staircase. The wings and her white gown made it appear as if she was an angel ascending.

She did not check to see if Eric and Kent were following, but they did and soon they were led down a massive, darkened hallway to an enormous bedroom framed by tall windows. Music played from an old school vinyl record player. Eric didn't know the track, but he knew Wagner when he heard it.

There were vintage FloridaWorld posters on the walls, along with black and white photos of water-skiers, framed in mahogany and old wooden skis mounted next to the heads of deer, boar, and bear. The light was sun-cutting through the stained-glass panes and reflecting off of wall sconces.

Eric had seen some things in his life, but he wasn't ready for what he saw inside the bedroom.

Irv Irving sat on a massive throne of black and gold. He wore a black robe, and there was a long black cane in his left hand. The robe was open at the chest, and Eric got the definite sense that the man was naked underneath. The old man's white hair hadn't been cut in years, and it spilled out over his shoulders like snow on a dark mountain. His face was a landscape of wrinkles and dark skin, one eye bright and green, the other covered with a black patch.

A raven sat atop the throne. A German Shepard, powerful and gray, rested at the old man's feet and watched Eric and Kent without blinking as they entered.

He's like a king. Or a god. Hell, he created this place, so in a way, he's both.

Eric struggled to reconcile the bizarre man on the throne with the cheerful "Founder of FloridaWorld" he'd seen in media.

Hilda stepped back, behind and to the right of Irv Irving's throne.

"The new waterski show driver, Mr. Irving," she said.

The old man barely moved when he spoke, and his lips quivered.

"Ragnarok is upon us. The end of times. Twilight of the Gods," he said and his voice was a hoarse whisper. The single green eye looked hard at Eric.

Eric was quiet. He didn't know what to say. He found himself speechless under the power of that watery green eye.

The old man spoke again, and this time his voice rose and came like a thunder crack.

"Are you a man who loves the petting zoo too much? You like to startle the ponies with your probing digits? Tell me now, because I won't have it, son. Not in my home. My God!"

Eric froze.

"A creeper, are you? Touching the goats, stroking the bunnies? Is that you? God's wholesome creatures will not be violated in my presence, sir. Not now, not ever. So, I ask you again, are you a petting zoo boy?"

Kent nudged Eric with his elbow and stared at him as if to say, "Speak, idiot!"

There was a big, scary dog staring at him. His first instinct was to play along. He hesitated and then said, "I have never touched an animal in an unusual or socially unacceptable way."

The Old Man made a pucker face and grunted. "Good. That's just fine," he said. A bony finger pointed at Eric and then curled up, beckoning. Eric stepped forward a step. The dog growled. Eric stopped and subconsciously covered his crotch with both hands.

"Od's blood, son, what you fondle on your own time is your own bailiwick, but this is a godly mansion, sir. There's a line. A big red line. No buggery of the innocent small things in my home."

Change the topic, thought Eric.

"Mr. Irving," Eric said and was interrupted.

"Irv."

"Irv. My name is Eric Walters. I'm a huge fan of everything you've done, and I'd consider it an honor to work here at FloridaWorld."

Irving held up an enormous hand. The fingers were long and skeletal, and his hand reminded Eric of a spider he'd seen while in Khafji. He pointed at the framed photos on the wall. Black and white shots, some color, all of skiers on the waters of Lake May during the glory days of FloridaWorld's water circus.

"Fallen warriors. Valhalla. Days of glory and innocence," said Irving. "Gods skied these waters and walked this Earth then. They were magnificent Golden Gods of the aqua circus."

"I'm sure they were," said Eric.

"Do you like organ players?"

"What's not to love?"

"Of course you do. Kent, you're employing an organ player for our show, yes?"

"Yes sir," Kent lied. "Many organ players."

"Fine. As it should be. Nothing pre-recorded.

Organs! And women with enormous breasts?"

"The biggest, sir."

"That's fine, too. I should get down there and see the show someday soon."

Eric noticed Hilda crack a slight smile. The grin was a strange one, almost frightening, and gone in an instant.

"That would be swell, Irv," said Kent.

Irving was silent for a moment. Eric was too disoriented to speak. Kent stared at his own tennis shoes. The Valkyrie stared at them both.

"Citrus was wearing us out," Irv continued. "I saw the end coming. I wanted to make people happy. Angels on skis and organ music and happiness. You cross the Rainbow Bridge and you drink the mead and eat the mutton, but we're ghosts now. And those days are gone."

Eric considered the strong possibility that old man Irving was a complete loon. One biscuit shy of a full breakfast.

"I should see a show soon," Irv Irving said again, but lower this time, as if to himself. There was a long moment when the old man stared at his hands and nobody moved.

In the silence, Eric noticed for the first time that the room smelled of cypress wood. There were faint sounds as well, as if voices in another room were laughing and singing.

Must be a television in another room.

When he spoke again, Irv's voice trembled.

"The doctor gives me how long, Hilda?" he asked.

The Valkyrie held up three fingers.

"Three days? My God, woman!"

"Months, sir. Three months."

"By gum, that's better but not good," his voice once again at a raging volume.

"Yes, sir. But he did say that it could happen more quickly. Time is short, I'm afraid."

"Short? So was that little rascal on Fantasy Island, but that never slowed his stride."

Irv Irving looked up at Kent and Eric then. His thin lips curled into a smile that made Eric's skin crawl.

"I won't hear them howl at night anymore when I'm dead. They howl, fellas, and it's a misery, especially on long nights when my bones ache."

"Yes, sir," said Kent. He clearly had no idea what Irv was talking about.

"But that's neither here nor there," the old man continued. "Here's the rub, boys. Something bad has corrupted my yam bag. Maybe too much sun, perhaps it was the happy spray we used on our oranges to keep the bugs away. Maybe it's a Voodoo curse from one of those chicken sacrificing bitches I took my pleasures with back in the day. Whatever the case, my time along the shore is drawing to a close."

"We won't hear of it, sir," said Hilda. Irv Irving glared at her for a long moment before continuing.

"Listen, I'm not entirely mad. I know it's been a few weeks since I've gotten out into the park to meet my sunshine friends. Maybe longer. So here's the scheme. A grand day. A celebration. Of me. Irv Irving Day at FloridaWorld, you bastards. Open the budget and put on a wing ding. You read me, boys?"

There was a noise in the hallway, beyond the bedroom chamber. A voice whispered "shit" and then there were some footsteps on the hardwood floor.

"Monkey boy! Get your ass in here!" Irv Irving's voice was thunder in the room's silence.

There was a pause, and then Eric heard footsteps creak toward the bedroom door.

Shiner popped his head in.

"Sorry, boss. Just stopped in to pick up some candy from your candy stash. For the piss monkey crew. It's Radford's birthday."

Irv Irving made a low, growling sound. Shiner smiled and waved and ran away as quickly as he could, his K-Swiss making tapping sounds down the hall as he went.

Kent cleared his throat to get the old man's attention.

"Sir," he said, "you were saying you want us to throw you a party?"

"Good God, you moron, yes. A farewell to kings before I fly beyond the bridge. And here's the thing. I want a ski show. Odds are, if you move me around too much, something might fall off, so Hilda will wheel me down to the shore to see the show. A final salute from the golden gods and goddesses of Lake May. Make it happen, Kent."

"Of course, sir. Big party. In a week. Got it."

Irving fell silent again, and they all stared at each other as the record played something stirring and Germanic. Eric heard those voices in the distance again, louder this time, as if someone turned up the volume on the television in the other room ever so slightly. There was a chill in the room that wasn't there before. The hair on the back of Eric's neck stood up.

Finally, the old man spoke, and his eye fell on Eric.

"You like to read?"

Eric nodded yes. The dog growled.

"Favorite book?"

"Moby Dick."

Irv Irving laughed then. He laughed long and hard, as if he were telling himself a private joke. He settled down and smiled at Eric. The teeth were the color of root beer jelly beans.

"What do you think my white whale is, young man?"

"Maybe yourself? Eric was proud of the answer and wanted to get out of the room as soon as possible.

"Not bad," said Irv with a frown. "But what if I told you the whale is all around us? What if I told you we were in the belly of the beast? Still, as everyone knows, meditation and water are wedded forever. Here by the shore I simply begat a dream."

Irv Irving snapped his fingers. The raven made a "caw" sound, and the dog walked to the corner of the room. Irv beckoned again for Eric to come closer. When he did, Irving reached out and touched Eric on the cheek. The old man was crying, and a tear fell from his one good eye. When he spoke, it was as if he was sharing new information.

"I'll be dead soon," he said, "My balls are eat up with it. Cancer of my nethers."

"So I'm told. I'm sorry, sir," Eric said, and he was sure that the scene couldn't be stranger, but in the next moment he was proven wrong.

Irv Irving stood up and shouted to the ceiling, at the top of his old lungs -

"I've wrestled the great serpent that strangles our world!"

The dog whimpered, the bird cawed, and the Valkyrie extended her fake wings in a grand theatrical gesture. There was a little squeaking sound, and the wings flapped.

Eric didn't know what to say, so he blurted, "That must have been quite a sight," then regretted it. The old man didn't appear to hear him, though. Irving went on, as if there was no one else in the room, his voice booming.

"It strangles us all in time, eating its own tail, always eating its own. But the sword will go deep on the day of atonement, on the day when blood washes the walls of Utgard."

"Of course, sir," said Eric, feeling even like he was listening to the ramblings of a confused child.

The Wagner record skipped. Nobody made a move to nudge the record player.

Irv Irving mumbled then. They might have been

words, but there was no telling. Then, his lone good eye focused on Eric.

"Always have a backup plan, boy. Always look five moves ahead. See, I own all this and treasure besides, but what good is that if your own balls turn against you?"

Eric was quiet.

"Do us proud, sunshine friend. Welcome to FloridaWorld," said Irv Irving. "And Kent, I want my tribute to shine across those glorious waters like the shows and days and times of old."

They walked out of the room as the Wagner continued to skip, and Eric wondered if this whole thing had been a trippy dream.

The sun hit them when they emerged from Tallahassee Commons. A queue line of tourists had formed, and they waited their turns at touring the grand old mansion.

Eric stopped and looked out at Lake May. Kent took a couple of steps, then stopped when he noticed Eric wasn't with him.

"What just happened?" asked Eric.

Kent looked like a man who'd passed wind in a crowded elevator. "Sorry, kid. If I'd warned you about crazy Irv and his weird bodyguard, I figured you might just skip it and we'd never see you again. And I wouldn't blame you. That's next level batshit crazy, I'll grant you that."

"I have no words."

"Copy that. It's a freak show."

"So he never comes out to see the park?"

"I haven't seen him outside of the mansion since Reagan was in the White House."

A dragonfly buzzed past. Somewhere a band was playing something by The Beach Boys.

"Damn it, I'm gonna have to find a fucking organ player," said Kent. "And we'll need to come up with some kind of special show. In a week, no less. Good gravy."

They walked along the path back toward the stadium.

"What happens when he dies?" asked Eric. The question came as if he were talking to himself.

"That's a good question. He's got no kids, no ex-wives that are still alive, no relatives at all, as far as we can tell. Hell, he might give everything to Hilda. Or that damned wolf. Who knows?"

Eric thought for a moment as they walked. *That's a terrible thing, being so alone, surrounded by all of this, all of his dreams and work. Just alone. Terrible.*

"Hey, let's get you squared away back at the stadium. We've got a show coming up," said Kent.

Eric shook his head and followed Kent down the winding pathway back to the ski stadium as the flag of a failed racist republic snapped in the morning breeze over the Antebellum whiteness of the Williams Mansion.

"Meditation and water are wedded forever."

Eric recognized the phrase from Melville's great book. He looked out over Lake May as they walked. Her glass calm waters reflected the clouds and blue of the sky.

So beautiful. So much crazy here, and so much beauty.

Irv Irving was a lunatic, and there was something strange beyond that happening in the old plantation home.

Eric was certain there was something more going on here, but he was also certain that it was none of his business.

There was a show coming up, indeed.

#

Eric's first un-official day at FloridaWorld was the day Kenny Jones nearly died at the bottom of Lake May, in front of hundreds of people.

First, though, there was some paperwork.

"This is just a liability form in case something happens to you during the show. Keeps us off the hook whenever we have visitors or folks from the media riding in the boat. Just sign and we'll be able to let you tag along today," said Kent.

Eric signed the form and handed it back to Kent.

"Let's go," said Kent. "Time for morning start up."

Kent led the way into the meeting room.

There were a couple dozen people in the room, some asleep on the floor, others leaning against the walls, most sitting in the plastic chairs. Almost all the team had changed out of their uniforms and were wearing a rainbow of bikinis, speedos, and board shorts.

The room was loud with talk and laughter. It smelled

of cologne, sweat, sunscreen, and last night's alcohol.

A beefy young man with a shock of blonde hair that nearly covered his face was reading a comic book and smoking a menthol. Kent snatched the cigarette out of his mouth as he walked past and took his spot at the front of the room.

He dropped the smoke and ground it out under his heel.

"No smoking, Kenny."

Kenny Jones moved the comic book up and in front of his face, an act of defiance to which Kent paid no attention.

Eric wanted to sit next to Paulina, but she was bracketed by a couple of women in t-shirts and bikini bottoms so he took a seat in the back of the room next to Gary, Commander Freedom, and a tiny woman who smelled to Eric like the entire perfume counter at Burdines.

Johnny Fig, the show announcer, was already dressed in his Army Lieutenant costume and he sat in the back of the room playing some kind of portable video game. There were beeps and blips aplenty.

"Good morning, team," said Kent. "Are we ready for the day?"

"Boats are gassed up and ready to go, boss," said Gary. "Schedule is on the board for both shows."

The woman next to Eric raised her hand.

Kent's eye roll was not subtle.

"Yes, Cicely?"

The woman's voice was a cigarette-smoke rasp. Eric thought she might be young, but the sun had done no favors to her skin, so she seemed mummified.

"My family is here first show, and Gary didn't give me star swivel."

"Gary, give her star swivel."

"She's not checked out. She'll fall all over the place out there."

Cicely raised her hand again in an unnecessary gesture that conveyed boredom, anger, and a certain ignorance all at once.

"Patty checked me off on star swivel last week."

"Patty's on vacation, you idiot, and this is the first I've heard about you getting checked off. How do I know you're not yankin' my beezer?"

Cicely punched Gary hard in the shoulder.

"Kent, I'm checked off and I want star swivel. My family is here first show."

"Give her star swivel, Gary." Kent said with a sigh, "But if you fall, Cicely, it's double dock for a week."

"And covering for a star swivel fall is the worst. I never know what to say. The music has lyrics, and the script they gave me is horrible. Don't fall, please," said Johnny Fig.

"Fig, you've been doing these shows long enough. It's high time you learned how to say a few things to cover for falls," said Kent.

Fig went back to his portable video game. "I say what's in the script. Write a new script and I'll say whatever you want me to as long as it's written down. You know, in the script."

Kent sighed so loudly that it sounded as if his larynx was going to burst.

Eric thought he heard Cicely's teeth grind.

"Ain't gonna fall," she said.

Someone in the back of the room laughed. Cicely turned around and glared at everyone and nobody.

"Ain't gonna fall!"

Eric glanced over to Paulina and saw that her eyes were closed and her mouth was open, a thin line of drool dangled from her lip.

She was sound asleep.

"Let's move on, for the love of mud. Alright, team, we have a guest this morning. Please welcome our visitor for the day, Eric Walters."

Eyes turned to Eric, and there was a smattering of applause. The sleeping remained asleep - and that included Paulina Campos.

"He's from the Dells. Eric will be shadowing for pick up boat duties for both shows today and we're hoping to have him ready for an official tryout PDQ. Billy, he'll ride with you."

A lean, tattooed man wearing only a pair of shorts and Oakley's with electric yellow frames raised his hand in acknowledgment.

"So, Eric, you ride with Billy. Watch what he does, help pick up skis and roll ropes. It ain't rocket science."

"Yes, sir," said Eric.

Fergus made a snorting noise from his spot in the corner of the room.

"Funny, Kent, I thought Mr. Aqua Pixie already had his tryout this morning. I remember something about a flipped pub boat and you nearly t-boning the sumbitch. Or am I mis-remembering?"

"I'm sure Eric here is going to ace his second chance. America loves a comeback story. Put a sock in it, Fergus."

Fergus said something profane under his breath and sparked up a cigarette.

"No smoking in here, Fergus," said Kent. Fergus grunted and dipped his smoke into his coffee.

"So, here's the big news," continued Kent, "and it's a whopper. The Old Man dropped a bomb on us when we were up there just now."

"He's selling the park," said Karen, the costume manager.

"No, damn it, Karen, but almost as big. The Old Man wants us to do a tribute celebration. He's getting along in years, and he wants us to throw a wingding in his honor. That means a special show. So, more to come on that."

"Do you think we'll get overtime?" asked Fig.

"He said open the checkbook, so who knows? Like I said, more to come."

"Open the checkbook, he says," said Karen, and her eyes rolled so dramatically that Eric was concerned for a moment that the woman might have harmed herself.

"Now," continued Kent, "only a couple more things. One, if I show up for an after-hours ski party, do not attempt to pass me a joint."

There was some laughter.

"I will fire the next son of a bitch who tries to pass me weed at a party. I make twice what you idiots make and I have a pension plan through the company and I'm not going to lose my job because one of you morons thinks it's funny."

"Boss, we don't drug test anymore."

"My luck they'd start it up again. Just don't. Two, I don't know who the Mad Crapper is but knock it off. Nobody appreciates finding a turd in their binders during the show. Three, the cheap beer and chili party is Friday night. Plan accordingly for Saturday morning. Any questions?"

Karen raised her hand. "There's a rumor going around that the park is being sold. Is that true?"

Kent sighed with a sound like a wet fart. "Again with that? You know everything I know, Karen."

"What does that mean?"

"I've heard that rumor too, and I don't know if it's true or if it's not. So let's just focus on doing shows and getting this big celebration squared away and we'll see what happens down the road. Good?"

"I seen the budget for this fall and I seen what we're cutting just to make it work."

"Where did you see the damned budget?"

"On your desk. Well, in your desk but never mind

that, Kent Westheimer. I seen it. No K-Swiss sponsorship, no Minerva work-out machines, and no end of the year party. I seen it all and more."

Kent's mouth was open wide, but nothing came out.

"Is this true, Kent?" asked Gary.

Kent shot an angry look at Karen.

"You shouldn't be digging through my desk."

"Well, I've got kids and a mortgage, unlike most of these teenage idiots, and if I lose my job after thirty years of this crap, I'm going to end up charging nickels for blowjobs behind Fudge-O-Rama. And that'll be on you," Karen said.

She then stood, pointed a long finger at Kent, spit, and walked out of the meeting.

"These shoes are garbage anyway," said Kenny Jones from behind his comic book.

There was some laughter.

"Look, this isn't how we wanted to share the news, but yes. There are some budget cuts coming, but we all have our jobs, and the park isn't being sold. So relax, and don't listen to Karen."

"But the Minerva machines," said Alexa Bodinger, a local girl with a physique like a bodybuilder and a reputation for taking zero shit from anyone.

"Sorry, but those Minerva folks have us by the short and curlies and they won't budge. Those workout gadgets will be gone by the end of the month, unfortunately."

"And what if Old Man Irving sells us?" asked Alexa.

Kent's morning meeting was spiraling out of control. He threw his hands up in the air.

"Then he sells us. Maybe Disney buys us and we all get raises. Maybe they bulldoze the place and put up condos. What do you want from me?"

Johnny Fig looked up from his video game. The beeps stopped. "I heard Irv's already dead. It's just his corpse up in that mansion, looking out over the lake with dusty eyes."

"Sweet baby Jesus, son, I just met with the man a half hour ago."

"Don't take the Lord's name in vain," said Alexa.

"Of course. Sorry about that. Alright, let's have good shows," said Kent and there was another smattering of applause.

Those sleeping continued to sleep.

Eric and some of the other team members wandered into the hallway outside of the meeting room. The one named Billy Natsume shook Eric's hand.

"We preset the pub boat out to the right of the show course a half hour before the show. Get your gear on and meet me on the back dock."

Billy was rail thin and sported a series of tribal tattoos along his arms, with skin tanned dark and hair cut short. He wore a pair of sunglasses with a frame so yellow that it seemed electrified.

Eric made his way into the locker room. A couple of the guys were already in there. Dave and Freak. They sat on the long metal bench and played cards. Both were buck naked.

Dave was an older man with some silver in his close-cropped hair and a reasonable beer belly. Freak had long brown hair and seemed to be made of nothing but skin and bone.

Eric couldn't help but notice Freak's massive member was flopped over his thigh like a tube of pre-made chocolate chip cookie dough.

Nobody's shy around here, that's for sure.

"Hey, newbie," said Freak.

"Hey," said Eric. He stripped down and changed out into his new board shorts, stuffed his gear into his locker, and went back down the stadium tunnel to the boat dock.

Billy Natsume was already there, electric sunshades in position, and he had the pickup boat tied to the dock. Skiers were moving more quickly now, getting ready for the show. A few were already in costumes. There were a trio of Nazis, a couple of hillbillies, and one man in clown makeup dressed as Hitler.

The sound of the pre-show banjo player blared from a pair of cheap speakers.

Eric tried to make small talk.

"How long have you been a driver?"

Billy Natsume spit and looked like he might lash out.

"Ain't no fucking driver. Skier. Tweaked my shoulder so can't ski for a few weeks. Gotta drive the damned pub boat and babysit newbies. Can't heal up fast enough. Pub boats the lowest of the low, fit for injured skiers and idiots."

Well, I'm not injured and I'm not a skier yet, so clearly I'm an idiot.

"Got it."

#

This was it, then.

Showtime.

Storm clouds on the far horizon, the Florida sun still hot and high, the wide expanse of Lake May, a stadium half-full of tourists steaming in the midday heat.

Eric sat at the bow of the boat while Billy handled the throttle on the Mercury outboard.

Billy pointed things out as they made a wide arc out to their preset position.

There was a line of old car tires tied together and strung out parallel to and just outside of the show course. To Eric, it looked like a barrier. Billy confirmed that suspicion.

"We keep the tire line for two reasons. Helps with the waves, which can get rough during the summer, and keeps the locals from getting too close in their Weekend Wally boats. They can watch the show from the other side of the tire line."

There were canals and drainage pipes, huge ones, along the shoreline next to the boat docks.

"Those canals wind along into the cypress trees for miles. We used to run tours through there until a kid fell out of the tour boat one day and lost his leg to a mama gator. That big drainage pipe there goes back years, and from what I understand, it'll take you all the way out to the other side of the parking lot. I wouldn't recommend swimming it, though. God knows what lives in there."

Eric made a mental note that he would not, at any point, go swimming in the drainage pipe.

After rounding along the show course, Billy throttled down, and they waited just outside of sight, bobbing up and down on the water, the motor at idle.

"Okay, newbie," said Billy. "Watch what I do and when I do it. Hold on tight. I'll try to toss you out of the boat. See if I don't. Don't fuck up."

Eric smiled and nodded yes.

And then all hell broke loose.

The opening of the show was a series of fast-hitting acts in rapid succession. A trio of skiers screamed in behind one of the ski boats, each on two skis, then they literally jumped out of those skis at forty miles per hour. It happened fast. They jumped out, they were barefooting, and then they were landing on the beach.

Two ski jump outs, thought Eric. *I tried that when I was a kid and nearly broke my neck. They just made it look easy.*

Three skiers jumping out of their skis left six skis in the show course that needed to be retrieved.

Even before the trio landed on shore to the roar of the audience, Billy twisted the throttle hard and they rocketed into the show circle, skirting one MasterCraft that was setting up for their next act to pull while launching over the wake of the first boat as it passed.

Eric's ass bounced hard up and down on the metal seat and he held on to the rail with a death grip.

He heard a sharp sound like wood slapping metal and turned to see a jumper perform a front flip off of one of the jump ramps in the center of the lake.

No random ski to pick up there, but the jumper and his boat were another high-speed obstacle to be aware of and avoid in the chaos.

If the audience felt a sense of danger while watching the skiers, they didn't know the half of it. To ride in the pickup boat during the show was a frenzy and Eric felt an adrenaline rush like he hadn't felt since he was in the Zodiac running hot under a sliver of a moon in the Arabian Gulf.

There were trick skiers who landed on the clamshell stage in front of the audience. There were jumpers who threw lofty acrobatics from the center ramp, then skied off to wait for their next act on the dock at the far left of the show site. There was a skier on a disc, then two guys and a girl in a kneeboard pyramid formation.

Riding in a boat during a ski show is a rush, a confusion, a chaos, a calculated risk. Divorced from the stage antics and the music, unable to hear the announcer, there were just the speed and tight turns, the spray and the wind, moments of high excitement and then moments when they waited for the next act to drop skis. Like aquatic vultures, Billy and Eric swooped in and grabbed whatever detritus was floating. Usually, they needed to move quickly, often just throwing the gear onto the deck and throttling out before another boat slammed into them. The lake was churned up and the little deck boat was tossed almost to the point of capsizing, but Billy knew what he was doing.

Throttle down again, through the crashing wake of a big MasterCraft.

Eric held tight.

Billy took a hairpin turn, hard on purpose, and Eric felt himself lift up and nearly out of the boat. The only thing that kept him from flying out into Lake May was the strength of his right hand.

Gravity slammed his backside down into the boat with a thud, and his teeth came together hard.

"Almost got ya," said Billy with a laugh. "Tight work, newbie."

"Nice try," said Eric.

"Heads up, we got crash and burn coming up. This one's fast. First thing we'll grab will be combo skis we use for ramp slam."

Ramp slam. Eric remembered the act from watching the show the day before. It was a comedy act. The whacky Nazi is pulled skiing into the side of the massive jump ramp, slams his skis against it, and sinks with a zany plop sound effect.

Billy had the boat at idle just to the left side of the clamshell stage, just yards away from where the skier would take off. It was Kenny Jones. He held onto the ski handle with both hands, the rope playing out to the ski boat's center pylon.

The announcer shouted something incomprehensible. The MasterCraft took off, and after the rope went taught, so did Jones.

Kenny Jones hit the water on two skis and pretended to flail comically as he skied towards the metallic side of the jump ramp.

Eric heard the announcer then, shouting directions to Jones.

Johnny Fig shouted, "Go left! Go right! No, left! Right! Left! Wrong!"

Kenny intentionally slammed into the side of the big aluminum ramp. There was a comedic sound effect from the audio system. The scene played out like something from a Warner Brothers cartoon and was usually a guaranteed laugh for the audience.

This time, though, Kenny's skis slipped out from under him and the back of his head hit the ramp.

Hard.

That wasn't supposed to happen.

Eric heard Billy mutter, "Shit" under his breath.

The pickup boat throttled down and came out fast toward the ramp. They were the closest, and they'd been the only ones outside of the audience and Johnny Fig to see Kenny Jones knock himself out and slide into the water.

Billy killed the throttle for fear of running Jones over with the prop, and the boat coasted fast to the spot where Kenny had hit.

Kenny Jones had gone under.

Eric didn't have time to think. SEAL training kicked in.

He jumped into the lake and opened his eyes.

Visibility was zero.

The lake water was dark with tannins, even on a bright day. Eric looked left, right, down.

Nothing.

The water made sloshing sounds in his ears. He could hear and even feel the other boats still going through their patterns.

Damn.

Eric came up, took a fast and deep breath, and went back down. He swam under the ramp and checked in the darkness.

Wasp nests and spider webs. Nothing else.

Eric swam hard, straight down. Lake May was deep here, nearly twenty feet in parts. Eric pushed his muscles to their limit, his eyes wide open, scanning for a kid dressed as a Nazi.

So hard to see and it was harder the deeper he went.

Son of a bitch.

A fish swam past his face. His lungs were burning. He'd used up his air with the strength of his strokes.

Eric came up again, this time with a gasp.

He heard Billy shout something, but his ears were full of water and he was too busy taking another deep breath to pay any attention.

That kid is going to be dead soon if he wasn't already.

Eric went down again and swam as fast and as hard as

he could. He felt like his heart was going to explode and his eyes burned from the lake water.

Bubbles.

Wait.

Silver bubbles drifted up from the depths.

Maybe.

Eric swam deeper. The glow of the white sand bottom came up on him fast. There, in the murk of the tea colored water, was an unconscious kid dressed like the Gestapo.

Eric didn't have any air left and his lungs were screaming, but he got to Kenny Jones in four strokes.

Shit, the kid's tangled up in some of the tape grass at the bottom.

Eric yanked hard and pulled Jones free. Some of the lake weed that was wrapped around his feet trailed mud as they ascended.

He came up out of Lake May just as he was about to pass out from the effort. He had Kenny Jones in his arms. Billy was there, and another boat as well.

Hands grabbed Jones and pulled him to the floor of a MasterCraft.

Eric treaded water as Billy pounded on Kenny's chest until the lake water came up and nobody died in Lake May during the first show of the day.

It was the trail of bubbles, really. Just a trail of bubbles and Eric Walters were the difference between Kenny Jones being alive and being dead.

FloridaWorld

14

Sunday Night

A1A is the spine that runs along Florida's east coast - or more accurately, it's the vein along the back of a shrimp, all curvy and congested and sometimes full of shit. That said, there are stretches of that road where the development bleeds away and old Florida is there again, miles of palmetto and cactus that form a wall of dark green against the turquoise of the ocean and the white of the sands, where pops of red from wildflowers spatter the side of the road and there are old motels and older fish shacks and motorcycles roaring into the morning.

Eric's left arm was resting on the open window frame of the Firebird as he pushed the engine along just such a beautiful stretch of road. The stars sparkled against the early night sky. He wasn't sure how it had happened or why, but Paulina was next to him, and she smelled fresh from her post-show shower and the sea breeze from the open windows whipped her black hair back from her face.

It all happened fast, he knew that for sure. What a day.

After they carted away Kenny Jones to be checked for skull fracture and concussion, the show went on, and Eric rode in the boat as if it was perfectly natural to save a man's life during a ski show. By the time he rode the second show of the day, he had a better understanding of the boat patterns and of the expectations, of where the skis would be dropped intentionally and where they might end up anyway because of boat wakes or wind. He rolled a hundred ropes and learned to set up the dock. He received more than a few "attaboys" and promises of beers because of his Kenny Jones rescue adventures.

Eric was almost to his car when he heard footsteps coming up fast behind him. It was Kent.

"Hey, brother, I never had the chance to make this official today, what with everything that's going on. You still want a job at the show?"

Eric's heart felt like it mule kicked his sternum.

"Yes, sir," he managed to spit out. Kent smiled and slapped him on the shoulder.

"Swell. I know a good kid when I see one and I knew you had the stuff, even when you fucked up your pub boat tryout. Saving Kenny Jones swung the deal with the rest of the team. Let's go do your paperwork and I'll hand over your gear."

"Thanks, Kent. I won't let you down."

"Hell, don't thank me yet. Park's probably going out of business in a month, so what have I got to lose by hiring a newbie who used to be an Aqua Pixie? Besides, this show for Irv is an all hands on deck situation."

"I'm supposed to be at Mid-Florida in the morning," Eric said.

"Look, I know the owner out there. I'll call him personally and ask if he's ok that we steal you for a few days. Are you comfortable with me making that call?"

Eric smiled.

"Well, this sounds like a heckuva lot more fun than wrestling rancid bags of beer cans, so, yes. I'll follow up with a call, too. Just to be square."

Kent laughed.

"Good deal. Let's go to my office and make it official."

I'll be damned. Just like that. Maybe things are turning around.

Once in Kent's office, the formalities were quick. Some paperwork, a warning that there was a sixty day out clause that allowed FloridaWorld to end the deal, and a handshake.

"Here's your gear. Wear this whenever you're out in the park. Once you're here at the stadium, you can wear whatever the hell you want. Punch time is 8 am tomorrow. Welcome to FloridaWorld, Eric Walters," said Kent with a smile and a wink.

It would be nice if Mom and Dad could see me now. Happy. Would be cool if they could see me happy.

Eric was nearly out of the stadium and on his way to the parking lot when Paulina Campos stepped in his path.

"I hear you got the job. Saving somebody's life apparently trumps nearly getting killed driving a pickup boat. Welcome aboard, newbie."

"Thanks," said Eric, "and I'll get better in the pub boat. Count on it."

"Remember that coffee you wanted to buy me?"

Eric was too stunned to speak.

"I don't want a coffee," Paulina said, "I want to get out of here and go to the beach."

"Sun's going down soon."

Paulina didn't smile or laugh, she just looked Eric straight in the eyes and said, "It's good at night. I want to get out of here. I want a beer and a fish sandwich, and I want to go to the beach. You drive, and I'll pay for gas, beer, and food."

Eric almost stuttered when he answered. "Absolutely. And that's appreciated because I get about twelve miles to the gallon. I could get us to the coast, but I might not make it back."

Paulina broke eye contact. "That would be okay too," she said, then she turned on her heel and started walking out.

And that's how Eric found himself with Deputy Paulina Campos on that beautiful stretch of A1A on a

Sunday night when the sky was clear and the moon was high. He couldn't hear the ocean crashing off to his right as he drove north through Ormond Beach and toward Flagler County because the Firebird's big engine was roaring and the radio station was playing the new song by REM called *"Man on the Moon."*

Paulina knew her way around the area, and she told Eric to pull in when they approached a brightly lit place on the edge of the shore, just past the line into Flagler Beach. He could smell fried seafood and hear the jukebox and the crowd before he stepped out of the car. His shoes crushed seashells as he followed Campos into the restaurant.

They grabbed a table outside where the breeze kept the no-see-ums away, and there was a bucket of cold beer between them within seconds.

"Cheers. Welcome to the team," Paulina said. She tapped his beer with her own. They drank as the sweat from the beer bottles ran down their wrists.

"Nice place," said Eric.

She didn't seem to hear him. She just looked out at the ocean and watched the waves roll in white under the light of the moon.

Well, this is awkward, thought Eric. He wanted to say "Do you come here often?" but that would have been awful, of course, so he struggled for an alternative.

"You a regular?" *Not bad,* he thought.

"Do I come here often?" the sarcasm in her voice was sharp.

"Basically, I guess."

"Yes," she said, "I do. Cocoa is closer, but I like it up here. If you keep going north, it gets pretty and quiet and then there's St. Augustine. This area works for me."

"I get it," Eric said. "This is what I think of when I think of a beach in Florida. Seems authentic to a guy from Wisconsin."

"It's too late now, but during January and February you can watch whales up here, right offshore. Right whales. They're rare. It's not easy to spot them either."

The server came with plastic menus. He wore board shorts and a tank top under his white apron, as if he might have just finished surfing a set before work. His bleached blonde hair was partially hidden under a baseball cap.

Eric and Paulina checked out the options. Seafood baskets, fish sandwiches, not a salad in sight.

"Fried fish sandwich with extra hush puppies," said Paulina, as she handed the menu back to the server.

"Grilled shrimp," said Eric.

"Righteous choice, dude," said the server as he turned on a heel and disappeared into the crowd.

The sound was country music from a jukebox, the chatter of sunburned and buzzed locals, a ballgame on the television over the bar, and somewhere in the distance the crashing roll of waves on the shore.

"Kent said you served. Army. How was your tour?"

Paulina shrugged and drank some beer before answering. "Better than yours, I guess."

"Ouch. Yeah. So you left on your own accord, I guess."

"I didn't get booted out, no. What was it?"

"Huh?"

"What did you do?"

Eric had been on better first dates, but then he stopped himself and began wondering if this really was a date. Paulina might as well have been a menu in a language he didn't speak.

"Long story."

"I thought you were an archeologist, Mr. Cal Berkeley. Story's probably not as long as all that if you break it down."

"Right. Being a cop suits you."

Paulina's eyes flashed, and she spoke.

"My money says you stole something from somebody, and it blew up into a fight. Maybe you hurt somebody during the fight, hurt them bad enough to get noticed. You tried to plead drunk and stupid, but it didn't work because you were a SEAL, and they have high standards. Am I close?"

"And what is it about me that makes you think I'm a thief?"

"You're smart, so you probably didn't do something stupid during a mission, and it would really need to be something massively stupid in order to get a less than honorable discharge. You have guts, we saw that today when you pulled Jones out of the water, so you're no coward. You have a hero complex, again, as we saw today, so you didn't commit some kind of atrocity against a local. Process of elimination, nothing else. Am I right?"

"To be fair, archeology involves a certain amount of theft. At least sometimes."

"Oh. Okay. That's a clue."

"Not really," he said, but then he realized that it actually was a clue, and he'd allowed the conversation to open up in ways he didn't expect.

"You're a SEAL, but archeology is your true love. So you come upon some relics during a raid or a mission or some shit and you decide to liberate a few things."

Eric smiled and felt a sheen of sweat pop out on his skin.

"Called it," said Paulina.

"Do you know how many priceless artifacts were destroyed during Desert Storm and the subsequent operations? How many are still being destroyed?"

"Quite a few, I bet."

Eric took a deep pull on his beer before he continued. "Yes. Quite a few. We're talking about the cradle of civilization and things that have been hidden by desert sands for thousands of years. And now let's introduce the biggest, deadliest, most destructive weapons of the modern world. Let's blow shit up. So yes, quite a few things that are priceless get lost in war."

"You stole something."

"Let's just say that a few important historical items were safely extracted from hot zones and this might have been done without military authorization."

"You sold relics on the black market and got caught."

"Your words, not mine."

The food came then and with it, another bucket of beer on ice.

They ate and drank and said little for a while. The food was good and the breeze from the ocean was fine so there was no need for discussion, no desire for an argument or a quip, there was just a beach shack seafood joint on a cloudless night and that was enough.

After the food and the beers and the tab were paid, Eric and Paulina made their way down an old wooden walkway to the sand. They dropped their shoes at the end of the walkway. Sea oats brushed against their legs as they walked to where the waves became white on hitting the shore. The lights of a shrimp boat twinkled just offshore, and the moon was high and bright now.

They walked north, the water to their right, and there wasn't another soul to be seen. Their feet crunched the sand and felt cool on their toes.

"You grew up in Bacopa County?"

"We don't need to talk," said Paulina.

"No, but I'd like to just the same," said Eric and he hoped that his irritation didn't come through in his voice.

"Fine. Yes," said Paulina. "I grew up in Bacopa County. At the park, really."

"How so?"

Paulina didn't respond at first, and when she did, her

voice was low. "Grandma Alma was Irv Irving's housekeeper. Mom was too, for a while, but she quit when I was little. We stayed in town, though. I was in and out of the mansion with my Grandma and in and out of places with Mom. Didn't have any money to go anywhere else. Then Mom died, and I moved back in with Grandma Alma. So, yeah, I grew up in Bacopa County."

It was Eric's turn to hesitate before he spoke. "I met the old man today, and it was strange to say the least."

Paulina was silent.

"Was he always so eccentric?"

"He was always a fucking bastard. I just didn't always know it. What's it like growing up with money, Eric?"

The question came out of nowhere, and he took a moment to respond. "We didn't have all that much, and it went away fast when they died, so I don't know how to answer that question. It's your perception, but it's not my reality."

"Did your parents clean toilets so little Eric could have enough food to eat?"

"No. They did not."

"They were good parents, yes? Your parents?"

"Yes."

"Sometimes those toilets are real dirty, and sometimes there's no food no matter what your parents do. Sometimes being good, and working hard, doesn't matter. That's reality, not perception."

She stopped then and pulled her t-shirt over her head

and threw it on the sand. Her fingers went to her jean shorts, and she unzipped them, stepped out, and kicked them away. The underwear came off next, and Paulina Campos walked naked into the water.

Well, this has been a day, thought Eric. *Some day.*

He considered his options. There were two, really. One, join her. Two, sit on the sand and wish that he'd joined her. He looked around. The beach was wide and empty. They were a half mile from the seafood joint, and there was nothing but tall sea oats and scrub brush between the sand and this quiet stretch of A1A.

She was knee deep, and he considered what might swim in those waters at night. Eric was a Wisconsin guy and the thought of dangling his bits in the ocean where a passing shark could take a chomp left him cold. He had a momentary vision of himself screaming and running out of the water with a crab attached to his sack.

Still, Paulina Campos was beautiful and naked and only ten yards away.

He took a deep breath and stripped naked. Eric walked into the water. He flinched at the cold when it hit his ankles and then made a little shrieking sound when the spray from a wave break dowsed his Johnson.

Damn, he thought, *it's cold and I'm going to look like I have a baby mushroom between my legs.* He covered himself with his hands as he went deeper and closer to Paulina.

He needn't have bothered. She wasn't looking at him.

Paulina Campos was half floating, half standing in waist-deep water, the little waves breaking around her in explosions of silver. Her hands were out, trailing along in the water, her head back. Eric saw then that she was looking up at the moon and the stars.

Something jumped nearby. A mullet or some other bait fish.

"Hey, I get bit by a shark that's on you," he said and his voice broke when he spoke. Paulina said nothing.

Still, though, the cold of the water was fine once he was in and the surf was light so that he could stay balanced and float. It felt good.

Paulina sang then. Eric didn't know the song, but the melody was simple and lovely and her husky voice was wonderful. The lightness, the joy in the song, made him think it must be an old Appalachian song, a lullaby she'd learned as a child.

He was next to her as she sang. There was water on her face and he could not tell if they were tears or if the water from the sea had splashed her face. She did not look at him as she sang, it was as if he weren't even there, as if Paulina were alone in the surf at night and she sang to the moon and the stars and to the vast blackness of the ocean.

When the song was done, Paulina turned to Eric and swam closer until their faces were only inches apart.

Those are tears, he thought, and then she held him by the face and kissed him. Her hands were rough, and her grip was hard. They kissed as the cold Atlantic swirled around them and then their hands found each other and they came together. Her body felt strong, warm in the chill of the sea, and they held, kissed, and touched each other until the cold was too much.

All thoughts of work, of the darkness around them and what might be in it, all thoughts of anything but the taste and smell of each other drifted away along the dark spine of A1A.

#

The old Plantation House on Lake May stood witness to the saving of Kenny Jones that day. As the sun faded and the lake grew dark, the place welcomed a certain Dr. Claude Bluford to her halls. Hilda greeted him at the door and motioned that he could enter and proceed on his way. He smiled at her, hoping to win her smile in turn, but Hilda grimaced and turned away.

She's wonderfully brusque, he thought, *what a day it would be if we were to embrace. Perhaps embrace and more.*

Dr. Bluford watched Hilda walk away for a moment, then shuffled quickly along as he knew the place well and was eager for the night's conversation. Up the stairs and around the bend he went, the creaks and groans of the old floors a chorus as he made his way to the foreboding bedroom of Irv Irving.

Dr. Bluford entered and sat in an uncomfortable chair a few feet from the side of Irv's large, ornate bed. The room was dim except for the amber glow of gas lamps and some light that spilled in between cracks in the curtains.

"Are you well, Mr. Irving?"

"I'm dying from ball cancer, you fuck-stick. What do you think?"

"Of course, sir."

"I am most certainly not well. I am anything but well."

"Yes sir. You are taking your medication, yes?"

"Your happy pills, doctor? They do nothing."

"I can increase the dosage, Mr. Irving. That can cause a bit of constipation, though, so we should consider our options."

"I shit tar balls now, you dumb fuck, so triple the dosage. I don't care."

"The medication should help to ease your anxiety, sir. Here. Take two."

Old Man Irving took the pills from Dr. Bluford and knocked them back. He chewed them.

"Water?"

"Fuck you."

"Sir, when last we spoke, you were telling me about the great golden globe. Do you remember that story?"

Old Man Irving glared at the doctor with his one good eye. Bluford continued.

"Yes, well, we were discussing what this golden globe might represent. Might it be your memories of the sun? Of oranges? Of the glories of the citrus industry?"

Irving spat a massive green gob onto the floor. It struck with a splat.

"It represents the soul of this kingdom, you idiot. The treasures of FloridaWorld. Of my father."

"Sheriff Irving."

"No. My father."

"Sir Reginald Williams."

"Yes."

"When did you first imagine this golden treasure, sir?"

Old Man Irving was quiet then for a moment. When he spoke, his voice was low.

"As a child. I saw it. It was a glory. Shining bright, a staff of jewels and an orange of gold. It was lovely."

"Why do you think you remember it now?"

"Alma died. She was there too. Poor old Alma. She helped me hide it. She helped me keep it a secret through all those days. Good old Alma."

"Your housekeeper. Yes?"

"More than that," Irv said, and then his voice rose again. "And less than that. I'm going to hell, you fucking head shrink and your happy pills won't stay the hand of the devil. I'm going to burn, Doctor Claude Bluford, as well I should. So fuck you."

"Where is your treasure, sir? This great golden globe? Do you keep it here in the mansion? Or perhaps it's just a dream?"

Claude felt that he'd overplayed his hand, but he was so anxious and time was so short.

"It's in the belly of the whale, you bastard. And it's not imaginary. I'm not mad. I'm just pissed."

Old Man Irving threw a thick book at Dr. Bluford and it struck him on the forehead. Bluford felt a sharp blast of pain, and then blood leaked from his thin scalp.

"Get out of here, you fucking quack."

Dr. Bluford held his wound with his hands and staggered out of the room.

Hilda was not there. The hallway was dark and quiet.

He looked at himself in one of the many mirrors.

Scalp wounds bleed. It was a superficial cut, and he'd be fine.

It's in the belly of the whale. And it's not imaginary.

Dr. Claude Bluford made tracks down the hall and then down the steps. He hoped Hilda wouldn't see him in this state. A bloody, frantic mess of a man.

He rather liked Hilda and often imagined what it would be like to surrender himself to her cruel yet tender mercies.

Thoughts of finding himself helpless in her powerful arms carried him out the door and away.

#

Hilda finished cleaning Irv Irving just as the sun set, when the shadows grew long and snaked through the darkness of the mansion like the spirits of the dead.

The tourists were gone and so were the tour guides, the teenagers who made six bucks an hour to walk guests through the lower levels of the old place, to repeat the scripted story of the mansion's glorious past and hopeful future, of the wonders created by Irv Irving here in this hallowed and sacred place, of the lives changed and the dreams brought to life and the sunshine friends made along the way.

Irv Irving intentionally integrated his old family home into FloridaWorld and always intended the place to feel like one of the park's premier attractions. As years had passed and guest expectations changed, the mansion experienced less and less foot traffic. Fewer visitors were willing to take time out of their day to be led through her dusty hallways.

Hilda's shift at the Monkey King attraction was done and had already been forgotten. She'd been Brunhilde for most of her adult life and each shift just blended into the next and disappeared into some dark closet in the back of her mind.

Irv's filth was a dark and sticky tar now, with a smell that had grown even worse as the disease ate away at his body. Hilda used paper towels dipped in soapy water to remove the mess from the old man's skeletal shanks and thick white pubic fur. She would tolerate his insistent penis, shockingly hard even in his decline. She would ignore his howls and laments, she would wipe and scrub and tug him off if necessary because she was playing a long game, and she did not need to upset the apple cart because of some shit and a handie.

"My music," said Irving in a voice like a flutter of a bat's wing. Hilda lifted him to the vastness of his bed and tucked him naked into the sheets. His mane of silver hair splayed out over the black pillows and he stared up at the carvings on the ceiling with his one good eye.

She tuned an old tube radio to the local FM "oldies" station. The warm glow of the set and the doo wop vocals transported them back to a distant time. Hilda washed her hands in the great porcelain sink of the old man's bathroom and considered herself in the tall mirror.

She was naked. It was best, she had learned from experience, to clean him nude. There was no telling when he might emit something foul, and she hated to soil her costume. Hilda was a strong woman, and she was proud of her strength. She was so tall that the dark diamond of her pubic hair could be seen at the lower edge of the mirror. She let her fingers run through the soft hair and then lower still.

It felt good.

Pulling the old man off was a chore and a bother, but there were times, like tonight, when she found herself aroused as she tugged on the silly flesh spigot. The whole thing seemed so dirty and in some ways that was fine. Nobody else knew what she did, and Irv Irving wasn't going to tell.

Not after all this time.

She was his favorite Brunhilde for a reason.

It had been days since she'd pleasured herself and years since anyone had been down there, really down there to do the serious work.

Who was the last one?

Hilda felt a moment of sadness when she couldn't

think of her last lover, but then she saw the face of that man from the power company, his firm hands, his breath that smelled like Mountain Dew. She didn't miss love making, not really, but she imagined that she'd make up for lost time when she was free to fly from here, the chains of Valhalla forever broken.

She pulled her fingers up from her groin and inspected the hairs in her fingers. There were a few silver ones now, but she wasn't afraid of growing old. She had a secret and her time was going to come soon enough.

Hilda flexed, and her thick muscles pulsed in the dim light. She was certain she could snap the old man's neck with one hand and cave in his bony chest with the other.

That wouldn't be necessary, though. Not at all. The disease was doing the good work and there was another plan ready to put into play when the time was right.

Hilda walked naked through the amber light of Irv Irving's bedroom and out into the hallway. There was no chance she would be seen. Not only were the tour guides gone, they kept everything above the first floor locked off from view for privacy. It was just Irv and Hilda and the ghosts. The many ghosts.

The air felt good on her skin as she walked past the framed ads for FloridaWorld, the mounted animals, the suit of armor from one of the films that had been shot here, "The Knights of St. Augustine", starring Tex Flannery and Poco the Chimp. She did not name the ghosts when she saw them or heard them. She just knew them as Fancy Man Dressed like A Mouse, as Flapper

Girl with a Cigar, as Bloody Black Man. They paid her no attention, and she'd known them for so long now that she paid them no mind, either.

The spirits were just there, like the Cypress Trees or the dust.

Hilda's room was simple, with large windows that looked out over the lake. The glass was made in such a way that nobody could have seen her, even if they'd had the interest to look, so she didn't bother putting her costume back on. The Valkyrie suit was on a costume post in the corner, the wings spread wide to air out. The metal needed a good polish, but she didn't want to bother with that tonight. An enormous terrarium held her snake, Jormungand, while several smaller exhibits were home to other reptiles.

Hilda sat at the antique mahogany desk and pulled the cord on the table lamp.

Under the glow of the light, she looked at The List. The first two names were crossed out, of course, because that vulgar Pub Boat Roger and that simple-looking Jiffy Mart clerk were dead.

There were only a few more names on the list, or at least, only a couple that needed to be tended to.

She considered calling the policewoman. Perhaps they could work together again tomorrow night. Yes, that would be good. Irv Irving wasn't getting any better and time was no longer a luxury.

Should I call her tonight?

Hilda chewed on this for a moment. The plush bench

felt nice on her ass cheeks, and she was comfortable.

What if Irv died tonight?

No. He was alive and kicking well enough. Not yet.

I like hearing the policewoman's voice though, she thought. Hilda didn't have many conversations with anyone other than Irv. Hearing another voice would be nice.

No. This is a professional business. There's time for pleasantries down the line. Tonight I sleep and I might even touch myself, but I will not cross the next name from the list until tomorrow. I will call Paulina tomorrow and we will do our business with the next one as planned and according to our schedule. Yes.

Hilda looked into the eyes of Jormungand as she pleasured herself, and then the Valkyrie fell fast asleep.

15

Monday Morning

Baby ducks quacked and rustled outside of Shiner's place, so Eric woke to that sound and the heat of the sun on his face as it cut through the living room blinds.

They had not stayed to watch the sunrise on the beach. Eric thought about the warmth of Paulina in the cold water, the taste of her on his mouth, the quiet between them.

That was strange, he thought, *the silence, even on the drive back to Winter Paradise, only the radio and the wind, no words, barely a glance.*

He suspected that he'd been a one-night stand and he wasn't sure how he felt about it.

Still. She had been crying. For someone who seemed so tough, it was unexpected, but Eric understood the power of the past and the cruelty of the present.

He didn't know what haunted Paulina Campos, and he wasn't sure that he would ever know.

But it might be worth the time to find out more.

Probably should have showered, he thought. The crust of the sea was thick on his skin and the sheets were rough with Flagler Beach sand. It was sticky sand, not the white of beaches he knew, sticky red sand of ground shells and coquina rock.

Eric checked his watch.

6:00 o'clock.

He was up and frying eggs when Shiner emerged from his bedroom with a cigarette in his mouth and a beer in his hand.

"Well, look at the newest member of the FloridaWorld ski team. From what I hear, congratulations are in order," he said.

"Thanks. Hope it's alright that I swiped a couple of eggs," said Eric as he slide some scrambled onto a paper plate. Shiner waved him off and clicked on the television.

They watched as the local news told the tragic story of a young clerk who was shot dead in an apparent robbery attempt at the little Jiffy Store near Lemon Pip Lane.

"Damn," said Shiner, "this town is getting worse by the day. He was a good dude. Marcus Traster. Always played along when I was acting the fool. Young guy, too. Fucking shame."

"Probably dead for fifty bucks and a carton of

smokes. They say being a convenience store clerk is one of the most dangerous jobs you can possibly have. I believe it."

"Hey, where did you disappear to yesterday after the show?"

Eric realized with a jolt that he'd been Shiner's ride home.

"Ah, I am so sorry, man," he said. Shiner jammed his cigarette into the empty beer can.

"No worries, dude, I got a ride with one of the piss monkeys and we ended up at The Tavern."

"Old Man Irving is a strange one, am I right?"

Shiner laughed.

"Yeah," he said, "that's an understatement."

"He keeps candy for employees?"

"Huh?"

"You said you were grabbing some candy for a birthday party?"

"Radford's birthday, yes. Sorry, I'm out of it this morning. The Old Man keeps some odds and ends in the kitchen for the crew. We don't often dig into it because, well, it means you have to interact with either the Old Man or Hilda and that's nobody's idea of a good time."

"Understood. Hey, glad you got a ride, though. Sorry again. I just spaced it after work. I took a long drive out to the beach. Up north, almost to St. Augustine. It was a nice night for a long drive," said Eric.

He chose not to mention Paulina.

"So you got, like, three hours sleep?"

"That's about right, yeah."

"I'll buy the coffee if you can give me a lift to Mid-Florida," said Shiner.

"Let's roll."

#

Eric gambled he could get into the park earlier than his 8:00 am call time, so he dropped some soap, shampoo, and deodorant into a Publix bag. He'd wash up in the locker room.

His FloridaWorld polo shirt and shorts smelled like chemicals when he pulled them front their plastic wrap, but he assumed that would fade with time and sunshine.

Did Paulina work today? He wasn't sure, and he wasn't clear whether this would be awkward or not.

He parked in the employee lot, left another note on his car explaining that he was too new to have a parking sticker, and made his way to security.

"You the new janitor?" asked Quillis, the old security guard with the face like a beagle's scrotum.

"Ski team. New guy. First official day. I was here yesterday?"

"You on the morning clean-up crew? You're late, boy," he said.

"Not a janitor. Not a boy. Ski team." Eric felt his jaw tense.

The guard made a show of scanning a clipboard list of names.

"Name's not on the guest list."

"That's probably because I'm actually an employee now."

"Open your bag," said Quillis.

Eric emptied the contents of his backpack onto the table.

The guard pulled out a long, thin stick and began prodding Eric's belongings as if they might explode at any moment.

"You know where you're going?"

"Yes. The ski stadium."

"Guess they'll hire anybody nowadays. Stay out of trouble."

Eric shoved his things into his backpack and chose not to say another word.

The walk to the stadium was a wonder of fresh morning air, a light breeze, and a touch of warmth from the rising sun. There were no guests in the park yet, but there were already other employees, or "sunshine friends," running here and there doing their work. Horticulture experts in khakis and ball caps tended to the lush landscaping, trimming hedges where they were getting unruly and watering the endless rivers of flowers that lined the paths. Kids with leaf blowers cleared clippings and sand from the walkways. Food Service employees in bright white uniforms pushed metal carts of food into snack huts and restaurants. The music of the park played in the background, everywhere, but the place was peaceful enough.

It's an entire ecosystem dedicated to keeping this place alive and running. It's been this way more or less for fifty years now and it's like a living thing. An enormous, weird living thing dedicated to happiness. I'm not sure how I'm going to fit into this. It's a machine.

Some employees, like the security guard, were veterans and knew every nook and crevice of the place. Others, he saw, were just kids, young teenagers, working their first job. There was a confidence, though, that everyone showed.

This is an enormous place to be the new guy.

As he rounded a turn to make his way into the north side of the stadium tunnel, he almost bumped into an older woman in white pushing a cart of hot dogs and buns.

It was the woman he'd met on his first visit, the one who'd sold him a bag of chips and given him a cup of water. Her tall, orange hair seemed even brighter in the morning light.

"Oh," she said, "I remember you. You were here to see the show."

Eric smiled.

"Yes, ma'am. I liked it so much I thought I'd join the team."

She laughed.

"Well, that's fine. It's a wonderful place. You'll see. I'm Audrey. I've been working the snack stand over there for going on thirty years now. Every day is a smile and a blessing."

Eric extended his hand. She took it and gave him a gentle handshake.

"I'm Eric. It's great to officially meet you, Audrey. Thanks again for the water the other day."

She waved him off.

"Honey, I know broke when I see broke. Almost gave you a hot dog too, but they've been counting things. Well, it's lovely to meet you. I can't wait to see you in the show," she said and with that Audrey, with the orange whip hair, pushed her little cart of dogs and buns toward the snack stand.

Eric made his way into the tall tunnel of the ski stadium as the park came to life and the sun rose over Lake May.

#

The pain was immediate and sharp.

Eric's eyelids felt like they'd been pulled back over his head. Water didn't just blast up his nose and into his mouth, it felt like the lake itself was drilling into the skin of his face.

He floated face down for a moment, unable to think, then rolled over and let out a gasp. Lake water went into his mouth again and he started sputtering and coughing like a cartoon character who'd been sucking on a firehose.

This was Eric's third fall while trying to barefoot and it was by far the worst of the three.

He licked the inside of his mouth, checking to make sure that all of his teeth were in their proper place and orientation. Water poured out of his nose.

"You alive?" Fergus's voice echoed down from the boat to Eric as he tucked and rolled and started treading water. His flotation vest kept him from sinking. The coughing eased up long enough for him to give Fergus a thumbs up and say, "let's go again."

Fergus laughed.

Eric coughed again and more water came out of his nose.

"Sure thing, tough guy," said Fergus. "Nothing I like better than driving barefoot practice for an Aqua Pixie while he face plants over and over again. That's a good time, in my book."

Eric floated and was vaguely aware that the handle of the barefoot rope landed in the water next to his head.

Face plant. Such a deceptively gentle way to describe what happens when you fall while trying to barefoot ski at forty miles per hour. Yes, your face plants onto the surface of the water with shocking, sudden, violence. At that speed, the water feels more solid than liquid. So, yes, my face literally planted itself onto Lake May. Again.

Eric grabbed the handle. A long rope stretched from the handle to a pylon on the deck of the MasterCraft. He leaned back and allowed the rope to play out between his legs as he floated, and the boat began to move away from him.

Barefoot waterskiing wasn't new, but it was difficult and a definite crowd pleaser. Back in Wisconsin with his Mom and Dad, Eric had worked hard over one summer to become proficient at the sport. Fall after fall, day after day, but eventually he'd been able to get from his butt to his feet and skim across the surface of the water at a high rate of speed. He became so good at it that he'd even done some backward barefooting in their last summer at the lake, that last summer before Cal Berkeley and that last summer before his parents died and everything went to shit.

That was a long time ago, however.

Fergus sat behind the wheel of the MasterCraft, cigarette in his mouth, and checked the mirror for a signal from Eric that he was ready.

Eric waited a few seconds for the water to calm down. Calm water was everything in barefooting. Finally, he gave a nod.

Fergus saw the nod and put the throttle down.

The engine roared.

The boat was a good one with fast acceleration. It exploded out of the hole and the rope played out fast. Eric held tight to the handle.

The rope grew tight and Eric felt the immediate power and pull of the boat. He was dragging, then skimming along the surface of Lake May on his arched back and his butt.

It was a timing and balance thing, really. Eric had to get from his butt to his feet and, once there, maintain the right body position so that his feet skimmed the water almost like a ski would.

There was a reason so few people could do it, and

even fewer could do it well. Barefooting was damned difficult.

Eric didn't want to fall again. Not only did it hurt like hell, he was the new guy who almost wrecked a pub boat. Saving Kenny Jones from drowning would only carry so much weight. Eventually, he'd need to prove that he belonged on the team as something more than a lifeguard.

This was it. Speed was right. The water felt hard enough to stand.

Don't think about it. Just go for it. Like back in the day.

He was up and barefooting before he even realized what was happening. The water began to heat up under his feet, the spray whipped his eyes, and he had a smile on his face that was so wide Fergus could see it from the boat's rear-view mirror.

This time he didn't face plant after getting up. Eric held on for dear life as Fergus took him on a wide turn through the show course. Seconds went by, and as they went, Eric became more confident. He could be in the moment.

Eric took a chance and lifted one hand off the handle. He pumped his fist in the air and let out a war cry.

That, of course, was the moment one of his toes caught the water awkwardly and he whipped face first into Lake May. Again.

Son of a bitch.

It was probably just his imagination because he was face down and underwater, but Eric would have sworn that he heard Fergus laughing.

He rolled up and let the flotation vest keep him from sinking. The universal signal for a skier to inform his driver that he's "done" is a tap to the top of the head.

Eric tapped the top of his head. Repeatedly.

#

The rest of the day was a whirlwind, and much less painful, both physically and mentally, for Eric. There were the routine duties of setting up for the show, then striking and resetting everything. Eric observed, pitched in where he could, and went out of his way to make sure that at no point was he just sitting around.

It was hard work, but it was fun, and he appreciated that day at FloridaWorld more than any day he'd had in a long time.

The only negative was the complete and total absence of Paulina Campos. When she hadn't been in the morning meeting, he'd assumed she was busy doing something else for the show. She'd been AWOL the rest of the morning, though, and it struck Eric as odd, especially after their time in Flagler Beach the night before. Alarm bells were going off, but he wasn't sure why.

He didn't want to sound like a stalker, so he was hesitant to ask Kent or any of the others, but eventually his curiosity got the better of him. Eric approached Kent in his office.

"Knock knock. Is Paulina working today?"

"Called in sick. What's up?"

"Nothing. Just wondering."

Eric pushed thoughts of Paulina Campos to the back of his mind.

Too much to do, too much to learn, too many ways to fuck up. I need to focus.

The alarm bells kept going off, though. Eric couldn't shake the feeling that something was off, that Paulina was carrying some weight that she wasn't willing to share.

Focus.

Eric knocked back his second smoke of the day and it helped him get his head back in the game. He shadowed Billy Natsume in the pickup boat again during the first show and between shows they gave him another tryout.

This time, he avoided ropes and didn't flip the boat. This was considered a success by all accounts, and Eric was met by an applauding Kent Westheimer on the back dock.

"You've got this, kid. Take the helm of that pub boat next show. Billy'll be right there with you, but I think you've got this sucker dialed in."

It was the lowest role in the show, usually reserved for injured skiers, but driving that pub boat during the second show that day made Eric feel like he'd won the lottery.

Billy Natsume and his electric sunglasses even gave him a high five at the end of the day.

Things are looking up.

* * *

FloridaWorld

16

Monday Night

The little radio on the kitchen counter was usually tuned to 1590 AM, the home of Bacopa County's merengue and salsa hits, but now it filled the room with the sound of David Bowie singing about some Chinese Girl, and Sarah Santiago danced to the song as she cooked. The AM station went off the air after sundown, so now it was 95.5 Mega Hits out of Tampa because the moon was high and the storms had passed.

Sarah Santiago was proud of her encocado de pescado. It was a simple dish, fish with coconut sauce and rice, but Sarah's recipe came from her family back in Quito, from her mother, who was dead some ten years.

Sarah's dog was named Fred, and he was a mutt that she'd found by the side of the road. He was old before his time, like Sarah, and he was no bigger than a purse.

He did not dance to David Bowie, he just rested in the corner and dreamt of days spent chasing birds in the field.

Her home was tucked away off of Highway 27 between a used car lot and an empty building that had once been a Golden Corral but was now just a hangout for crackheads and sex workers.

Sarah did not have bars on her windows, and she rarely locked her doors because Sarah did not want to live in fear. Her husband has passed, but she still felt his presence, her protector, her champion. Anyway, if she died, then that was the will of God and she would die knowing that she made a fine coconut fish and the world could go fuck itself for all the miseries it inflicts on the innocent.

Tonight she used frozen cod for her dinner because the pescataria up the street was out of the good white fish she preferred, and catfish would not do. She just peeled the breading from the frozen fish sticks and didn't look back. Fred enjoyed the breading. Sarah's meal would taste wonderful, and it was cheap.

She was the stage manager at Winter Paradise's community theater and had been there until midnight for rehearsals of "Oklahoma." The pay was lousy, but she loved the place, and this late dinner would fill her belly and warm her memories of better times.

Her degree in stage management would pay off eventually, of that Sarah was certain.

Sarah's home was a bright green one-bedroom with a chain-link fence and a garden of cactus and roses. There was a rusty push mower next to the front door, and the old air conditioning unit on the west side of the place was the perfect ledge for Hilda the Valkyrie.

Hilda knelt on the broken old AC unit and peeked into the kitchen as Sarah cooked and danced.

The dog was frail, Hilda could see this much, and would be a yapping little thing, so she would need to be quick.

I told Paulina that I would not harm the animal, but I just might, anyway.

Jorgumand was back in the patrol car, curled into the backseat. Hilda loved animals, but she would not let a yapping little dog change her plans.

Maybe Jorgumand would enjoy eating the little dog. That was a thought.

The coconut fish simmered in the bright yellow sauce. Sarah used the old cast-iron skillet that had been with her family for generations. It was heavy and well-seasoned and made wonderful meals.

Sarah was a big woman, but she had a grace when she moved. As a teenager, she'd been popular with the boys, but she never felt at home in their arms until her husband swept her away. Sarah imagined his face as she danced, swayed to the music, and let her mind go blank.

The door opened. Sarah looked up and saw a muscular woman dressed as a refugee from a Wagnerian Opera.

The muscular woman had a gun in her hand.

Fred looked up at the woman without interest. The ancient dog's eyes were gray with cataracts, his senses dulled by age, so Fred was no longer a yapping dog. Fred loved his mistress, but he could not see or hear well enough to be concerned.

Hilda raised the gun to fire, but Sarah had her hand on the handle of the skillet within an instant. Her old skin sizzled because the handle was hot, but Sarah did not care.

She brought the skillet up and around, spraying coconut sauce and fish sticks around the room. The strange woman cursed as hot liquid spattered her face, and then Sarah brought the skillet down hard. She aimed at the strange woman's head but missed and caught her on the shoulder.

There was a heavy thud, and the invader grunted in pain.

This is not going well, Hilda thought. The shoulder of her gun hand was numb. The sauce was boiling on her skin. Then the fat woman swung the skillet up like Arnold Palmer hitting a drive, and the cast iron caught Hilda in the ribs.

Hilda's metal chest plate saved her from broken ribs, but her breath was knocked out of her lungs, and she dropped to her knees in shock.

This is a disaster.

Sarah stood over Hilda with the skillet burning her hands and her heart pounding in her heavy chest. There was encocado de pescado everywhere.

Fred stood and stretched. He sensed that something was happening, but now all he could smell was coconut fish and all he could see were gray shadows.

"Who are you?" Sarah asked.

She did not want to kill this strange woman. What if she was mentally challenged? Why else would someone dress like this? She had wings, like an angel of God, and this was a blasphemy, and this blasphemy was in her home, interrupting her midnight meal.

Hilda fought to breathe.

The gun wasn't in her hand. It was on the floor to her right, not within reach. She held her hand up, as if to ask for peace and forgiveness. She then brought her other hand up in an uppercut that caught Sarah in the groin.

Sarah was no killer, but she would not die this way, not to this blasphemous lunatic. The blow to her privates was hell, but she had been through much worse in her days, so she found the rage to bring the skillet up again to strike a killing blow.

This would end.

And then the 9mm round tore through Sarah's skull and she dropped to the floor. Fred heard this noise, and it was a terrifying sound to the dog, so he scampered under the coffee table to hide.

Hilda looked up. Paulina stood with the weapon in both hands, her legs wide in a proper stance, her eyes wide too, and her mouth was open as if she gasped for air.

"Let's go," said Paulina. The deputy wore her uniform, and she turned on her heel and left the little green house as quickly as she could.

Paulina's pulse was racing, and her hands trembled as she stepped into her patrol car.

Hilda was in the car then.

There were no sirens.

Just crackheads out here, nobody calls the cops, thought Paulina. *This is Bacopa County, I'm empty inside, I feel nothing, and this was a lost neighborhood and a poor old woman whose neighbors were crackheads and whores and nobody will call the cops.*

Would there be evidence? Paulina had been careful with her shoes, had been sure she left no trace, but Hilda's DNA was all over the room. Not ideal.

"My blood is in that house," said Hilda, as if she was reading Paulina's thoughts.

Fuck.

Hilda stepped back out of the car and hurried into the home. She returned a few minutes later with Fred the dog snapping and yipping in her arms.

Paulina saw a glow from the kitchen window. The light grew brighter as she watched.

Flames.

No evidence.

Her blood was pumping hard, but she didn't feel like throwing up this time. Not at all. She looked at her hands and they weren't shaking.

They were steady.

I wonder if Mama's ghost is watching. I wonder what she thinks of me?

The smell of the food that was being cooked in the little house made Paulina hungry. She thought about what the dead woman might have in the fridge, and then she thought about Irv Irving's neck in her hands. It would be a brittle, old man's neck, and it would snap like a dry chicken bone.

Or a 9mm right through the old man's forehead.

Paulina did not think of the dead woman and she did not think of her mama. She pushed Irv Irving from her mind as well, and did not think of anything except what was in the fridge and how quickly she could cook it when she was safe in her single wide trailer.

Paulina pulled out, no headlights, and took a left turn on the little side road that led back out to 27. Fred, the old blind dog, trembled and whined next to her.

The home of Sarah Santiago was modest and made of simple things that would burn fast and burn well.

17

Tuesday

The brainstorming session for "A Tribute to Irv" ski show took place in a little conference room just behind the clamshell stage where the Beach Boy tribute band played.

The clamshell stage was tucked away in the "Daytona Sands" section of FloridaWorld. Here you entered a place of white sand beaches along a water-slide area, of a mini-race car track, and of snack stands that sold "Decapi-taters." These were tater tots molded into the shape of the heads of famous NASCAR drivers who had died in horrific crashes. There was a little boardwalk of carnival games and salt-water taffy, not realistic as the real Daytona boardwalk offered lively drug dealers, interactive pedophiles, and sunburned Brits trying to avoid vomit puddles. The FloridaWorld version was sanitized, and this robbed it of much character and charm, but created a decidedly safer family experience.

The conference room behind the stage was cooled, barely, by the window AC unit and a ceiling fan. The walls were a mural of marine life, everything from smiling sawfish to purple octopus.

The team assembled to create the Irv Irving Extravaganza was seated seven strong in plastic chairs and they faced a chalkboard. Kent Westheimer stood in front of the chalkboard with a cup of coffee in one hand and a chunk of chalk in the other.

Eric wasn't sure why he'd been invited, but there he was between the show announcer Johnny Fig and Karen, the costuming manager. Fig smelled of Polo by Ralph Lauren. Karen smelled of Kools and gin. The combined scent was a roundhouse to Eric's nose, and he chose to mouth-breathe until he'd acclimated.

Gary Peppers and Carol Champlain were in the room too. Gary had already taken off his shirt and was smoking a cigar. Carol, the captain of the women's side of the team, was a muscular woman with the requisite skier tan and short black hair. Eric thought she looked like the cartoon character Betty Boop if Betty was an ass-kicker. Top boat driver Fergus the mustache and lean Billy Natsume with his neon shades were there too.

The show course was drawn on the chalkboard and above it, in thick chalk letters, was "For Irv!"

"Alright," said Kent, "let's kick it off. We have a week to come up with a tribute show for the Old Man. That means we need boat patterns drawn up, costumes, something for Fig to say, the whole deal. It's a load, folks, and we need to walk out of here with a plan."

Eric could sense the energy in the room. He wasn't sure if it was excitement or annoyance.

"I'm gettin' overtime," said Karen.

"Goes without saying," answered Kent. "Now, you've been invited because the seven of you are the brain-trust that I suspect will cover the bases. We're keeping this in-house."

Eric leaked a light sheen of nervous sweat, and his stomach rumbled. He raised his hand.

"Yes?"

"One of these things is not like the other," he said, indicating himself.

Everyone turned and looked at Eric. Carol Champlain raised an eyebrow and smirked. Fergus made a fart noise.

"Yeah, why the hell is Mr. Aqua-Pixie here? Can't even drive a pub boat," he said.

"He did alright saving Kenny's dumb ass," said Billy.

"Look, Eric is a big resource for two reasons. One, he's young and that'll be a good perspective. We're so old we can't see the forest for the trees. And B, he's from that hippy school out in California so he can help come up with all the crap that Fig needs to say. Script and words and such."

"Hippy school? Oh Christ," said Karen. "What are you, a socialist?"

"Archeologist."

"I don't know what that is, but it doesn't sound American to me," she said with a shrug.

"At least he went to school, Karen," said Kent. "Will anyone in this room who has written anything other than a grocery list please raise your hand?"

Not a hand was raised.

"Then compared to us, he's Steven Spielberg."

"So what's the theme?" asked Johnny Fig.

"I love that Top Gun movie with Tom Cruise," said Fergus with a broad smile and a slap of his knee.

"That's the ticket. Ski Gun. No, Top Ski. That's a winner," said Kent, and he started scribbling on the chalkboard.

"Where do we get planes?" asked Fig. Fergus shrugged and tugged on his impressive mustache.

"Who gives a shit? The boats are the planes. Hey, I know a guy who's in a model plane club. They fly those things all over down by the city dump."

"I love it," said Fig.

"I don't have Top Gun costumes," said Karen. "We only have what we have in the warehouse and there's no Tom Cruise suits in the bin."

"What's your point?"

"My point is this thing is in a week, and we can't make new costumes. Use what we've got."

"So let's do that nudie show Shiner's always talking about. No costumes required," said Billy.

Eric wasn't sure if he was serious.

"They do a nudie show at Delray Beach. It's a spectacle. The sliding beach barefoot start is a show-stopper," said Billy, sliding his neon shades down to the brim of his nose for emphasis.

Kent stopped writing on the board.

"Stop dickin' around, fellas. We need ideas," he said.

"Don't we still have our western costumes? From the *Hang 'Em High* ice skating show?" asked Gary.

Kent returned to scribble on the board with renewed enthusiasm.

"Now we're cooking with gas," he said, "A Rooten' Tooten' Salute to Irv Irving. That's gold."

"We can use those new Garth Brooks songs as the soundtrack," said Johnny Fig, "and some bluegrass to cover when I need to talk."

"Oh, boy!" shouted Kent.

This was all new to Eric, and none of it sounded very good. He sat quietly, listening to the others pitch ideas and shoot them down.

None of this, none of these ideas, reminds me of the Florida World I fell in love with back in the day, he thought. *Those ski magazines, those tv shows filmed at the park, they all had some charm, some hard to describe style, that made me fall in love.*

Carol raised her hand. Kent's back was to her, and he didn't see, so she cleared her throat.

He turned.

"Yes, Carol?"

"What does any of that have to do with Irv Irving?"

That's it, thought Eric.

Kent's face dropped. "Hell's bells, you're right. I was so excited, too."

Eric raised his hand. His voice was tight, and it cracked a bit when he spoke. "Look, I'm the new guy, but wouldn't he want to see something that looked like the old shows? From back in the day?"

All eyes turned to Eric at that moment. Fergus's neck even gave a dramatic little creak as he looked over.

"I mean, wouldn't he want something that brought him back to his glory days?"

"An organ player. Jantzen shorts. A white-faced clown. All that and more," said Kent.

"Sure."

Karen raised her hand. Eric caught another whiff of gin and Kools, but this time it was laced with body odor.

"You know," she said, "we only have what we've got in the warehouse, but we've got a shit ton. We never threw out anything. Ever. There's costumes from the 1950s buried in there. So this ain't a terrible idea."

Kent chewed on his knuckles for a moment. "Now, we might never have been in those old shows, but we all sure as hell grew up here and saw 'em as kids," he said.

"Every weekend," said Fergus.

"Brother, those crowds back then. Filled the stadium and the overflow lawn besides. Everybody dressed to the nines and having the time of their lives," said Kent.

"Maybe some of those old farts could ski for the

show," said Billy.

Kent waved him off. "Jesus God, son, the liability. Some geezer pops out his hip doing a slalom pass and we're all cruising shit creek with a lawyer up our ass. No. We can do this."

"They had kites back in the day," said Carol. "Those boys strapped into kites and flew right over the audience. Like birds."

"I know a guy," said Billy. "There's a place out near Lake Wales where they do those hang gliders. He could do it for us. Aerial Daredevil Stevie Piston. He's legit. Once got drunk, had a threesome with Evel Knievel and a lady acrobat."

"More liability," said Kent.

"Grow a set, Kent," said Billy Natsume, "that would kick some kind of ass, pulling a kite flyer in the show. Why the hell did we ever stop doing that, anyway?"

"You know that big cypress tree just to the left of the stadium?"

"Yeah."

Kent's voice dropped low as he spoke. "Back in '69 it claimed the life of top kite pilot Pappy 'One Eye' Jackson. His depth perception was off, and he zipped into that tree like a dart into a board. Pieces of Pappy went everywhere. His tally-whacker fell into a kid's popcorn bucket. You should have heard the screams."

"We can't let one weird incident ruin a good thing, boss," said Gary.

"True. Hot damn," said Kent and he clapped his

hands together. "This is a good plan."

"Helluva idea, kid, going old school with this whole thing. Credit where credit is due. Damned fine idea," said Fergus to Eric.

"Now, let's head out. We've got a field trip," said Kent.

"Where?"

"The Waterski Hall of Fame. Out on Citrus Drive. They have movies of those old shows. We need to do our homework."

#

The field trip to the Waterski Hall of Fame was a good one.

It was a small place tucked away next to an orange grove and behind a church. The curator was thrilled to have visitors, and he knew his way around a 16 mm film projector.

The team spent the better part of the day reviewing the archive's deep stash of FloridaWorld ski show movies from the park's 1960s glory days. Some were advertisements for the park with a focus on the ski show. Others were short documentaries intended to be played before the feature at the local drive-in. There was an episode of some old television show where Ron Ely was trying to solve a murder mystery at the park and he ended up doing strap doubles with Angie Dickinson. Another reel was from a Tonight Show skit that ended with Ed McMahon on waterskis at FloridaWorld.

Eric felt a rush of nostalgia for his own childhood as

he watched the images pass by on the little pull down silver screen in the back of the building. The colors were so vivid, the vibe so positive, and everywhere there was the blue of the sky, the orange and green of the citrus groves, and the colorful antics of the performers at the aqua circus.

Just digging up treasures from the past again. Maybe this isn't a scroll from Judea or a tablet from the Valley of the Kings, but it's history and now we're going to bring a piece of it back to life, if just for a day.

So when the viewing was done and notes were taken, the team left the Waterski Hall of Fame as the sun dropped below the church and the bats swooped. Their mood was far different, Eric noticed, than when their meeting began that morning.

They're happy. Excited. That's cool.

Eric smiled as he slid into his car and powered up the engine. He was almost out of the gravel parking lot when a man stepped in front of the Firebird and held his arms up in the air.

It was the doctor. Bluford. He wore a short-sleeved button-down shirt tucked over a round belly and a pair of shorts that hugged his hips. There was a large adhesive bandage on his forehead. His glasses were round and too large by half.

The man was a caricature of a pedophile.

Eric grabbed his second cigarette of the day and killed his engine. He lit up the Marlboro as he stepped out of the car and approached the little man.

"You're in my way, Doc. I told you I would call you," he said.

"Time grows short, and I think we need to talk now. Right now, please."

Eric took a long pull on his smoke. It felt good and gave him time to think.

"Sure. Here?"

The doctor glanced around. The others were gone and the parking lot was empty except for Eric's car, a truck that might have belonged to the Hall of Fame curator, and a bicycle that had Dr. Bluford's style written all over it.

"Perhaps in the church," he said. "There is a little garden behind the building where we can have a bit of privacy."

Dr. Bluford led the way to a tall oak tree behind the church. There were a couple of stone benches and a circular garden of flowers and tropical plants. A small fountain made soft gurgling sounds.

Eric sat on one bench, and Bluford sat across from him on the other. The doctor looked around again, his eyes shifting.

"I think we're alone," he said.

"Tell me the story, doc, but I don't have much time or much patience at this point."

Dr. Bluford's voice was soft. He didn't look at Eric as he spoke. He stared at his hands and the ground the flowers of the garden in turn.

"I am a small man, Mr. Walters, as I'm sure you can

tell. My achievements are few. Some might think that my doctorate is significant, but I have not advanced beyond that at all, really. That was the high point, as it were. This is nobody's fault but mine. I am a small man with small motivations, sir. I have no family. I have no friends. This is not self-pity, this is fact. But I have a dream that has until recently been just a fantasy. My retirement to paradise. Beyond my means, to be sure. So, when I tell you I am ready to take a risk, you understand that I have given it considerable thought."

"This is going to be something criminal, I suppose."

"Not necessarily. My oath as a physician will be broken almost certainly, but the law, perhaps, will not."

Eric was surprised. "I'm listening," he said.

Bluford adjusted his glasses. "A man is dying, Mr. Walters. That man is one of many that I meet with during my day. I listen, I offer comfort or advice, I document, I prescribe medicines, and that's the extent of it. This dying man has verified something that another dying man once told me. Something I'd dismissed as madness until now."

"Specifics, please."

"This dying man has told me of an item that holds extraordinary value. It is a treasure in the truest sense of the word. This item, once broken down, melted, transformed for sale, could be worth a great deal of money."

"And you think this is on the level?"

"Yes. As I said, it confirms something that another

told me several years ago. So, I know it to be true."

"Do you know where this item is located? Wait. You don't. That's why we're having this conversation," said Eric with a smile. His cigarette was done, and he ground the cherry out with his foot. He wanted another one.

"I have few clues to the item's location, but you are correct. I do not know where it truly is at this time. There's my proposition, sir. Are you willing to look for this item?"

"And it's not illegal for me to do this?"

"I suppose that depends on where it is," said Dr. Bluford. "You might need to break and enter. You might not. This I cannot say for sure."

"And it will need to be broken down before being sold? What does that mean?"

"It is an object of value not because of what it is but because of what it is made of, Mr. Walters. Gold. Silver. Diamonds. Some jewels."

"It's not criminal for you to destroy this item?"

"I will not destroy it, sir. I am reducing it to core components, if you will," Bluford said, and then he barked a loud, awkward laugh.

"And my payment for this treasure hunt is going to be?"

Dr. Bluford took a deep breath and sighed before he continued. "Five hundred dollars cash now. I am willing to forfeit ten percent of the ultimate sale of goods once that comes to pass. Should be a princely sum."

Eric laughed.

"Forty percent. After all, the risk is mine, Dr. Bluford."

Bluford was quiet. He still didn't look across the little garden at Eric. His eyes closed, then reopened, and he stared at his hands. "I enjoyed reading your paperwork, Mr. Walters. When you were booked. You recall I mentioned that it's my professional responsibility to gain an understanding of those unfortunates and ne'er-do-wells who pass through Bacopa County Jail."

"Where are you going with this?"

"Quite an adventure you had in Iraq. Unfortunate ending, though. A less than honorable discharge clings to a man for a long time, from what I'm led to believe. The stench of such failure makes it difficult to make a real living in this cold world, Mr. Walters. Most of those discharged without honor from our military eventually wind up incarcerated. Such a difficult road ahead of you, sir, if fortune does not smile upon you in some way."

Bluford paused for a long moment. He did not look up, did not meet Eric's stare, simply gazed at his hands and smiled.

"Fifteen percent, Mr. Walters. Please accept this sum as it will be substantial and this sacrifice on my part should certainly fund my plans and aspirations. I have such exquisite plans, sir."

"To do what?"

It was Bluford's turn to smile then. "To live my dream. You do not want to know what that dream is, nor will I share it with you."

This whole thing stinks to high heaven, but the son of a bitch isn't wrong about my future. It's going to be tough to make more than pennies with that big red "less than honorable discharge" hanging around my neck. Difficult road, like the man said.

"Fifteen is fine. Done."

Bluford pulled out a roll of cash from his pockets and handed it to Eric.

"So, where do you think this thing might be? Where should I begin?" Eric asked.

"The dying man told me that it is hidden in the belly of the whale at FloridaWorld. That is exactly what the other gentleman said several years ago. The belly of the whale. Somewhere in the theme park. I do not know what that means, but that's as much as I have. Believe me, I have looked for whales and have found none. I hope you are up for the job, Mr. Walters, the man who finds things. The clock is ticking."

"That's all you can tell me?"

"Sadly, yes."

"Sadly, no. Who's the dying man?"

"That isn't your concern and it will not help in your quest."

"You don't know that. In fact, I'd argue just the opposite. And you said there was another dying man who knew at some point. I can't help you if you don't give me names."

Bluford chewed on his lower lip.

"The sound you hear is my oath as a doctor being broken."

"Your oath is standing in the way, Doc. Make a choice."

"It doesn't matter, I suppose. The first man who told me of this secret was a patient of mine at the sanitarium. He died in 1987. For many years, he was the Sheriff here in Bacopa County. He suffered delusions and dementia as he grew old and I listened to his many stories. Many hard to imagine stories about terrible things that might have or might not have taken place in the Williams Plantation. Horrors, really, but who knows what was real."

"So this Sheriff told you about a treasure? At FloridaWorld? In the belly of a whale. And then this other man confirmed it?"

"Yes. The treasure was not - is not - the raving of a confused mind. I'm certain now. The sheriff was the adoptive father of Irv Irving."

Eric could almost feel the heat from the lightbulb that went on over his head.

"And Irv Irving is the dying man who told you the treasure is in the belly of the whale at FloridaWorld."

Bluford smiled and nodded. "Yes."

18

Wednesday

The car horn woke Eric out of a sound sleep. Eric staggered up from Shiner's couch and went out into the yard.

It was Paulina. Her truck was an old Ford, red with rust and paint, and its horn was loud. Eric waved his arms in the air to get her attention. She stopped pounding on the horn and stuck her head out of the driver's side window.

"Get your uniform on and let's go," she said.

Eric was still half asleep. The air was so thick he could feel it weighing him down. He didn't understand what was happening.

"Huh?" He looked at his watch. 6:00 am.

"I know it's early, but I need your help. I'll give you a lift in my truck. Let's go."

"Help doing what?"

She hit the horn again.

"Ok," Eric shouted. She stopped.

Eric brushed his teeth, threw on his FloridaWorld uniform, and grabbed his backpack. He was in the passenger side of her truck within five minutes.

"I need my coffee," he said.

"I'll buy. We can pull through Mickey D's when we're done."

"Done with what?"

Paulina turned the stereo up loud and hit the road. Eric was still groggy. He looked around the interior of the truck. It was disgusting. There was trash piled up on the floorboard, cigarettes spilling out of the ashtray, and a layer of dust on the dash. He also noticed that she was in her FloridaWorld uniform, but her police belt and holster were around her waist.

That's weird, he thought. Eric's mind went to his conversation with Dr. Bluford and the roll of cash in his pocket. *The belly of the whale. What was it Irving said about Moby Dick and the white whale? It was all around us?* Eric couldn't wrap his head around it. *Too vague. The mansion? The park? The bedroom? All around us is meaningless.*

Paulina drove out past the main road for a few minutes and took a hard right onto a dirt trail that led into a patch of grassy swamp. The sky was dark gray and heavy with clouds. It looked like rain would soon come down. There were fewer trees here, just an expanse of grass and muck that stretched off into the horizon.

A quarter of a mile down the trail, she stopped.

"I need you to drive," she said as she stepped out of her truck.

Eric slid over into the driver's seat.

"Now what?" he asked. He needed caffeine, he was hungry, and he wasn't sure this wasn't a weird dream.

Paulina went to the back of the truck and reached into the flatbed. She pulled out a watermelon.

"What the actual heck is going on?" asked Eric.

She didn't answer.

Paulina walked over to a long dead tree stump about ten yards off the side of the road and placed the watermelon on top. She came back to the truck and hopped onto the flatbed.

"I need you to back up about a hundred yards and then go forward at about twenty-five miles per hour," she said as she pulled her Beretta 92 from her holster.

Eric went with it. He backed up along the narrow dirt road, stopped, and moved forward again. He looked in the rear-view mirror. Paulina stood in the bed of the truck and was fiddling with her weapon.

Is that a scope mount? Sure looks like scope over the slide, Eric thought. *That's weird. Definitely not standard.*

Paulina stopped adjusting the scope and stood with her weapon in one hand.

Eric focused on the dirt road, but glanced back at her as often as he could.

They were closer to the watermelon. Only yards away. She raised the weapon with one hand and aimed.

The sound of the gunfire was loud. It made Eric jump even though he expected it. He slowed the truck to a stop.

"Shit," she shouted, "a miss. Let's do it again."

Eric saw the watermelon was unscathed.

"What kind of target practice is this?"

Paulina didn't look at him when she answered.

"Conditions aren't always ideal. I train this way. Just need a driver sometimes. Let's do it again."

Eric was wide awake now. Gunfire at close range will do that to a person. He backed up again, then hit the accelerator until he was at twenty-five miles per hour.

Paulina took a wide stance in the flatbed and leaned back a bit. Just like being on top of the human pyramid during the show. The road was bumpy, and she bent her knees to absorb the motion, kept her back straight, and only turned to aim and fire at the last possible moment.

The watermelon exploded. Eric braked and brought the truck to a stop.

"Nice shot," he said.

Paulina spit into the flatbed and reached down to grab another watermelon.

"We've got time to do it again. I need to hit it from further out. Let's go."

Just like the top of the pyramid.

#

It was the rain. It had to be the rain.

Almost everyone blamed the falls and the confusion and the boat patterns that nearly caused a half dozen high-speed collisions on the rain. The sky was a gray steel that blended with the waters of Lake May, and there was a light but steady rain that made everyone cold, even though the air was warm.

It wasn't the rain, though. The team skied in the rain, in the sun, in the wind and the waves and everything but snow because it didn't snow in Florida. Well, there was that one Christmas, but that was more like dandruff on a shirt.

The rain wasn't the problem for the skiers or the drivers. The real problem was pressure, the pressure to put on a show in four days, one that would be in the news, one that would pack a stadium, one that would be performed in front of the dying owner of FloridaWorld.

Everyone felt pressure.

The near-electrocution of Rutherford Fig as he did lines of coke under his jacket and noodled on a Casio CT 680 while the rain came down was, however, absolutely weather related.

But that's just common sense.

The day began with cups of coffee, doughnuts, and hangovers in the ski stadium meeting room. Kent, his face beet red save for the stripe of white zinc oxide on his nose, stood in front of the chalkboard and chain-smoked as he tried to explain the show rundown.

Eric sat next to Paulina at the back of the room. There was an awkwardness between them that Eric felt, and he was certain that it wasn't just his imagination or his hormones. Paulina barely spoke after the target practice session from the back of her truck.

She's beyond preoccupied, but that's not my business, thought Eric. *Just give her space. Damn. Get a grip, Walters. Be a grown ass man.*

"Real traditional stuff, folks," said Kent, tapping the chalkboard. "Ballet, barefoot, jump, pyramid. You know the drill."

Kent started drawing up boat patterns in swirling scratches of chalk. Skiers shouted suggestions, drivers shouted options, and Kent kept drawing, erasing, drawing, erasing, until the board disappeared in a cloud of chalk dust.

Now and then Costume Karen would shamble into the room, grab a skier by the arm, and pull them away for a fitting. Her arrival came with a hint of menthol, and her departure seemed to carry a whiff of gin.

Eric kept his mouth shut because he was new and he wasn't sure that he could add anything to the discussion anyway. Paulina just stared straight ahead, as if she was in a different world, doing different things with different people.

The back door to the meeting room kicked open then, and Johnny Fig entered, his skeletal frame a chaos of bones under the wet polo and shorts.

"Excuse me, folks," he said in his best announcer voice. "Allow me to interrupt so that I might introduce you to our special guest keyboard player for the big show. This is the multi-award-winning electronic music artist Rutherford Fig, also known as DJ Cybernetic Jones."

The room went quiet, and all eyes fell on the lanky figure of Rutherford Fig. The pale man was dressed in a black duster, like a villain from an old Western, a black bolo tie, and a derby hat with an ostrich feather. He wore round black sunglasses that gave him the look of an emaciated owl.

"That's just your brother, you idiot," said Kent. "Multi-award-winning? What the hell are you talking about?"

DJ Cybernetic Jones sniffed and assumed a pose that he must have considered intimidating. He held up a single hand and waved it, serpentine, revealing dazzling blue fingernail polish and silver rings on every finger.

"The world is plastic. I am your salvation, your Jesus of the digital dance. Fear me. Fear the future."

Johnny Fig stared at the ground, uncomfortable. "My brother's been mixing at a club in Orlando for a few weeks, and they love him. Alternative stuff, all electronic. He has his own gear, all digital. It's the next wave."

"What does that have to do with our show?"

"He plays the keyboard, and he's agreed to help us for a nominal fee."

Kent smiled. "Welcome aboard, DJ whatever the hell you are. Grab a seat."

"There are no chairs."

"On the floor, you idiot."

Rutherford Fig remained standing in his pose of intimidation as the meeting resumed, and, eventually, spilled out onto the stage and the waters of Lake May.

The weather forecast was not forgiving, but the heaviest of the storms wouldn't arrive until the afternoon. So, the team went about their business of setting up the ropes, the skis, and the boats as required by the proposed show rundown.

They were a well-oiled, if hungover, machine.

Eric made his way to the boat dock and started inspecting his pickup boat. He fired up the engine with a yank on the pull start and twisted the throttle. There was a cough, a belch of blue smoke, and the Mercury outboard fired up.

The light rain made soft sounds on the aluminum roof of the boat dock. Eric watched as the other drivers, *the real ones,* he thought with a smile, went to their boats and started their own routines.

The moment brought him back to days in Wisconsin, with his Mom and Dad, as the frost and ice melted away and the summers took hold.

"Hey," said Paulina.

Eric hadn't heard her approach through the sound of the rain and the motor. She stood next to him, close, on the old wooden planks of the dock.

She seems so tired.

"Hey," answered Eric.

Eric throttled the motor back to idle and looked up at

her with a smile. "Mom and Dad and me, we never felt like we belonged back home until we started skiing with the little amateur team. And then, it was just nice. Really nice. They accepted us."

"It was transactional. You gave them something and then they opened up. You think that was real? Or was it because you could ski and had a boat?"

Eric looked up at Paulina. She was beautiful, but so troubled. The way she looked out into the distance over Lake May was as cold as the rain.

"What's bothering you? You can talk to me, you know. Something is eating at you and I'm here, if you want to talk."

She turned to Eric and her eyes were dead. "Who do you think you are? Just because we fucked? Come on, new guy, step off," she said. Then she turned and walked away.

Eric watched her go and was reminded that, when we look out to the waters, we're only seeing the surface and sometimes there are sharp things just beneath.

Shit, he thought, *I have no idea how to move forward with her.*

#

Johnny Fig introduced his brother DJ Cybernetic Jones to Mr. Harold, one of the techs at the stadium, a 75-year-old ex-Navy mechanic who'd been with FloridaWorld since opening day.

DJ CJ pulled his Casio out of its black carrying case and began setting up on a portable keyboard stand as the light rain fell.

Harold scratched his head and stood to his side as DJ Cybernetic Jones went about his work, bobbing his head to a beat that only he could hear.

"My good fellow," said DJ CJ, "can you finish energizing my gear while I go powder the old nasal cavities? There's a proper gentleman."

DJ CJ left Harold holding the power cable as he sashayed off to the men's room, sniffing and chewing his lower lip as he went.

Harold plugged the Casio into a wall socket and wandered off as well, less concerned about electrical hazards and more interested in catching *The Price is Right* in the break room.

When DJ Jones returned from his visit to the restroom, he was met at his gear rack by Kent Westheimer. Kent handed Cybernetic Jones a stack of laminated papers. The lanky musician shuffled through them.

"What are these? This is nonsensical gibberish to a digital mind," DJ Jones said.

"The original music sheets used by the old FloridaWorld keyboard players. They're labeled according to the show act, just the way we're doing for our tribute to Irv. So, there's opening, underscores, ballet, jump act, and so on. Should be easy for you to follow along."

DJ CJ sniffed and rubbed his nose. "What do these have to do with me?"

"Son," Kent said, "these are the songs you need to play. Didn't your brother explain what we're doing here?"

Another sniff, followed by a dismissive wave of his thin hands. "I'm an artist, my fellow. I create. I imagine. I transcend. I abominate."

"You won't get paid if you don't play this stuff, dipshit."

DJ CJ looked over the sheet music again, more slowly this time. "Well, perhaps I can transform this retro nonsense for a digital age," he said.

Kent smiled and slapped him on the arm. "There you go, sport!"

"The sounds of the 1950s as interpreted by the cyber frontier. An evolution. A revolution. A new musical constitution for a more enlightened time."

Kent slapped him again, harder this time, and walked away as he sparked up another smoke. Westheimer walked fast through the light rain, his eyes shifting back and forth as he went. The practice continued, a frenzy of activity, pockets of chaos and concentration, a riot of color and noise in the drizzle.

There was Johnny Fig at center stage, going through his script and saying his lines to nobody, gesturing and presenting and posing as he practiced. There was a ski boat on the water, running a practice barefoot pattern in a wide circle, pounding through water that was growing choppier as the day went on and the weather grew worse. The dock was a bustling hive of activity with most of the team setting up skis, measuring and setting ropes, and arguing over the proper sequence of the show rundown.

"I love this shit," Kent said just as he bumped into a short, stocky man in a white jumpsuit.

The man grumbled something unintelligible. He was a bulldog with white hair, skin the color and texture of fake leather, and a pronounced gut.

Kent stared at the man for a second, didn't recognize him, and asked, "Who the hell are you?"

The man said something that might have been "I'm your mother's boyfriend, you nut job," or "I've just caught the bus from Arkansas and need a drink." The Australian accent was thick, the vocal cords were fraught with polyps, and the man's teeth were tea-colored nibs.

"What?"

The man spoke again, this time slowly and with an effort to enunciate, "I'm Stevie Piston, Mr. Superfly. Kite pilot, mate."

"Kite pilot? You're the guy who used to fly here?"

"Same, mate. Pilot here some thirty aught years back. I fly, you buy. Pop the top on a tinny and away we go."

Kent held out his hand and Stevie Piston gave it a proper shake.

"Nice to meet you, Mr. Piston," said Kent. "Welcome to the show. Irv Irving's gonna be thrilled to see you take to the skies once more. Just stay out of the trees."

Stevie Piston said something that Kent didn't

understand and walked away, arms held wide to either side, as if he was an eagle soaring over Lake May.

"Helluva business we're in," said Kent as the strange old man flew away, "but it's never boring."

The popping sound came then, followed by a screamed profanity and a weird, whirring noise that sounded like the sort of thing one would hear in a 1950s sci-fi movie.

Do I smell burnt hair? Kent turned and saw Cybernetic Jones lying flat on his back in a cloud of billowing smoke.

He ran to the musician, taking care not to slip in his old K-Swiss shoes, and leaned over him.

Dammit, if this sumbitch is dead, we're never going to get this show off the ground by Saturday.

The keyboard was smoking, and so was the unfortunate DJ Jones.

"Are you alright, son? Never should have plugged your piano into the wall socket during a rainstorm."

The wall socket was charred black. The air smelled of fried hair and ozone.

Cybernetic Jones held up his thumbs and smiled.

"Living the dream, my good man. It's not the first time I've danced with Lady Electric."

"How about your piano?"

DJ Cybernetic Jones staggered to his feet and made his way to his Casio. The keyboard wasn't smoking anymore, but the smell of fried electrical gear was overwhelming.

"Looks like you're buying me another one, kind sir."

Kent's face flushed a deep red. "What kind of idiot plugs in a gadget while it's raining?"

DJ Jones smiled. "That would be your idiot, my good man. His name was Harold."

"Aw, shit."

"Tallyho the fox, we're off to Circuit City!" The lanky keyboardist turned on a heel and exited with a flourish of his still smoldering duster.

Harold emerged from the tunnel holding a bagel. He looked puzzled. "Power's out. I'm missing my Bob Barker show. What happened out here?"

Kent Westheimer took a deep breath and exhaled, thinking of peaceful things, as his doctor advised.

The rain and the rehearsal continued, deep into the day.

19

Thursday

Dr. Claude Bluford lived in a pleasant home in a pleasant neighborhood on the outskirts of Winter Paradise. Here the lawns were green, the hedges well-trimmed, and the flags always flew on the 4th of July.

Bluford was fortunate that he never had the neighbors over for cocktails because they would have looked askance at the porn collection that was strewn about his otherwise tidy place like a canker on a tangerine.

It was after midnight and he was naked in his leather recliner, sipping hot tea from a fine porcelain cup. The Technics audio system played the *Dirty Dancing* soundtrack. The lights were dim. A Kodak eight-millimeter silent film projector sent images of "The Nurse's Surprise" onto the white wall.

There was a slight haze in the room from the joint the good doctor had burned, and the smell of reefer lingered. One of the orderlies at the hospital kept him well stocked with the good stuff.

Dr. Bluford's eyes were shut, so he didn't see Hilda come into the room.

"Claude," she said. His eyes shot open, and he spilled his hot tea onto his pale, flabby legs. Bluford let out a shriek and covered his genitals with a handy copy of "Thrust."

"It's movie night. I want to watch," Hilda said. Bluford reached for his glasses with one hand, but kept the other squarely on his manhood.

"What are you doing here?"

Hilda tilted her head to the rear of the house. "Your back door was unlocked."

Bluford had his glasses on now. He tried to reach the projector and shut off "The Nurse's Surprise," but he couldn't quite touch the switch. "Hungry Eyes" played from the stereo. The projector clicked.

"Leave it. I like movies," said Hilda. She moved in front of the projector's beam so that her body became the screen. Images of a nurse being rudely surprised by a vigorous patient played out on her metal chest plate.

"I didn't ask how you entered. I asked what you are doing in my home, Hilda."

"How long have we known each other, Claude?"

"Please throw me that quilt so that I can cover myself."

Hilda looked at the lovely red quilt on the couch but ignored the request. She smiled. "I like your magazines. I love your movie, though."

"Get out of my home."

"I'm not passing judgment. Nothing to be ashamed of, Claude. How long have we known each other?" She repeated.

Bluford made a sputtering sound.

"Since I was an intern at the old sanitarium, I suppose. Yes, so nineteen years. Why do you ask?"

Hilda's armored chest plate gleamed in the light from the movie. "And you've known Mr. Irving just as long."

"Yes, of course. And his father as well. Please tell me what you want."

"I've watched you watch me, Claude." Hilda moved closer, almost to the foot of the recliner. Bluford tried not to make it obvious, but he couldn't help himself from looking at her sturdy legs, her thick arms.

Hilda reached out and stroked Bluford's foot. He flinched, then settled back and let her touch him.

"What is this about, Hilda?"

"Do you think about me sometimes, Claude? You know, when you have dirty thoughts?"

Bluford's pale skin flushed red. Her fingers traced along his almost hairless leg.

"Claude, did you know how much Irv Irving cares about you?"

"What?"

"Did he ever tell you how much he thought of you?"

"No," said Bluford, "not in the slightest. I always felt that he has a strong dislike for me. A strong dislike."

"You're wrong. I was surprised as well, but he truly appreciates you."

Hilda's hand was at his thigh and Bluford's hands gripped the magazine over his groin.

"Oh," said Hilda, "are you shaking because you're afraid or because you're turned on?"

"Hilda, you know I've always held you in the greatest admiration."

"I've thought about you, Claude. I have. I've thought about you when I've been naked. So now you know that I've had sex thoughts about you, and you also know that Irv Irving cares for you very much. Isn't that nice?"

Bluford's shaking became more pronounced. The projector clicked and Eric Carmen sang.

Hilda let her fingers trace his skin as she moved around the recliner. She stood behind Bluford and massaged his shoulders.

"Oh, Hilda," he said and his voice trembled.

"Irv Irving thought enough of you to name you in his last will and testament, Claude. You're in select company on that list."

"You're joking, surely."

"I'm serious, Claude, and don't call me..."

Silence.

"You don't know that one, do you, Claude?"

Paulina Campos entered the room. She made no sound and stayed well out of sight.

The little man moaned and shivered. Hilda's fingers were deep into his shoulders, working and kneading the flesh.

"What does it mean? What will I get? Do you know?"

"The park, Claude. You'll receive a significant stake in FloridaWorld. Treasures beyond imagination."

Bluford's eyes rolled back in his head and he felt the courage to move his copy of "Thrust" away from his now rather active crotch.

"Hilda, this is wonderful news. You have no idea. It's a dream," he said, and his hands reached up to touch hers.

"Yes, it's a dream, sunshine friend. Watch the movie. Let's watch the movie together, Claude," said Hilda as she moved her hands to either side of Bluford's head and rubbed his temples.

Bluford moaned again and closed his eyes.

"You can hold yourself, if you'd like, Claude. Don't be shy. We're friends. Have a little tug."

Claude's trembling hand reach down between his legs as Hilda continued to rub his temples.

"It feels so good," he said only a moment before Hilda tightened her grip and twisted as hard as she could.

There was a sharp crack as the man's spine snapped. Hilda leaned into her work with all of her considerable strength. Claude Bluford was already past resistance. His crotch remained active, but the rest of him did not. He evacuated onto the leather recliner as the house absorbed his ghost and the smell was enough to make even Hilda recoil.

Paulina turned away at the sight.

"My God," she said. Hilda walked away from Bluford's corpse, stepping over porn mags as she went.

"He was a sweet man. I didn't know the others, but I knew Claude well, and I liked him very much. That's it, though. The last one," she said.

"Not the last one," responded Paulina. "Not the last."

"Of course, Paulie. You'll get yours and I'll get mine, and what a merry world it will be."

Paulina reached out so quickly that Hilda couldn't respond. She had her left hand around Hilda's throat, and the grip was strong, stronger than Hilda could have imagined.

"There's nothing merry about this," said Paulina through clenched teeth, "and after this is done, consider yourself lucky that I don't come for you."

Hilda felt her heart race. She struggled to breathe. The smaller woman was powerful and angry and her hand was crushing her throat.

If she squeezes any tighter, I might have a problem.

Paulina was in a side stance, and she drew her Beretta from the holster at her waist with her free hand. She held it up, the barrel pointed right at Hilda's face.

"This ends Saturday. You do anything stupid or greedy before Saturday, before I get mine, and I will kill you. Do you understand?"

Hilda couldn't speak, so she nodded her head.

"It's going to come around for both of us, you know," said Paulina.

Spit flew from Hilda's lips as she struggled to breathe. The Valkyrie made whining sounds, like a wounded pup.

"Karma, justice, fate, whatever you want to call it, it's going to come around for us. I just hope it gets to you first, and I hope it hurts like hell."

Paulina released her grip. Hilda stepped back, gasping. The weapon went back into the holster.

Stay by Maurice Williams & The Zodiacs played as Hilda and Paulina left the house and the projector clicked long after the reel of "The Nurse's Surprise" ran through.

The bulb projected nothing then but white light onto the white wall. A day later, the bulb burned out and even the light was gone. A couple of days after that, the shocking circumstances of Irv Irving's glorious final celebration at FloridaWorld prompted the police to check on Doctor Claude Bluford.

Although the lurid scene became a bit of a legendary tale back at the Bacopa County Sheriff's Office, the graphic details of the late Claude Bluford's messy demise were kept from the public.

He never escaped to the life he wanted and the quiet privacy of the life he led was maintained beyond his passing.

The films and magazines, of course, were passed around the sheriff's office and kept the department entertained for many years.

20

Friday Night

Dr. Claude Bluford was in the final phase of rigor mortis when Eric Walters clocked out of the last show practice before the big day.

The last day of rehearsal had been a train wreck of epic proportions. Boat drivers forgot their patterns, a late thunderstorm chased the team from the lake for a few hours, costume changes proved impossible despite Karen's best efforts, Johnny Fig couldn't remember his lines, and Aerial Daredevil Stevie Piston encountered an unexpected air burst and dropped to the water from thirty feet in his Delta Wing kite.

The saving grace was the Casio noodling of DJ Cybernetic Jones, who found unexpected and contemporary life in the old sheet music from the glory days of FloridaWorld. His droning, thumping, electronic reinterpretations energized half the team to dance along onstage at points during the rehearsal.

"Well, the show's gonna sound good, even if everything else falls to shit," said Kent as the final boat pulled into the docks at the end of the day.

Paulina Campos said little to Eric throughout the day, but they were all busy and there weren't many opportunities to chat. He looked for her before he made the long walk to the employee gate to leave for the day, but she was nowhere to be found, so Eric clocked out and hit the road back to Shiner's place.

#

"Bad practice, great show. That's what they say," said Shiner through a puff of smoke. He offered Eric a hit and Eric waved him off.

"It's going to be an amazing show, then. An all-time classic," said Eric with a smile.

"It'll be fine. Even if it goes balls up, the crowd is going to be amped to say goodbye to the Old Man one last time."

"True."

They sat for a while listening to Shiner's cassette mix of southern rock tracks. There was a cool breeze from the lake that felt fresh on Eric's skin as the sun fell below the horizon and the frog chorus sang.

I have five bills in my pocket and I have a bad feeling about the whole thing, Eric thought, *a feeling that there's a helluva lot more to the Doc's story than he's telling.*

Eric looked at Shiner. The little man was nodding off

in his plastic chair, eyes shut and leg twitching like a dog having a dream of chasing a car.

"Hey."

Shiner jolted awake.

"Sorry," said Eric, "wanted to catch you before you were out."

"Fucker. I was dreaming about putting at the Masters. What's up?"

"You golf?"

"Absolutely not. What's up?"

Eric hesitated.

"Must be scary. If you have a crush on me, you gotta move out. Ain't gonna work," said Shiner.

"How well do you know Irv Irving? I mean, you seem to come and go to the mansion."

Shiner laughed. "I know him about as well as anybody, so not very well at all," he said.

"What about that weird assistant? The woman in the viking costume?"

"Hilda's always with him. They probably even do the nasty. She's one scary woman, my friend. I keep a wide berth from her over at Monkey Kingdom."

"So you don't know Irving well."

"Look," said Shiner, "he lets me hang around more than most. Let's put it that way. I do odd jobs around the mansion and he'll let me dig into the fridge now and then. A couple of years ago, I started trying to have conversations with him, but even then he was going soft in the melon. So I just say hi and bye and let it go at that."

"And that's more time with him than most people get, yes?"

"Sure. I guess so. What's your point?"

Eric was quiet for a long moment.

If I tell him anything about Doc Bluford and it goes south, I couldn't live with myself. This whole thing just feels dangerous, Eric thought. Then he smiled at Shiner and said, "No point, my friend. Just getting the lay of the land around here."

Shiner grunted, farted, and closed his eyes.

Eric sat on the darkening patio and listened to the frogs.

What if I just drove over to Paulina's place? Is she going to refuse to open the door? Is there going to be some other guy there? Maybe she'll just shoot me and get it over with.

Or maybe, Eric thought, *we might have a nice time.*

He considered his options for a few more minutes as the sun disappeared and the moon took its place on the horizon over little Lake Michelle.

\#

She was a silhouette in the door of her single-wide trailer, an amber light from behind her and just a sliver of silver from the moon on her bare legs.

Eric killed the ignition of his car, and the rumble died fast. He walked to her, unsure of what he was going to say or do, but certain that he wouldn't be the one to lead the way.

Paulina lifted her left hand, and there was a bottle in it she brought to her mouth.

Eric stood at the bottom of the three aluminum steps that led up to Paulina and the inside of her trailer. He was close enough now to see that she was wearing a pair of tight cut-off jeans and an old OP polo that was much too big for her.

"I didn't bring anything. I hope you're not hungry."

She drank again. "I'm not hungry," she said and turned back into her trailer.

Eric was up the steps and into the place before she turned around and when she did, he thought she looked like someone who had just come from the funeral of a friend.

She spun in a circle and presented her home. "Welcome to Casa Campos," she said. Her voice was husky and slurred. "Where dreams and hopes come to dance and die."

She laughed then, as if to say *It's okay, I'm just joking,* but her eyes didn't track with the laughter, and Eric wasn't sure what to say.

The place was a mess. Empty bottles, fast food bags, and clothes were everywhere, as if they'd all been caught up in a whirlwind. The smell was dank, a punch to the nose stink of rotten food and that single wide chemical scent that was halfway between pine and formaldehyde.

There was a small television on a stand in the corner. The old Disney film *Pinocchio* was playing out on the screen. There was a whale as big as the world, and that spelled trouble for the little wooden puppet. Eric remembered the movie from a Wisconsin drive-in theater with his Mom and Dad on a cool summer evening.

It was a warm memory, and he smiled as he watched the movie for a moment.

"Good movie."

"Great movie," said Paulina and they both watched the adventures of the little wooden boy as he struggled to escape Monstro, the great whale.

Eric heard a strange sound and noticed a little ball of fur on the far side of the living room, half hidden underneath some clothes.

"You have a dog?"

Paulina didn't respond for a long moment. She just stared at the television. When she spoke, her voice was so low that Eric could barely make out what she said.

"Watching it for a friend. Name's Fred. At least that's what the collar said."

"Your friend didn't tell you the dog's name?"

"Nope."

The station cut to commercial. Paulina continued to stare at the screen.

Eric gestured to Paulina's living room.

"You didn't have to tidy up for me," said Eric, trying to joke but failing in the effort.

"Drink," said Paulina.

She handed him the bottle. It was a cheap tequila he'd never heard of, so naturally he tipped it back and swallowed.

The stuff burned, but then she pulled the bottle away and came to him.

Paulina walked to him on unsteady legs, and her hands reached out to his belt. She started trying to work it loose, tugging and fumbling.

Eric stopped her and pulled her close.

When he kissed her, the burn of the tequila disappeared and all he could taste was the metallic warmth of her mouth, her tongue.

She shoved him back and fell into a chair.

"How about that tribute to the Old Man? All the bells and whistles, all the pomp and circumstance, all that and more," she said, and her eyes focused on nothing.

Eric sat down in front of her on the floor.

"Yeah, how about that? Some show. Some week."

"Some week," Paulina echoed, and then her eyes locked on his and they were laser focused. "What brought you here, new guy? I bet I can guess. Well, someone is going to be disappointed. Probably me," and she laughed again.

Eric ran his fingers along her strong, dark calf. She didn't stop him.

"I'm here because I thought it might be a good idea," he said.

Eric's hand moved up and along the skin of Paulina's bare leg, past her knee and now along her thigh. The skin felt smooth and warm.

Paulina reached out and held his hand, pulling it away from her leg and wrapping it in her own grasp, as if in mutual prayer.

"You need to go away."

"You want me to leave?"

"Here's a secret," she said, leaning in as if to spill something confidential. "I feel good when I'm on the water. Like, really good. Fuck the show, fuck all that. But on the water, behind a boat, I'm so glad I learned how to do that. It's like being free. I know that sounds stupid, but it's like being free and that won't last much longer."

"Why does that need to be a secret? And why isn't it going to last?"

She pulled his hand to her mouth and kissed his knuckles. "Thanks for coming by, but you need to go."

Paulina stared off into the corner of the room then, and it was like Eric wasn't there. He knew something was wrong, but he also knew that the door of this conversation was closed.

This night was over. Eric left without saying another word and made his way back to his car.

The Firebird's windows were down and the stereo was loud on the drive back to Shiner's place. The wind was on his face and the local R&B station pumped out the latest from Naughty by Nature.

Eric felt that something was wrong with Paulina Campos, something that he didn't understand. It felt dangerous, that she was in danger, and what if he didn't find a way to help?

There was more, though. The movie, *Pinocchio,* there was something about the movie that nagged him. He loved the story of the little wooden boy who just wanted to be real, but tonight there was something about the movie that he couldn't shake.

Just anxiety, he thought, *so much going on right now. I need to sleep. Clear my head.*

He killed the engine and coasted into the driveway of Shiner's place. The engine was loud and he didn't want to wake the little guy. Eric made his way into the place in stealth mode, careful not to make a sound. A piss, some sips of water, and he crashed out onto the futon.

Sleep came quickly. The nightmare swept over him almost as fast.

He drifted in a darkness that felt like loneliness, a loneliness so intense that it choked him, strangled him. But no, he wasn't really alone, there was someone else with him in that darkness, just out of sight and reach. There was someone there that wanted to hurt him.

Eric knew then that he was adrift in the blackness of his night terror, that there would be a shimmering figure or a young man with a colorful backpack full of explosives, or a spider the size of his head, just out there, in the dark, waiting for him. He knew it wasn't real, he wanted to wake up, but he was paralyzed as he always was, and completely alone. Drifting. Detached from everyone that could help. If he could just scream loudly enough, he would wake up, but he couldn't catch his breath. If he could just scream, it would all go away, but he had no voice, no air.

His nightmare whispered to him that he had been swallowed up in darkness by a monster and there was no way out. He was in the monster's belly. He saw the great teeth from the inside, from in the gut of the thing. It was here, in this lonely place of darkness and horror, that he would suffocate and die.

Monstro. The whale. The great white whale.

Eric gasped and woke up from the nightmare so quickly that he almost fell out of the futon. His skin was cold with sweat and his heart was a jackhammer in his chest. His breath came in gulps.

He sat for a long moment in the darkness, then reached for his pack of smokes and treated himself. The smoke felt good in his lungs. His pulse slowed, but his mind raced.

An hour later, when he finally drifted away again, his thoughts went not to Paulina, but to the five hundred dollars in the pocket of his pants and the little wooden puppet who took a trip into the belly of Monstro.

Into the belly of the whale.

21

Saturday Morning

"A Sunshine Day Celebration for Irv Irving."

The brilliant Florida sunlight cascaded through the tall windows of the mansion on Lake May and dust motes danced along the light beams.

Irv Irving sat in his gold-framed wheelchair, resplendent in his finest white suit and a dapper white hat. His long white beard splayed out over his bowtie and coat jacket. The old eye was alert, and the bushy eyebrows seemed to move with a life of their own. Those huge hands clapped together in rhythm as if he listened to a song only he could hear.

Hilda pushed him to the window so that he could enjoy the view before they descended and joined the celebration. This was quite a day, a sunshine day with sunshine friends, and Hilda was beside herself with excitement.

She wore a silver scarf around her neck to hide the bruises from Pauline's grip. It didn't coordinate well with her Valkyrie ensemble, but Hilda didn't care what others thought of her fashion choices.

Hilda didn't need to care what others thought.

In a few hours, this will be mine. Every bit of this will be mine to do with as I please.

She smiled as the sun warmed her face.

The scene beyond the windows of the mansion was extraordinary, a bustle of arriving guests, media trucks, excited FloridaWorld employees, and there was even a plane in the sky over Lake May, writing in smoke as it went and the words were a blessing, "Thank You Irv!"

"They love you, sir," said Hilda.

Irv smiled, and it was the smile of a wolf in its last dying moments.

"My sunshine friends, Hilda, they love the idea of me," he said and then he winked at her with his one good eye. "If they knew me, they wouldn't be so thrilled. They'd burn me at a stake of cypress wood."

He laughed then until his laugh rattled and became a wet cough. Hilda wiped the Old Man's mouth with the handkerchief that she always kept for just such an occasion.

"Shall we go, sir? It's going to be quite a show and we won't want to miss anything."

Irv waved his hand as if swatting at a fly.

"No. Where's the little man? Where is he? He's

supposed to be here, too."

Hilda didn't understand. "The little man?"

"You know, the little fucker they call Shiner."

The sound of fast footsteps and Mike "Shiner" Thomas came through the vast front doors as if he'd been shot out of a cannon.

"Sorry, boss, I got tied up setting the dock for the show," Shiner said as he came to Irv and Hilda. He was slick with sweat and little veins pulsed on the sides of his forehead.

"Oh." Hilda said, "This one. I wasn't sure who you meant, sir."

Irv smiled again, and this time, the smile held a trace of warmth. "Shut up, you brute, let me say a few words to the little man before we go. Make yourself useful and go fill up a thermos with a martini. Off you go," said Irv Irving.

Hilda muttered "little bastard" under her breath as she walked away to the kitchen. Shiner went to Irv Irving and knelt down on one knee in front of the Old Man.

"What did you need from me, Mr. Irving?"

"Setting up dock for the show, huh? Are you in the show, too?"

Shiner laughed. "No sir, they don't want any falls today," he said.

"Fair enough."

The Old Man pointed to the elevator.

"Wheel me over there. Let's go up to my office.

There's something you need to know before we go enjoy today's little spectacular, Mr. Shiner Thomas. There's something we need to discuss."

Shiner felt like someone had kicked him in the jimmy and splashed pickle juice on his face. In other words, he was confused.

"Sir?"

"I know you, boy. Known you for years, haven't I?"

"Yes, sir."

"You ever do anything to piss me off?"

"Not that I know of, Mr. Irving."

"Irv, you fucker."

"Irv."

Irv Irving laughed again, louder this time, and even more wet stuff came flying out of his mouth. When he could speak again, Irv Irving leaned over so that he was close to Shiner. The Old Man's voice was low.

"They said I was crazy when I pitched this thing, this FloridaWorld. Didn't give me any money, but that was fine. Didn't need it. You know what I really wanted, boy?"

Shiner shook his head no, and now he was really confused.

"I wanted a place where there would be happiness, where there would be joy, where there would be sunshine and sunshine friends. And that's what I fucking built, so the joke was on them. I did it, boy. I did it."

"Yes, sir. It's a great place."

"It's turning into a shit hole. Whole thing is going to die on the vine, die from the blight, just like the citrus, unless we keep her warm and keep her safe. Now, a smart person would sell this property for more money than Midas ever knew. Are you a smart person, boy?"

"No sir," Shiner said with a fair self-awareness.

"Bullshit," smiled Irv. "Only a smart person would say that, in this situation, confronted with a frightening deity like yours truly staring down at them. You might not be smart, but you're clever."

"That's fair."

Irv Irving took a deep breath then, and his lungs made rattling sounds.

"Elevator?" Shiner asked.

Irv nodded affirmatively and Shiner wheeled the Old Man to the bright brass doors of the mansion's elevator.

They weren't gone long and when they returned Hilda stood ready with a thermos of martinis and a long black umbrella that could shield them from the damaging rays of the Florida sun.

Hilda the Valkyrie's wings were clean and her chest plate was polished for the day's festivities. There was even the hint of perfume in the air, a scent Hilda kept for special occasions that smelled of orange blossoms.

"Would you prefer the little fellow be responsible for your wheelchair, sir?" Hilda asked. There was more than a hint of sarcasm in her voice.

"Hell no. I need someone with heft to push me around. Let's roll. I don't want to miss anything."

Hilda guided Irv Irving's wheelchair through the vaulted mansion doors and out into the park, with Shiner following behind.

The colorful and lush grounds of FloridaWorld spilled out before them. The sky was so blue, the grounds were so green that the colors seemed to vibrate. Lake May was calm and the wind was just a light kiss on the skin.

"Do you hear it, sir? The music?"

Irv Irving heard it. The songs of FloridaWorld's past carried along the wind from the stadium and down the pathways and lanes. There was a new beauty to the sound, to the songs, and Irv Irving would never know it, but DJ Cybernetic Jones was pleased with himself, pleased with his interpretations of the old tracks and how he married the vintage melodies with a contemporary sound.

"A kite, Mr. Irving," said Hilda. She pointed up to the deep blue sky at the Delta Wing kite soaring against the sun.

The process of flying a hang-glider on the show course seemed simple enough. Imagine strapping a G.I. Joe to the underbelly of a traditional kite. That was the essence of the thing. The pilot strapped into a large kite harnessed to their back like great wings. They were then attached to a long line and towed behind a boat until the kite's wings caught air and the kite was lifted aloft, higher and higher, until the pilot released the rope and achieved free flight.

Aerial daredevil Stevie Piston caught the thermals over Lake May like an eagle and he swooped back and forth in widening arcs. He was easily five hundred feet above the lake. Voices exclaimed and shouted as the gathering crowd watched the kite paint its brush strokes along the breeze as it descended.

"Yes," said the Old Man, "just like in the day. Glorious stuff, my friends. The stuff of dreams."

Guests noticed them then, the unmistakable Irv Irving and his strange entourage, and there were shouts of encouragement, thank you's, and the occasional "We love you, Irv!" The excitement built as Hilda guided Irv along the emerald green grass, the flower beds of countless crayon colors, and on toward the waterski show stadium.

Irv waved and smiled as they went. He saw the guests in their FloridaWorld t-shirts and hats, but he also saw those who had come before, the thousands who brought his dream to life since those early days. Irv thought of his cooter farm, of the early days when it was all dredging, construction, concrete, steel, and imagination. There were glorious times, so long gone, when Irv Irving used every bit of his wit and cruelty to bend the world to his will so that FloridaWorld, that great sunshine place for sunshine friends, could become a reality.

A moon-faced woman wearing Mouse ears and eating a corndog shouted, "Thank you, Irv Irving!"

Irv's weepy green eye rested on the woman, and he

forced a smile.

"A fucking Disney hat," he said low under his breath, "ungrateful cow."

#

There was a *Sunshine Day Celebration for Irv Irving* ceremony before the ski show, of course. Irv sat in his golden chair along the shores of the lake and at the edge of the stage, Hilda and Shiner at his side. The words spoken by a parade of well-wishers, including the outgoing and disgraced mayor of Bacopa County, were effusive in their praise. DJ Cybernetic Jones played jaunty electronic melodies as underscore during the ceremony. The ski team emerged en masse from the stadium tunnel and came to the stage in a grand salute to the Old Man of FloridaWorld. A noted animal trainer and her chimpanzee "Mr. Bingo" performed an adagio in tribute to Irv until the animal became aroused and attempted to mate. This brought the festivities to a brief halt as Mr. Bingo was sprayed with a hose and the trainer was tended to by medical professionals.

It was quite a celebration, and the show hadn't even begun, but when it began, the crowd roared approval that drowned the sound of the four ski boats as they throttled through the front stretch of the stadium at top speed.

And what a show. Kent Westheimer and the team outdid themselves. There was no nonsense, no theatrics, only the skiers doing what they did best, and that was more than enough.

Irv Irving watched the waters of Lake May erupt into a pageant of color and excitement. FloridaWorld came back to life as well, all around him, with the sounds of the organ player and the power of the engines and the beauty of the ballet on the liquid stage.

There hadn't been a ski show like this at FloridaWorld in years and it seemed as if the ghosts of the past were rising up in applause to recognize the moment.

Of course, the most impressive moment of the show was always the arrival of the human pyramid, that grand formation on water, that ultimate display of teamwork and waterski showmanship.

Eric Walters would be at the throttle of the pickup boat, trailing just behind.

Paulina Campos would be the woman at the top of that pyramid. At just the right moment, as was tradition, Paulina would stand proudly atop the grand formation and she would raise the flag of FloridaWorld high above her head.

It was guaranteed to be a "goosebump" moment.

22

Saturday Afternoon

The pyramid was the only thing left, except, of course, for the thunderous applause and the standing ovation.

There was wind, the roar of the inboard engine, and a hard splash as skis hit the water, but there was no music to be heard. That's the thing about the theatrical timing of the human pyramid on skis, that's the tricky bit. If you're one of those holding tight to a handle and working as one to build this grand aquatic acrobatic formation, you're relying on your driver to sync the pattern with the music so that when you raise that flag high, at just the right moment, the audience applauds and stands, lumps are in throats and tears are in eyes.

So, Paulina and team had their hands full building the pyramid and the sound of DJ Cybernetic Jones's Casio noodling out the FloridaWorld anthem was there for the audience and nothing more.

The team's women dropped their skis and began climbing up onto the shoulders of the men, one hand on a handle, the other finding purchase. It was complicated and dangerous enough on land, but building a human pyramid, four tiers high, on the water in wet conditions traveling fast, well, the waterski pyramid was borderline insanity and injuries were not uncommon.

Eric followed the teams as they formed the pyramid, his hand on the throttle of the outboard, watching for falls and skis. He stayed distant enough that he wasn't a part of the scene, but not so distant that he couldn't provide help if someone needed it. He watched Paulina as she clambered higher and higher up the scaffold of bodies.

His focus was the pyramid, but Monstro the whale ate away at the back of his thoughts.

Eric had spent the better part of the morning wrestling over the best path of action.

Do I just reach out to Dr. Bluford? Call the cops? Check it out for myself?

Because Eric was damned sure that this white whale he'd been paid to find was a big stuffed alligator in the middle of *Splashy Springs*.

The focus needed to be the tribute show, though. The safety of the team demanded that he focus on his responsibilities in that pub boat. Eric knew there would be time after the tribute was done to make his next move wherever that move might take him.

He continued to watch Paulina as she climbed to the top of the pyramid. She was strong and fast and showed no hesitation making her way to the top. Her left hand kept a tight grip on the braided rope as her foot found a thigh, her hand found a shoulder, and she was at the top of the four tier.

I love this feeling, Paulina thought. The wind smacked her face. The setting sun painted the distant shores of north Lake May in gold, and she could tell that the driver was on target with the timing of the boat pattern. *I love it and I'll never feel this again.*

To her right, the grandstands, full of FloridaWorld's season pass members, curious locals, and random fans. Onstage was Jimmy Fig, microphone in his left hand. When he raised his right arm to present the pyramid to the crowd, that was the signal for Paulina to hoist the FloridaWorld flag with her free right hand and for the entire team to turn and smile as they passed.

Paulina spotted Irv Irving in his place of honor, his wheelchair throne sitting at the base of the broad green grass expanse that led to the white sand beach and shielded by the sun only by Hilda's black umbrella.

Shiner was next to Irv as well, and Paulina didn't understand that, but it didn't matter to her, not at this point.

"What a sight," said Hilda as she stepped to her left along the grassy knoll. "I must move over here for a better photo."

Irv didn't remember Hilda carrying a camera, but he was too engrossed in the moment to care.

"My sunshine friends," said Irv Irving, "here you see the most photographed act in all of waterskiing. The by-God human pyramid. Stand at attention, boy. This is FloridaWorld."

Shiner tried to stand taller, and a cascade of sweat poured down his hairy back.

It all happened so fast. Paulina reached back into her costume and pulled out, not the FloridaWorld flag on a wooden dowel, but her scoped Beretta 92.

She kept the gun tight to her back, just as she would the flag, but she wasn't waiting for the signal from Fig. Paulina was waiting for the moment when the pyramid turned the corner and the boat straightened out for the front stretch. There would be smooth water and her legs would be locked.

Fig's right arm went up, presenting, and that was the signal for Paulina. The team turned and smiled as one. The audience held its collective breath, waiting for this iconic moment in celebration of the most notable figure in the history of Bacopa County.

Irv Irving smiled and thought about a day in 1946 when he had convinced himself that FloridaWorld would be his wonderland, his Valhalla, his dream of a perfect place with perfect friends. He thought of the warmth of many suns, the taste of many wines, and he did not think of Alma, Rose, and so many others who had just been there for him to take as he wanted. He did not think of what he had done, only of what he had enjoyed.

There was a flash of distant memory, of blood and gold and naked people doing naked things, but the flash was just that, and Irv dismissed it as he'd always done.

For a moment, though, there was the ghost of a whisper in the soft Florida wind, and it asked, *"This is some swell party, isn't it, son?"*

What a fine day at FloridaWorld, thought Irv Irving. *Just fine. Drink today and drink all sorrow. You shall perhaps not do tomorrow. Best while you have it, use your breath. There is no drinking after death. The anchors up, the sails are set, and off we glide.*

The music swelled, the four-tiered pyramid began to pass the grandstand, and the audience started to cheer, the sound a building wave of white noise.

Paulina leveled her service weapon, steadied her breathing, aimed through the scope, and fired twice.

The first shot sent a 9mm round into the center of Irv Irving's forehead.

The second shot carved a shallow trench along Shiner's cheek on its way into the grassy knoll and would be found later by the forensics team, along with chunks of Irv Irving brain pan.

The back of the old man's skull flipped out and slid down the back of his neck. Hilda heard a champagne bottle pop sound and smiled for the briefest of moments before she focused on the sloppy mess that was Irv Irving's head and feigned horror.

She ran back to his side, tossing the black umbrella as she went. Shiner felt little pain, just some wetness on his face, and he ran his fingers along the wound.

What just happened? he thought.

The crowd saw Paulina fire, heard the shots, and a few souls were witness to the immediate aftermath of Irv's unlikely demise. It was all so odd, though, that it took several seconds for anyone to acknowledge or comprehend what had just happened.

Hilda was screaming and attempting to pop Irv's skullcap back onto his head. Blood and tissue flowed, she screamed, and the theatrics, she thought, were a wonderful touch.

Johnny Fig stared at the mess of Irv Irving and his immortal words, "Ladies and gentlemen, holy shit," echoed out over the scene powered by amps and woofers and underscored by the synth noodling of that state-of-the-art Casio keyboard.

There was panic, then. Shiner dropped to his knees because the pain hit too and the confusion made him dizzy.

What the hell?

He looked over at Irv Irving through a star field of dancing white lights. The Old Man was well and truly dead.

The pyramid was already past the grandstands and in front of the inside dock. Skiers, unaware, were bracing for Paulina to come down, and with her, the rest of the pyramid so that they could circle back around, women in front of the men and balanced together on their skis, for their landing and final bow.

Paulina, of course, had a different plan.

After the second shot, Paulina took a deep breath and bailed out the back of the pyramid, tossing the handle and doing a double back to Lake May.

When she hit the water, it felt like concrete, but she kept her breath, the weapon, and her wits.

Paulina was under the dark copper lake water and swimming hard, swimming as fast as she could to the drainage pipes to the south of the inside dock.

She knew there would be roots and spiders and mud.

She hoped there would be no alligators waiting in that long, dark pipe to freedom.

#

Eric recognized the weapon the moment Paulina pulled it from the back of her vest and aimed it toward the crowd. He recognized it, but he didn't acknowledge the reality of it until he heard the Beretta as it fired.

Was she firing back at someone? Was it part of the show?

Eric couldn't wrap his head around what he saw until, a moment later, he watched a patch of panic erupt along the grassy beach where Irv Irving watched the show.

She'd fired into the crowd. Toward the old man.

He thought of watermelons and the back of a pickup truck and his stomach flipped.

"Holy shit," he said through clenched teeth, echoing

the unfortunate Jimmy Fig's reaction.

The pyramid was in front of the inside dock, where it would normally begin to disassemble from the top down. Instead, Paulina tucked and back flipped and Eric saw her hit the water.

He torqued the throttle and the pub boat rocketed toward the dock, toward where Eric had seen Paulina disappear.

It took a moment to get his boat on plane and stable. The waves from the pyramid were massive. Eric was nearly launched out of his seat until he got the bow down and the boat to speed. His shades kept the spray out of his eyes, but it made it hard to see in the late afternoon shadow of the stadium, so Eric tossed them to the floor of the boat.

He killed the throttle to stop the propeller, but not his forward momentum as he reached the choppy water twenty yards from the inside dock, where Paulina fell.

Nothing. He couldn't see her, couldn't see a sign of her, no vest, nothing.

Wait.

A FloridaWorld flag on a wooden dowel floated to the surface of the dark copper water.

Eric looked off to his left. The pyramid was coming down and the boat pattern took that hard loop out to the far side of the show course.

They don't have any idea what just happened, Eric thought.

Did she swim under the dock? Where the hell was

she?

For a second, he remembered the hidden scuba gag used by the mermaids at various tourist traps he'd seen.

Surely not.

Then he saw the yawning black mouth of the large drainage pipe that ran from the shore by the back dock all the way out to the parking lot and beyond.

No way.

He scanned the water, looking for any sign. Bubbles, blood, anything.

Just chop from the boat pattern.

What was more likely, a hidden scuba tank or a trip through a gator infested cement death tube?

No bubbles. Not a scuba tank.

If she was unconscious, she would be floating by now. They all wore flotation vests under their pyramid costumes in case of an emergency.

Eric looked back at the stadium and saw people scattering in every direction. There was no music, no announcer, just the sound of screaming and chaos.

He pulled the kill cord, shutting down the motor, and knifed into the dark water. It was warm and felt good, but he realized what this really meant. She had a thirty-second head start on him, and if she was in that drainage pipe she could always turn around and fire at him if that was her preference. Eric hoped Paulina wouldn't do that, but he also didn't think, until a few moments before, that she was capable of opening fire into a crowd during a waterski show from atop a four-tier human pyramid.

He swam hard to the dock.

Not going into the pipe, he thought, *don't need to.*

Eric got to the dock and pulled himself up and out of the lake. Staggering, almost falling but catching his balance, Eric ran as fast as he could.

The other side of that drainage pipe opened out into the retention pond that sat in the center of the FloridaWorld parking lot, and Eric was pretty damned sure that he could run faster than Paulina could crawl.

#

The service semi-automatic wasn't the only thing Paulina had hidden in the back of her vest. A small flashlight was the other, and she held it tight in her shaking left hand as she scrambled fast through the drainpipe.

Mud, roots, and trash. Her knees scraped against concrete and cypress roots that were tentacled into the pipe. Cobwebs plastered her skin and at first it was a horror, but then she knew that there was only one way forward, and this was a price she would pay.

The gators were her biggest concern.

The air was still, and Paulina struggled to breathe. The gun was back in her vest and scratched at the skin of her back. Panic and adrenaline made her muscles shake.

Her right hand dug into the mud as she went.

A root? No, it moved, and it was thick as her wrist.

She screamed and scrambled fast, her flashlight

glimpsing the fat water moccasin she'd just released as it slithered back into the darkness.

Gators weren't the worst thing down here, she realized, but it was too late now. The path was set.

Paulina had planned carefully, and this was no exception, but there were always going to be risks. She knew the distance from the inside dock to the pond in the parking lot, and she knew how long it would take to crawl that distance. Paulina knew also that the gunfire and the death of Irv Irving would panic the crowd and there wouldn't be anyone even thinking of where to search for a good, long time. It would take time for the witnesses to make sense of what they'd seen.

She also knew that Eric was in the pub boat and he would have seen everything. So there was a good chance he'd assess the situation and determine that she'd made her way into the drainpipe.

After all, he was a man who found things. And he wasn't a fool.

Paulina paused. The echoes of her breathing and scrambling drifted into a silence of dripping water and nothing else.

He wasn't following her.

Maybe he was confused. Maybe he was diving into the lake where he'd seen her fall, looking for her in the grass and sand twenty feet down.

Or he was running for the parking lot and the other end of the storm drain and Paulina would need to make a hard decision.

She crawled, fast and hard, flashlight scanning ahead for anything scaly and prehistoric nestled beyond her in the black.

#

Sirens.

There were sirens getting louder and louder as the squad cars and emergency vehicles fought their way down FloridaWorld Drive to get to the scene of Irv Irving's last waterski show. Cars were pulling fast out of FloridaWorld's parking lot, jockeying for position and rubbing rails as panic took hold.

Everyone wanted to get away as quickly as they could.

Who knew if there were more people with guns? The good folk of Bacopa County didn't want to find out.

Eric leaned against a small tree that stood next to the retention pond and caught his breath. He'd run as fast and as hard as he could and was sweating in the evening humidity.

If I'm wrong, and Paulina doesn't pop out of that drainpipe, then I have no idea where she went. Maybe she was hurt from the pyramid fall and was stuck at the bottom of Lake May under some dead limbs and roots. If I'm wrong, I don't know what to do next. Just no idea, he thought, his eyes trained on the two-meter-wide concrete pipe that fed into the pond.

Right or wrong, he didn't know how to feel. Didn't know what he was going to say, but then came Paulina, covered in mud, clambering out of the drainpipe and into the scummy green water of the retention pond.

She looked up and saw Eric. Their eyes locked.

"Give me a second," she said in a quiet voice. She reached down and scooped up some of the water and used it to rinse mud and cobwebs from her face.

When she looked back up at Eric, her face was blank, a clean slate.

"My Grandma taught me that song. The one I sang in the surf at the beach the other night. Then my mama sang it too. It was a pretty song, and now it just runs around and around in my head, and it won't stop. I love that song and it won't stop, Eric. It's like a ghost in my head."

Eric couldn't help but notice the service weapon in her right hand. Maybe the mud would jam the trigger and maybe it wouldn't.

"We need to lower the temperature on this before the police show, Paulina. Put the gun down," said Eric. His voice trembled as he spoke.

"Great shot, right? I mean, I was top of my class, but that was a great shot. You have to admit it," said Paulina, and she was somewhere between laughing and crying.

"Helluva shot, but why?"

"Let's go off together. This is it. Last chance. Come with me. Mexico. Sunshine friends, right? Let's go and drink on the beach and live happily ever after."

The sirens were close now.

"Not going to happen, Paulie."

Paulina raised the Beretta 92 and aimed it at Eric.

He didn't move.

"Fine. You let me climb out of this pond. I traded my truck for a car this morning. A real piece of shit. You let me get to that car. I hit the road and am out of town before anyone knows to look for me."

"That's it?"

"That's it."

"You won't make it, Paulina."

"I know. But what a shot."

Paulina kept the weapon on Eric as she made her way up the bank of the pond, unzipping the front of her wetsuit costume as she went. She pulled the vest back and let the water pour out.

The sirens were so close that the noise hurt their ears.

Paulina started to say something, took a deep breath, opened her mouth again, and then dropped to her knees. The barrel of the semi-automatic went underneath her chin.

Eric's stomach dropped.

"No."

She sang then, that old song from the green hollows of Kentucky, a song of her mother and her grandmother. A simple prayer of dreams sung low and sweet.

Eric walked fast towards Paulina. There was the taste of copper in his mouth and his legs felt numb. Like a nightmare.

She aimed the weapon at Eric again, but he came on anyway, fast and low.

He didn't think. He just dove for her and the 9x19

round grazed his back, but he didn't feel it at first. His hand caught her right wrist, and he pushed for all he was worth.

Paulina was strong, but there was no fight left in her at that moment, so Eric pinned her with little effort.

She released her grip on the weapon but kept singing low and steady.

Eric's question repeated, and it was one word: "Why?"

Paulina locked eyes with Eric.

She just kept singing.

They stared at each other until voices surrounded them, angry, frightened voices, police officers telling them to put their hands behind their backs and to lie still on the soft green grass.

Eric did as he was told, his forehead on the damp grass, his hands open and low on his back.

Paulina did not do as she was told and when she stood, weapon in hand, the low-paid and terrified officers of the Bacopa County Sheriff's department opened fire at Paulina Campos.

Eric couldn't hear because the gunfire deafened him, but he sensed the ground tremble as Paulina fell.

He turned his head and opened his eyes. Paulina was there, and they were face to face.

She smiled and sang for a few brief moments before the blood filled her lungs and her eyes lost their light.

Paulina's hillbilly lullaby would haunt Eric Walters for the rest of his life.

23

Saturday Night

FloridaWorld was closed, the moon was out, and Hilda quickened her pace as she made her way along empty paths toward the employee gate to Monkey Kingdom. She'd been this way thousands of times in the past few years, and she knew her way in the dark.

Hilda's hands were still sticky from Irv's brain matter, though she'd scrubbed and washed several times. She'd become annoyed with the police after more than an hour went by and they still insisted on questioning her about Paulina, about Irv, about everything and nothing all at the same time.

Finally, she pretended to tremble uncontrollably, and they'd released her with vague apologies and questions about her fitness to drive.

"We'll be in touch, ma'am," the skinny one who

seemed in charge said as Hilda feigned tears and staggered away, back into the park.

Her boots were loud on the concrete floor, too loud for Hilda's comfort, but it was pitch black in the back of house hallways and there was nobody around to hear. She slowed her pace. No need to rush after all this time.

The gators of Monkey Kingdom were fat with the day's chicken, so they might as well have been statues, or stuffed, like the legendary Monstro, the largest gator in the world. The music was off, so the only sound in the place was the whine of mosquitos.

There he was. Monstro. Nearly twenty feet of stuffed reptile that loomed out of the darkness like a dinosaur.

Hilda smiled and pulled the machete from where she'd hidden it in a bunch of ferns. The moon shone through the glass above them and the big lizard's waxy belly shone white.

She drew back and whacked the enormous stuffed gator as hard as she could, right along the belly. The machete dug in, but not enough. Hilda hacked at hit again. Again. She dropped the machete and tore at the thing's belly with her hands, ripping it open.

The jewels that fell out made a wonderful tinkling sound as they hit the concrete floor. Hilda looked up into Monstro's gut cavity and smiled at the enormous golden orange inside.

So much gold. So many jewels. It was even more than she'd been told, more than she'd ever expected. There were ingots, coins as big as silver dollars, a necklace of pearls, a crown of bright red and green gemstones, diamond ring after diamond ring, a sea of treasures she would swim in for eternity.

Sure, Irv Irving's will and testament would hand over the park to Hilda, especially now that she was the only one on the list who was still alive. That was never the plan, though. That was never the endgame.

Her hands ran along the smooth golden orange, and they trembled as they went.

I'll be gone before morning and in the islands before noon, she thought with a smile. The sun was going to be warm, the beach was going to be beautiful, and Hilda Rosenblatt would never be heard from again. The park? The park could burn for all she cared.

She was too preoccupied in her dreams of an island retirement to hear Shiner sneak up behind her. The little man, a bright white bandage on his cheek, brought the baseball bat down hard on the back of Hilda's head and the metal helmet she wore made a solid, sickening, thud sound.

"That's for PBR, you bitch," he said.

Hilda shook her head as if clearing her ears of water after a dip.

"Oh shit," said Shiner as Hilda reared up and turned, not only conscious but now pissed.

Not hard enough. Shiner was frozen in place with fear and confusion. And a little weed.

She had him by the throat and was lifting him high off of the ground, her fingers digging into his neck just as they'd been digging into Monstro only moments before.

Shiner's eyes bugged, and he made little hacking sounds. The white bandage blossomed red.

Hilda squeezed. Shiner, the piss monkey, felt the warmth along his thighs as he lost control of his bladder.

"Your face is turning purple, little man, and in just a few seconds my hands will crush your trachea and then you'll be dead," Hilda said, her voice deliberate and low.

"Let him go."

Hilda didn't recognize the voice. She turned to look, but she kept the pressure on Shiner's neck.

Eric stood in the gloom only a few feet away. Paulina's service weapon was in his hand and it was aimed at Hilda.

"I won't miss from this distance. Put him down."

Something rubbed against Eric's ankle. He looked down.

The snake. Her enormous snake. It moved quickly and coiled around Eric's leg.

"Nope," he said, and stepped away from the thing. The distraction was enough. Hilda tossed Shiner, and the little man slammed into Eric like 120 pounds of bone and gristle.

She came toward him. Eric was off balance, but he brought the gun up hard to Hilda's chin and she staggered.

Eric had seen enough movies to know that the gun in his hand was a liability, as he had no intention of shooting. He wasn't even sure why he'd grabbed it from the weeds in the chaos and confusion after Paulina had been shot. He'd tucked it away before the police had seen the damned thing. Maybe a hunch, maybe something else, no idea. It had been a stupid risk and thank God they hadn't searched him before they let him go.

Now, though, Eric had a raving mad Valkyrie coming for him, and he did not want her to get her hands on that gun.

He tossed it into the gator pond. It bounced off of a sleeping alligator's snout, and the weapon sunk into the foul water.

Hilda came at him again. Eric dropped and swept her legs. She toppled and fell with a loud thud, but she was scrambling toward him again in an instant, this time on all fours.

Eric kicked out and caught her in the teeth with the heel of his K-Swiss. He heard a crunch and was pretty sure she'd lost some Chiclets. He crab-walked back and away, then jumped up as Hilda bull-rushed him. She screamed as she came, and it was one of the most terrifying sounds Eric had ever heard.

That scream, though, was nothing compared to the noise Hilda made when Eric sidestepped and used her own momentum to send her spinning into the gator pond.

Rather, the sound she made when the gators woke up and felt the need to eat.

Hilda's tortured shriek was a dinner bell. First one fat gator woke up and took a chomp, then another, and within seconds it seemed to Eric that every big lizard in the exhibit was tucking in for a piece.

They were accustomed to chicken, so this new meat was a delight.

Eric grabbed Shiner by the back of the shirt and pulled him into the hallway. It was too dark to see anything. There were just the sounds of the alligators enjoying Hilda, and the tortured breathing of Shiner.

"Talk if you can," said Eric. When Shiner spoke, his voice was a rasp. "Park was gonna be mine. All of it. But, she killed all of those people, man. Thought it was gonna be hers. Killed PBR. All of them. For nothing."

"I don't understand," Eric said. "You weren't here for the gold? The belly of the whale?"

"Huh?"

Eric didn't necessarily trust Shiner at that moment, but he wanted to know more, and the only way to get the information was by asking. He thought of the old movie playing on the television at Paulina's place and of the night terror that opened his eyes to the whole insane thing.

"Monstro. The name of the whale in Pinocchio and the name of this giant stuffed alligator. Irv Irving hid his treasure in the belly of the whale. Did you know?"

Shiner coughed and then spoke, his voice barely above a whisper. Fresh blood dripped from the bandage down his chin.

"Not about this. Something else. Something bigger. Come with me."

The grand mansion was black against the silver of Lake May, and the moon was nearly full, so there was light along the trees and topiaries of the path that led to her grand entrance hall.

Shiner opened the door and let Eric into the place. The little man was walking slowly and couldn't stop rubbing his neck.

Probably hurts like hell, thought Eric.

They walked up the wide, elaborate staircase. Moonlight knifed in through the many windows and dust motes danced. The floorboards creaked, and there must have been a draft because there were other sounds as well, almost like whispers.

Shiner led Eric into Irv Irving's bed chamber. He pulled a framed photo of a human pyramid, labeled "FloridaWorld 1967" from the wall and dropped it to the floor.

A safe, an old one, cast of iron and sporting a dial lock.

The little man manipulated the combination lock dial. There was a series of clicks, and the cast iron door opened with a metallic snap. Shiner reached in and withdrew a couple of documents.

"Get a load of these," Shiner said in a voice like an angry frog.

The first document was a will and testament, duly

notated, and Eric scanned it.

Irv Irving left everything he owned to a list of names. Some he recognized, some he didn't.

"I'll be damned. Dr. Claude Bluford. He's going to be surprised," Eric said.

"Not really. He's dead. Just like everyone on that list except, until a few minutes ago, Hilda."

"Hmm."

There goes my fifteen percent, I guess.

"Read the other one."

Eric scanned the second document.

A will, just like the first. Signed, notated.

Only one beneficiary.

It was Shiner.

"What?"

Shiner coughed before he spoke. "The Old Man didn't trust Hilda, so he had a fake will drawn up. His lawyers never saw it. It's a phony. The real one is the one with my name on it. Apparently Irv Irving showed Hilda the fake and she bit, hook, line, and sinker."

"Why those names? Why those people?"

"The people on the fake list? I haven't had much time to think about it, but I guess he hated them. Different reasons. Hated the Doc, maybe because the Doc was after his money. Hated the others because maybe he knew they were his kids."

"What?"

"There were always rumors that the Old Man had a bunch of illegitimate kids running around Bacopa

County. He never married, you know, so that's how rumors start. People need something to talk about, especially when it comes to the weird millionaire on the hill."

"Do you think they were his kids?"

"No idea, but if they were, they sure as hell didn't know the truth and he was afraid that someday, somehow, the truth would come out and tarnish his legacy. Maybe PBR had a suspicion, but no proof. The others? They were just trash he'd never cleaned up, at least in his mind. But I'm guessing. I don't know."

"Trash."

"The Old Man thought there was a chance Hilda would do something drastic. She did."

"It was a game to him."

"A game. Yeah. She played it out better than he'd ever hoped, at least until the end. I don't think Irv saw Paulina coming."

"No," said Eric, "I don't think he did."

Shiner sat down on the hardwood floor beneath the safe, his back against the wall, and pulled a pack of cigarettes from his shorts. He drew one to his mouth and reached for his lighter.

"Shit. Dropped my Zippo."

"I'll trade you for a smoke."

Eric needed a cigarette. Badly.

Eric pulled his Bic and tossed it to Shiner. The little man tossed a Marlboro red in return, sparked up the cigarette, threw back the Bic, and took a deep draw.

"What's it gonna be, Eric?"

Eric sat down across from Shiner, his back against the frame of Irv Irving's massive bed. He lit his cigarette and drew a deep pull. The room was dark. Drafts and floorboard creaks spoke to each other in the hallway outside.

He had Paulina's song in his head and he felt his eyes get moist. He squinted hard and chewed on the inside of his cheek as he exhaled the smoke.

"My friends, in the service, over in Iraq, they knew about some things I did. I always knew I was guilty and didn't think about them and the things they might have done, too. Their guilt. That was on them. Mine was on me. We own our guilt, I guess, if we're honest with ourselves."

"We own our own guilt. Yeah. I can get behind that," said Shiner.

"Did you know what was happening? That Hilda killed PBR and the others?"

Eric could see Shiner smile and shake his head, even in the darkness. "Of course I didn't know."

"Really?"

"He showed me the will...the wills...when I went to see him before the show. He sent word that I had to go see him at the mansion, so I went quick as I could."

"And you said you didn't know him that well."

"Maybe we were closer than I thought we were," said Shiner.

"Go on."

"I didn't know a damned thing until I met him at the mansion. He showed me the will. I was too freaked out to process it at the moment. I think I would have spilled it to the cops, I think, but no, I was clueless as fuck. "

"Can you prove that?"

"Fuck no. But nobody can prove otherwise. So, what's it gonna be, Eric?"

The moonlight was brighter now on Shiner's face and the cigarette cherry glowed orange, but Eric couldn't read the little man's expression.

"As it stands, I think you're in the clear."

Shiner said nothing, he just hiked a haunch and passed wind, a high-pitched squeaker that lasted for a few seconds and ended with a wet punctuation mark.

Eric couldn't help but laugh, but he instantly felt that the laughter was obscene, a terrible thing. He shook his head and looked down at the hardwood floor, focusing on the knots and swirls of the cypress. How old was this place? When were these trees felled to build it? What ghosts still called the mansion home? Eric was quiet for a long moment and when he spoke, his voice felt too loud.

"So, if everything holds up, you're the owner of FloridaWorld," said Eric.

"Looks that way."

Eric looked up and saw that Shiner was crying.

"How fast are you going to sell it?"

The little man shrugged his shoulders and started to speak, but his voice caught in his throat and he just sat in the darkness.

They both thought they heard music then, not the song of Paulina Campos but a ragtime tune from a distant time, faint but there and coming from downstairs, but because that was impossible neither man said anything about the music, the voices chattering in the wind, or anything else.

24

Three Months Later

The waterski stadium was full and so was the grassy field to the left bank. The summer sun was high, and the clouds were cotton candy. They would grow dark in a couple of hours, as clouds do during a Florida summer, and there would be lightning and a show cancellation and even some hail that would dent more than a few cars in that packed parking lot.

Now, though, the first ski show of the day was packed with people who were there for FloridaWorld's grand reopening on a beautiful Saturday afternoon in June.

Light winds meant calm water and Lake May was almost glass, reflecting the sun and clouds like an oil painting.

Shiner did not erect a monument, plaque, or statue, nor did he even do so much as plant a garden in memory of Irv Irving. The Old Man had been his friend, but he had been a terrible bastard and he'd gotten what was coming. There would be no fond memory of him at this place. His voice, his image, his presence was erased from the park during the weeks they'd been closed and as the years went on, fewer and fewer would remember Irv Irving. They would just know FloridaWorld, for what that was worth.

During the down time, Kent and the team crafted a theme worthy of their talents. It was no theme at all. The show was an exhibition of the skiers and the drivers doing what they did better than anyone else in the world. And if what they did seemed trivial or with little grand purpose, you weren't paying attention.

Because on the shores of Lake May the women and men of the FloridaWorld Water Spectacular thrilled and amused and even brought the audience to their feet when that pyramid came through or when those acrobatic ski jumpers did their spins and twists and when those beautiful Aqua-Maids performed their ballet on the liquid stage.

This was not trivial, nor was it without grand purpose. No entertainment, when done with such a pure heart, is ever without purpose to the audience ready to receive it.

So, Eric could not hear the show's music nor could he hear the impassioned announcing of Johnny Fig when Eric's face was inches from the surface of the water at 45 miles per hour and the soles of his feet were burning from the friction.

Eric Walters brought himself up backwards, hands hard behind him on the tow handle, and opened his eyes. There was Lake May, carved and churning in his wake and in the wake of that ski boat. There was that blue sky, the green of the Cypress Trees on the other side of the lake, and the dark copper of the water.

This was the first show of the season. He had trained hard to do this, to be the show's back barefoot star, and he didn't want to fall, but he knew what had to come next. Outside the wake, at just the right moment, when his balance was secure, Eric spun forward and was facing the boat, facing the wake, and facing the 5000 people sitting in the audience, watching the impossible.

He released the handle and glided, standing up and leaning back, all the way to the sand.

The roar of the crowd was louder than the thunder that would come later that day. It was one of the loudest and most wonderful things Eric had ever heard.

His parents would be proud. He smiled. They are proud, he corrected himself, as he waved to the audience with the "catch a fly" ski show wave he'd learned as a kid. *Somewhere, they're proud.*

After the show a few of the team stayed out onstage, as they always did, to meet the guests for a few photos, signed "FloridaWorld" souvenir books, and a passed along phone number or two. It was Eric's first time handling the meet and greet, and it was not something that came naturally. He felt more than a little uncomfortable playing the celebrity.

When the last of the guests drifted away Eric and the rest of those left standing onstage made their way to the dock to drop off their gear and then into the tunnel, past the weight room, and down to the meeting room where everyone was already gathered.

Kent stood in front of the team, his face a ripe tomato slick with sweat and his white polo soaked through. A cigarette dangled from his lips. He removed his Oakleys, and when he spoke, his voice cracked.

"Damned fine show. No falls. Drivers were on point, top-notch work."

The applause from the team was genuine and loud.

"Everyone. Helluva job out there, and over the past few weeks. It's a new day, right?"

There were a few "right" shouts, and Gary screamed "harrumph" at the top of his lungs.

Shiner came into the room then, holding a can of Bud and smoking a fat cigar. A long white scar ran the length of his cheek. There was silence, then he flipped the team the finger and there was laughter and a few obscenities.

"So, one more show today," said Kent, "then we're going to have a mandatory team drunk fest at The Tavern until everyone passes out. The new owner of FloridaWorld is buying."

More cheers and applause then. Shiner looked stricken. "I never agreed to that," he mumbled, then he stepped next to Kent.

"What Kent said. Great work out there. Couple of things," said Shiner. His voice quivered, as he wasn't comfortable being an authority figure or delivering anything more than a joke to the team. "I'm going to keep things running, but it's up to you fuckers to keep the crowds happy once they pay their ticket and buy their popcorn, so keep it up."

"We gonna stay open? Rumor is this place is gonna crash and burn," said Carol through a cloud of smoke.

Eric smiled. The little guy was out of his lane, but he was driving as fast and as straight as he could.

"We're not dead yet," he said, "and I'm working on some changes that might help us stay afloat for a while."

"How about changes to our paychecks? I can't afford my smokes," said Karen in a voice that sounded like she would be better served stopping the smokes entirely.

"I'll buy you a pack," said Shiner, "and let's just keep the place alive before we hand out bonuses."

"That's fair enough," Karen said, which was as pleasant a thing as anyone had ever heard her say.

Shiner took a sip of his Bud and cleared his throat.

"Look," he said, "we have some guests coming to the next show, all the way from the Middle East, if you can imagine that, a place called Aqaba, in Jordan. One of the guys used to be a big deal waterskier back in the day, the other is related to a king or a queen or something."

Kent took a long drag on his smoke and asked, "They looking to buy the place?"

"No," said Shiner, "they want to put on a ski show

over there as part of some big celebration for royalty. A FloridaWorld ski show. So let's stick those landings, and maybe we'll get to do some traveling."

Eric smiled. He'd visited Amman, Jordan, when he was in the service and he liked the place. He'd never had the chance to visit Petra or the Wadi Rum while he was there and those were big archeological itches that he would love to scratch. It would be fun to go back, this time with a bag of ski gear rather than automatic weapons.

He looked around the room.

Mostly kids, really. Nobody was making enough money and there was no telling how much life the park had left, but they were birds of a feather along the shores of Lake May and that was good enough for now.

"Yeah," he thought, *"traveling overseas to do a ski show for a king? Sign me up."*

FloridaWorld felt more like home to him with each day, and these people felt like family.

Hell, he even had a dog now. An old blind dog, but still a dog. He'd never been able to track down the owner, with Paulina gone, but he liked the little furry fella well enough, so now he was a doggie daddy.

Fred was feeble and blind, but he was a very good boy, and it was nice to have someone to come home to after the day's shows were done. Fred wasn't perfect, but he would do just fine.

Eric didn't know how long this would last, but he knew he would always remember these days.

These days in the sun on Lake May at FloridaWorld.